D0324284

A Good Life

A Good Life

by François Gravel

Translated by
Sheila Fischman

A CORMORANT BOOK

This translation is for Jan Geddes.

Fillion et Frères was first published in French
by Éditions Québec/Amérique in 2000.

The publisher gratefully acknowledges the support of the Canada Council for the Arts and the Ontario Arts Council for its publishing program. We acknowledge the financial support of the Government of Canada through the Book Publishing Industry Development Program (BPIDP) for our publishing activities.

Printed and bound in Canada

National Library of Canada Cataloguing in Publication Data

Gravel, François
[Fillion et frères. English]
A good life

Translation of: Fillion et frères.
ISBN 1-896951-34-1

I. Fischman, Sheila II. Title.

PS8563.R388F5413 2001 C843'.54 C2001-901542-9
PQ3919.2.G75F5413 2001

Cover design: Bill Douglas @ The Bang
Text design: Tannice Goddard
Cover images: Joehari Lee and Patricia McDonough/Photonica

Cormorant Books Inc.
895 Don Mills Road, 400-2 Park Centre
Toronto, Ontario, Canada M3C 1W3
www.cormorantbooks.com

A Good Life

1

JAM

I no longer know what is true in this story and what isn't, but I do know that in one way or another I'm always talking about him. About myself too, of course, but differently.

And I know that it all begins in the fall of 1929, when a handful of men in black tear up pieces of paper and fling the scraps to the ground somewhere on Wall Street. At the end of a long line of dominoes stretching across the continent, my grandfather Étienne, until then foreman in a canning factory, ends up on the street.

Étienne was only thirteen when he left his parents' farm in Louiseville to strike out on his own in Montreal. Since then he's done nothing but work. Work all day and come home late, worn out. And begin again, day after day, never stopping. Save as much as he can, marry, then give his wife everything he earns. His whole pay, every week, except for a few cents for the collection plate on Sunday, and enough for streetcar tickets. Work is something he knows. It's all he knows.

When evening comes, he stays at the table just long enough to eat and smoke a pipe. After that he patches the plaster walls, stokes the furnace with coal, repairs some drawers and chairs or makes wooden toys in the shed. He always knows how things work or why they don't and he has what's necessary to fix them if need be. His workbench is covered with various kinds of planes, with files and handsaws, braces and squares, and with dozens of tobacco tins brimming with nails, screws, bolts and hinges. He is permanently surrounded by the smell of sawdust or iron filings, turpentine or varnish. He likes these smells, which make him feel that he's alive, that he's useful.

But ever since those men in black tore up their papers, he doesn't know anything; he's nothing more than a ghost who walks the streets from morning till night, tiring himself much more by looking for work than if he'd really been working. When he comes home he doesn't even have the strength to fix things.

He spends a year trying to find employment, then he gives up. In November 1930, he doesn't have the courage to stay outside, to look for jobs that don't exist. Who would hire a man who's well over forty and can barely read and write? He resigns himself to staying home, and that's when he discovers that the only place less welcoming to a man like him than the street is the kitchen. The kitchen ruled over by Annette.

I didn't know my grandmother very well, but my father, my

uncles and my aunts always straightened their backs when they pronounced her name: a proud woman, they'd say. If you asked about her they'd go into long circumlocutions: strict, yes, I suppose she was, but no more than any others, there were lots worse if you took the time to look, and anyway you had to be tough to make it through such hard times. During the thirties it was always November, it was always cold, you can't understand, you mustn't judge.

Unwelcome in his own kitchen, Étienne takes refuge in the shed as often as he can, but he's no longer in the mood to saw wood, sort nails or repair anything at all. Sure, he's got all those tools and plenty of time, but fixing things isn't about tools or time, it's about mood, inner peace, an urge to smile, to whistle, to do something good for himself, and that's what he can't do any more. And so he pretends to be puttering, without conviction, then comes back to the kitchen with nothing to do. He makes a place for himself between the window and the radio. A place on the sidelines so he won't get in Annette's way. He shrinks, he shrivels up.

When he tries to help his wife by shelling peas, hulling strawberries or washing dishes, Annette sends him packing:

"Not like that, my God you're awkward, give me that knife and go and sit down, there's nothing as useless as a man in the kitchen, always underfoot, a big nuisance, hasn't got half a brain, dear God, what did I do to heaven to deserve this?"

Étienne goes back to his rocker, looks out the window, listens to the radio, sometimes he'll light a pipe, inevitably provoking a long series of sighs from Annette, like a locomotive pulling out of the station.

"Funny thing, wife, wouldn't you say? I'm the one smoking but you're the one puffing like an engine."

What's the use of being married if you can't even goad your wife a little? thinks Étienne. But Annette doesn't find him funny. She's got other things to do: cook a meal out of practically nothing, a daily miracle, not even Jesus could have done it, what did I do to You, God, to deserve this? She doesn't find him amusing but she shrugs, makes a little less noise as she puts away her saucepans and even stops sighing for a moment. There's that at least, thinks Étienne.

Étienne knows it's hard for Annette to put up with him in the kitchen, particularly when he smokes his pipe, but where can he go? After all, he can't sleep all day; he'd get bedsores and he'd be no further ahead. The children's bedrooms are always full and the parlour is off limits to him — and to everyone else, for that matter: the armchairs are permanently shrouded in dust-covers that will crease if you sit on them. What's the good of having chairs if you can never sit on them? Étienne sometimes wonders. But, all right, the furniture comes from Annette's family so it's up to her to decide. There's always the shed, of course, but you have to work hard if you don't want the cold to get you; besides, the boys have taken it over, now they're the ones who use the handsaw and the plane; so long, old shed. Outside? Outside it's cold and there are taverns at the corner of every street. Maybe you'd prefer that, Annette?

Étienne likes listening to the news on the radio and he likes even more to comment on it, but Annette doesn't understand a thing about politics. She prefers love songs and soap operas, which make her heave great melancholy sighs. Étienne no longer does anything. He smokes, he rocks, he looks out the window and that's all.

And it's been going on like that for days and days, for weeks and months, when Louis's story begins.

It's a day like any other: Étienne is smoking his pipe and listening to the radio while Annette is banging around on the counter and three or four children, the girls especially, are sitting at the table. The girls scribble, draw or do their nails, depending on their age. Philippe and Léo, the oldest of the boys, have known for some time that they don't belong in the kitchen, so they play outside, putter in the shed or look for work; maybe they also hang around the port, explore the world — it doesn't matter. For the time being, all that matters is that there's just one boy in the kitchen. A ten-year-old boy who's been given one end of the table so he can finish his homework.

Louis is neither the youngest nor the eldest of the boys, he's no more handsome or ugly than the others, he doesn't have jug ears or flat feet or any other distinguishing characteristics, as the police would say. If he does stand out from his brothers it's on account of his shyness: the slightest thing makes him blush.

And he's my father. He's the one I talk about, one way or another. At the moment he's ten years old. Which means that I'm talking about a stranger. But nonetheless I know his story really begins on that day, around that table.

Annette is trying to unscrew the lid of a jam jar and the jar is sealed so tight that she can't open it. Annette is strong but, whether she's sick that day or she's having one of her bad days, or maybe she's thinking about something else, the fact is that the lid resists her.

Her gaze travels from the jar of jam to Étienne, then from Étienne to the jar, finally settling on Louis, who is colouring a map of Canada and doesn't suspect anything.

Rather than hold out the jar to her husband, Annette gives it to Louis. A little boy who's already big, but a little boy all the same. Ten years old. She entrusts the stubborn lid to Louis, aged ten, rather than to her husband, though he's ten times stronger. She holds out the jar of jam and says to him:

"Open this for me, son, you're strong. . . ."

Louis's mind is still on his geography when he sees the jar of jam appear before his eyes and he sits there for a moment, bewildered. He looks at his father, a smallish man but still bigger than he is, and a bundle of nerves, and so hard-working, and so strong that none of his sons has ever beaten him at arm-wrestling. Why me? wonders Louis.

He finally gets down to the task, still disconcerted by this unexpected sign of confidence. The jar is hermetically sealed with paraffin, but he'll do it. He has to. Muscles tense, the veins standing out on his neck and his heart about to burst, he persists; he has to succeed, it's a matter of life or death, this is no ordinary jar of jam in his hands, it's a grenade and he has to pull the pin and hurl it at the Germans, if he doesn't his own people will die. . . .

He's close to fainting when at last he feels the lid yield imperceptibly. He steps up his effort and slowly continues to unscrew the lid, then finishes the job with his fingertips. As if it's the easiest thing he's ever done.

His mother looks at him. She doesn't say anything. She just

looks at him, but Louis can read the message that appears in her eyes, in capital letters: I knew you could do it, you aren't like your good-for-nothing father. She adds a postscript that's just as easy to decipher: From now on, try not to disapoint me.

Annette goes back to her counter and heaves a sigh. It's not one of her great dry sighs, indicating anger, nor is it one of the great melancholy laments with tremors and shuddering throat; it's light, floating: she's proud of what she has done.

Étienne hauls himself out of his rocker and leaves the kitchen without a word. He'll come home very late that night, vaguely drunk.

Louis goes back to his geography book, but he has trouble concentrating. Something important has happened, something essential, irreversible, and he doesn't know yet if he ought to be happy or unhappy about it. For that matter he doesn't know that such words can be useful, that such things can be said. And he never will.

2

The Crash

"If you ask me, it's more than just the stock exchange," maintains Wellie. "It's all because of the Jews. They've got a plan, that's for sure."

Wellie is a distant cousin of Étienne's who runs a grocery store a few blocks away. Since the beginning of the Depression, his business has had more employees than customers; all the jobless in the neighbourhood have come to see him at some point, suggesting the same kind of deal. "I can do anything, Monsieur Wellie, wash windows, deliver orders, lift boxes, I'm not afraid of hard work, Monsieur Wellie, I don't even want any wages, just something to keep myself busy, and if you could give me the odd bit of food for my family now and then I wouldn't say no, but you don't even have to do that, Monsieur Wellie, I just want something to do with my time. . . ."

So Wellie put four chairs in back of the store for his volunteer employees, on whom he imposes strict rules: they must never walk through the store where the real employees work and, while they can smoke all they want, liquor will not be tolerated. Unless it's Wellie who offers it, of course. They're also allowed to play cards — in fact, it's encouraged — as long as they just play for toothpicks (there's never any money circulating in back of the store, but there's hardly any in the store itself, no more than anywhere else in the country), and it's a tacit rule that Wellie will be allowed to win more often than he deserves. It's the least they can do.

Whenever a volunteer employee does some little service, Wellie puts an X in chalk under his name on the blackboard. After a certain number of Xs (the number fluctuates according to Wellie's mood and the general state of business), the employee is entitled to take home a little sugar, some flour, even some canned goods, in order to soothe his wife's temper. That way the day won't have been a total waste.

Everyone has finally adapted to the situation: the men, glad to find a place more hospitable than their own kitchens; their wives, finally rid of their husbands; and Wellie, to whom everyone is grateful and who expects that gratitude to be translated into spending, no matter how negligible. Perhaps too he sees it all as an investment: he's preparing a clientele for the day when business picks up again, and it will, one day or another, when the Jews decide that it's in their interest. The factories will have to open their doors again, before all the machines are rusted. . .

"You're full of baloney with your Jews," replies Laurent, the only one who can talk in such a cavalier way to Wellie, who happens to be his brother-in-law. "The more unemployed there are, the less folks there are that can buy, so the companies kick out even more people, which makes even more unemployed, it goes around and around like a big wheel. Things will start up by themselves one of these days, and the Jews have nothing to do with it!"

"But what about that big wheel? Who controls it? Who is it that owns all the banks, the corporations, the finance companies? As soon as there's money there's a Jew nearby, everybody knows that. They're conspiring to take over the world, I tell you, and the Wall Street crash is just the first stage in their plan. When everybody's ruined they'll buy it all back for chickenfeed, and that's when the prices will start to climb again, guaranteed, I give you my word."

"But if they've already got everything, like you say, and if they're so smart, why would they start a Depression that's ruining them? It doesn't make sense! Nope, Wellie, it's not the Jews that caused this Depression, it's the Anglos in general. Because they're too materialistic."

"The Anglos aren't all crooked," says another man. "There's a few that are decent. I know some Irishmen . . . "

Louis often drops in at Wellie's after school. At ten he's obviously too young to join in the discussions, but he's sometimes allowed to stand and watch the men play. He'll settle into a corner, make himself very small and unobtrusive, then listen and look at these men he can't recognize even though he's always known them. They are his neighbours, his uncles, his own father; as long as they're at home these men are usually discreet and silent, barely shadows, but once they're at Wellie's they start to grow, to come alive, to talk and laugh. Louis closes his eyes and listens: it's as if his father's voice has changed or, rather, as if someone has added another voice that he doesn't recognize, an extra voice that only operates in a world of men, a voice that swells and rages, especially when it's time to play cards and the players use passwords and secret codes: they say *blackjack*, *royal straight*, *aces wild*, *bluff*, *stud poker*, and the words bounce off the four walls of the store. It can't be just a game of cards, Louis thinks, it has to be something grave and mysterious, an exercise for the intelligence, training for military strategy, something along those lines.

The men talk even more loudly when it's about what's wrong with the world, with politics, money and war. These are the conversations Louis prefers.

Only yesterday, all over the continent, there were big brand-new factories packed full of brand-new workers, strong young guys with muscles in their arms and their hearts in the right place. Those men earned salaries, they spent their money, they were happy, they were entitled to dream, and then suddenly, bang, nothing works any more. They're the same factories, the same muscular dreamers, only now they can't work. Louis doesn't know yet if it's the fault of the Jews, of Anglos in general or of the big wheel that goes around and around, but he does know that the Depression may not be inevitable, that it may have causes, understandable causes. And that's something he owes to the men.

It's from listening to the men that Louis learns how to distinguish between the different kinds of Anglos, which is always useful for getting along in society, or even just comprehending what's going on.

First of all there are the English from England, who are like the French from France, but worse. Those Anglos are very fond of money but they fix things so it doesn't show. Next there are the Anglos from the States, who also like money a lot but don't hide it. They're big children who eat badly and drink undrinkable beer; they're superficial and materialistic, but you can't really hold it against them. They're friendly and some of them are Catholic.

Then there are the Irish, who aren't real Anglos because they're poor and Catholic, and you have to watch yourself around them; they drink too much, they're bad drunks and they beat their wives. If there's a Depression it certainly isn't their fault, on that everyone agrees; they're too uncouth to do anything so complicated.

There are also the Scotch, who are the stingiest Anglos of all, besides being alcoholic and Protestant, which is a very bad mixture. A Protestant's like an Indian: he can't hold his liquor.

Finally there are the Jews, who are as stingy as the Scotch but don't drink. And they're the only Anglos who take the trouble to learn French.

"I know some Irish who marry French Canadians," says Étienne, "and twenty years later they can't even say merci. The Jews though, they talk to you in your own language when you go into their stores. They try, anyway: *For you mine friend I'm make a special price*. If you want my opinion, we ought to do like them: when a Jew's successful, other Jews buy at his store to encourage him, instead of shooting him in the foot like French Canadians. If we were Jews, Wellie, you'd have more people in your store. . . ."

"Could be," Wellie replies, "but they're still the ones that control finance, and this Depression started with the stock exchange so you aren't going to tell me that . . ."

And they're off, louder than ever, wondering if you really can put the Jews with the Anglos or if they're a separate race like the Polacks, and then they move on to Stalin, who destroys churches, to airplanes and submarines, to the Grits and the Tories, to bribes and telegraphing votes . . .

Louis is proud to be a man when he hears them talk like that. Men like logic and they use complicated words like *materialist*, *telegraphing* and *double clutch*. They know the chief characteristics of every race on earth, which makes life a lot simpler: since there are billions of human beings on our planet and it's impossible to know them all, it's better to use categories. Thanks to his father, Louis has learned that the Germans are cold and disciplined, that the Poles are always as drunk as Poles, that the Italians are crybabies and scaredy-cats, and that the Russians kiss each other on the mouth. All that could be useful some day, especially if there's a war.

Wars, depressions, money, peoples, races: the men want to understand problems so they develop theories, they search for solutions, they reflect on things. The only problem is that they're used to thinking but not really to talking, so it doesn't take long for their throats to go dry. Besides that, they like eating salty food and smoking cigarettes, which doesn't help matters. So they drink; it's normal. But the more glasses they empty, the less logical they are. Maybe their minds need a holiday. And maybe too they need liquor to fuel some kind of motor inside them. Something insatiable and very profound. Maybe this motor is what makes them men. A big eight-cylinder one that guzzles gas but works hard.

Louis could spend his life listening to them. He always learns something about politics, wars and sports, but above all he learns to think like a man, which is much more important.

As for the women, they always seem to talk a lot faster than they think, if they actually do think. Louis sometimes has to listen to them when he's doing his homework in the kitchen. There are sisters, aunts, sisters-in-law, neighbours and cousins who set each other's hair, knead dough, fold towels and talk, all of them at the same time. Any excuse for chit-chat is good and they only stop to eat chocolates or cake or doughnut holes, saying every time that they shouldn't but . . . maybe just one more, they're so good. They gulp down a mouthful of sugar, eyes rolling in ecstasy, and then they talk some more, they talk all the time, they never stop to wet their whistle, they talk the way bees beat their wings, to cool the hive.

Louis doesn't like women's gab. They natter so fast it makes your head spin and there's never any logic to it; his mother just said that his big sister Margot missed two days of school because she had a visit from Aunt Gertrude. That doesn't make sense: if anyone had come to the house Louis would have known, wouldn't he? And besides, they don't even have an Aunt Gertrude. Who is this aunt who only visits girls and only comes to see them when they're sick? For two days now

Margot's been closed up in her room, never leaving it except to close herself up in the bathroom. And her mother, instead of taking care of her, yells at her for leaving her bandages lying around. What bandages, for that matter?

None of it makes any sense, the women know that, but they go on talking as if nothing were the matter, even adding to it: one fat neighbour says that Aunt Gertrude doesn't visit her any more and it's a big relief, because seven children is quite enough nowadays. He doesn't understand any of this gobbledygook, but the women still send Louis out of the kitchen: go outside and play, these aren't subjects for children.

Louis may be just a child but he already understands how men and women are different. Men like salt, women prefer sugar. Girls shut themselves in their rooms or in the kitchen or the bathroom, which boys aren't allowed to do: they have to go outside and play.

Men and women don't *talk* the same way for the simple reason that they don't think the same way. While the men try to find what causes depressions and wars, while they think and reason, the women wonder why Madame Turcotte doesn't leave the house now that her husband has come back from the lumber camps, and whether it's true that her sister married an Irishman, poor girl, what a terrible thing, honestly, and what's the idea of parading around in white dresses that make her look twice as big, at her age, honestly, and so on and so forth.

Men think far, women think close. Men mull over the big ideas while women are only interested in the details, that's the main difference. Men talk about humanity in general, while women only talk about particular individuals. That's why they chatter so much: individuals are inexhaustible; general ideas are necessarily more limited.

• • •

In the kitchen or at Wellie's, at school or on the street, Louis learns. And I know perfectly well how he feels when he goes to Wellie's; I had the same impression, exactly the same impression, when I saw my father, so discreet and silent at home, come alive the minute he set foot inside his store. I watched, stupefied, as he suddenly began talking loudly, laughing, joking, and I couldn't understand why men seemed to be extinguished as soon as they came home, why they fell silent as soon as they'd set foot inside the house that they'd paid for, and sometimes even built with their own hands.

3

DECLENSIONS

Of all the boys in the family, Louis is without a doubt the one with the most aptitude for the priesthood. He's docile, he respects authority and he's got nothing against either God or the godly. He never needs to be coaxed to go to church, where he loves the gold and stained glass, the incense and hymns and even the reassuring drone of oft-repeated prayers.

He is equally fond of school, and he'd have no trouble pursuing lengthy studies. Mathematics, music theory, French, drawing — nothing puts him off. Serious and diligent, he collects good marks, medals, stars and honours. That's his way of opening jam jars to elicit a smile from the nuns.

In bed at night, he always has his nose in a book. Everything interests him, newspapers or magazines, the lives of the saints or adventure novels by Jules Verne or the Comtesse de Ségur, even if hers are for girls; but what he likes most of all are the novels of Jack London, his favourite author, for which he'd be willing to sin.

According to his big sister Margot, his taste in reading is the logical extension of his shyness: books are for those who're afraid of the real world. Louis shrugs; he likes words, that's all.

You read one word and then the next one, the sentences follow one another and, without really knowing how, there you are in the Yukon behind a dogsled, or in a ship braving a thousand storms at sea; you go up in a balloon to travel around the world and the next day you go down twenty thousand leagues beneath the sea. You open a book and you're excited, even if you never know just where you're going. You do know that you're going somewhere, which is all that matters, and that you're going there with a friend. You use the journey to get to know each other better. Late at night, when everyone's asleep, Louis devours the books he's borrowed from the school library till his eyes smart, and he continues until the book drops from his hands.

But he won't read for very long. Life won't give him enough time.

Nor will he spend much time at school, even though he came close to starting classical college. The teaching brothers, impressed by his skills, have sung his praises to the parish *curé*, who has agreed to enroll him at the Collège de l'Assomption, a boarding school where he has some contacts.

But no sooner is he enrolled than the *curé* changes his mind, and Annette has to explain to Louis why someone, somewhere, has decided without a word to him that he won't be able to become a priest.

Louis is summoned to his parents' bedroom. A mysterious room filled with strange odours, which he never enters without permission.

Annette is sitting on her worn-out bed, sunken in the middle and covered with a chenille spread, and she doesn't dare look her son in the eye. Instead she focuses on the rosaries wound around the bedposts as if to ward off some strange evil.

Louis stays on his feet. He doesn't know where to look either.

Annette picks up a rosary to give her hands something to do and lets everything out at once, without stopping to catch her breath. She says to him: "Now listen to me, my boy, I know that you're good at school and you'd make a good priest, the *curé* thinks so too, but we can't always do what we want in this life, that's something I know very well, you have to think about the family, my boy, you're bright but you're also strong, strong enough to make your way in life come what may, but for your little brother it's not the same, he's so thin you could knock him over just by breathing on him, you look at him sideways and he bursts into tears, he's the feeble type, it's not his fault, of course, it's the Good Lord who made him like that and speaking of the Good Lord, the curé was telling me the other day it might be a better idea if the family sent him to the seminary instead of you, what else could he do in life anyway, I ask you, school's expensive and we can't afford it for everybody, of course if your father was working instead of spending all his time at Wellie's it would be different but what do you want, my boy, we have to accept the trials heaven sends us and if the priests want Édouard we can't stop them, especially when they're the ones that pay, so anyway that's what I had to tell you, it's your little brother who's going to be the priest, he's the one who'll pray for us, and God knows we need prayers."

She takes a deep breath, heaves one last tremulous sigh, then goes back to the kitchen.

It would never occur to her to ask Louis what he thinks about all this. He couldn't object in any case: if the *curés*, his mother and most likely God Himself have decided that's how it will be, what's the good of objecting? And Louis has known for a long time that he doesn't have the right to suffer or even to be annoyed; his mother has an absolute monopoly on unhappiness and she wouldn't let anyone encroach on her territory, especially not her own son.

Louis is disappointed, but he's not angry with Édouard. You can't be angry with your own brother. If you could, you could also be angry with your family, with your parents who've given you life. That would be simply inconceivable. Besides, all things considered, Louis doesn't really see himself as a priest. Giving communion or the last rites, hearing confessions — that would be all right. But saying Mass, writing sermons . . . Talking makes him uncomfortable, but even more tricky is knowing what to say. How do the priests do it, how do they always know what to say in every circumstance?

Louis loved the Good Lord and he loved words. He should have gone to school for a very long time, but all they could offer him was a few years of commercial school. At the time that was a lot, but it didn't stop him from having a lifelong complex around people who had learned a few words of Latin. Including, unfortunately, his own children.

• • •

My father never learned Latin, he didn't go to school for very long, he stopped reading novels very early, but he always loved words, till the very end of his life. The words that made him see wolves, torrents and the gold of the Klondike much better than if he had really seen them.

The old man I knew would settle into his La-Z-Boy at night and read almost all of the newspaper, ending with the crossword puzzle. He'd write *convent* (seven letters down) and he'd hear behind him the rustling of the nuns' robes; words never come by themselves, they arrive with their baggage and their smells, their sounds and their dust and their light.

He would write *school* and he'd see again the sunbeams coming in through the window, bouncing off the inkwells and lighting up the pictures of the Virgin Mary. When that happened he'd say a prayer to the Blessed Virgin, and the next morning we'd find him asleep in the living room with the newspaper on his lap, his pencil lost forever in the innards of his chair.

My father never finished his crossword puzzles, but it wasn't because he lacked the vocabulary. Quite simply, he loved words, and that no doubt explains why he used them so sparingly.

4

The Boards at the Laurier Wharf

In the mid-1930s, the Fillion family is getting along as best it can — a significant improvement compared with the beginning of the Great Depression. Philippe, the second-eldest boy, is working in a cigarette factory, while Margot, the oldest girl, has a job as a secretary. Both give their salaries to their mother in exchange for a hint of a smile, and it's enough to take care of their everyday needs. Léo, the eldest, spends his days at the Maisonneuve market, where he helps farmers unload their produce. Sometimes they give him a few cents, but more often they pay him in kind. When he brings home a bag of potatoes or carrots, he too is entitled to a hint of a maternal smile. Which is something. The other children — Juliette, Louis, Hélène, Édouard and Thérèse — are still at school. As for their father, for a long time now he hasn't brought in anything — maybe a can of something from Wellie's now and then, which earns him only a sarcastic sigh.

But in the fall of 1935, Léo brings home something besides a few vegetables past their prime. In fact, he's heard on the grapevine a valuable piece of news: apparently there are mountains of boards rotting away on the Laurier wharf in the port of Montreal and they're there for the picking. Once the longshoremen have transferred the ships' cargo into trains or trucks, they either throw away the crates that held the merchandise or break them up, Léo's not sure which, but the point is that there are huge piles of boards near the wharves and warehouses that aren't being used for anything, a real waste. . . .

Léo's contribution stops there: he heard the information and he repeats it for the simple pleasure of having something to say. No doubt he never expected that Philippe would practically jump on him: "What? What did you say? Boards? How many? Where? Let's go!" No sooner said than done: he heads straight for the port, with Léo at his heels. An hour later he comes home to give an account of his reconnaissance mission to all the Fillion brothers, who've gathered in the shed for the occasion.

Philippe paces as he speaks, terribly excited:

"There aren't mountains of boards like Léo said, they're more like hills. And of course it's not high-quality wood. They don't make crates out of oak or rosewood. But still, the information was correct and it's worth its weight in gold. Take a look at this. . . ."

This is a rough piece of wood, poorly squared, the kind of board you just have to look at to get slivers, but Philippe is holding it up in front of him as if it were a monstrance, so that the others nearly feel they should kneel. And Philippe speaks while he looks at his board, or rather *through* it, like a saint having a vision:

"Every day, boats arrive in the port. Every day, their cargo is unloaded. Every day, crates are broken up. True, it isn't the best quality wood — but it's free, absolutely free! I'd be very surprised if we couldn't at least use it for firewood. Maybe that would only bring in a few cents, but five cents here and ten cents there, that's how fortunes are made. We'd start our business with one advantage over Henry Ford, who had to pay for his materials and his employees. We'll make a profit from the start! We can't lose! We just have to bend over! This board is gold. Better than gold: this piece of wood is freedom! First expedition, next Sunday at dawn. Meanwhile, not a word. Do you swear?"

"We swear," the three others reply in chorus, spellbound. They'll remember this oath till they die: and that's how, with no contract or legal jargon, no signatures or witnesses, the very first version of Fillion et Frères was founded.

Philippe is the instigator, the visionary, the incontestable and uncontested leader, that goes without saying, as does the fact that all profits will go to the family. Sharing was never discussed and the very idea of a percentage is totally foreign to them.

It's just as natural that Léo should yield to Philippe. It's always been like that. Léo is the oldest, but not by much; he was born in January and Philippe in December of the same year. When it's a matter of standing up, of walking, running or talking, though, Philippe always takes precedence. Léo is a bit slow, shall we say, while Philippe is the best at everything. So he's the leader and no one will ever challenge his title. It's an advantage of big families that you don't try to go against your characters, which seem to have been handed out at the start. Why should Léo try to cut through the waves when others will do it better? He'll position himself in their wake, that's all. As long as the ship is advancing, he's happy, especially because his brothers and sisters will always show him the respect that's due his rank: thirty years later, when the business sees its hours of glory, they'll take every opportunity to drink to the health of Léo, the true founder of Fillion et Frères.

For the time being, Louis and Édouard are content to play the role of younger brothers: they do as they're told and don't ask questions, pleased just to be there with the big boys.

And so the following Sunday at dawn, we see Philippe in the lead, like a conqueror, followed by Léo, who's pushing a wheelbarrow, and finally by Louis, who has never been so proud, so excited to be going with his brothers to some place other than school or church. He's on his way to the Laurier wharf in the port, that mysterious place where only men work, men who've built themselves a world made to measure, with cranes and sheds, boats and railways, a world where nothing is pretty, smooth or easy, a universe where everything is grey, metallic, solid, rough and dangerous; maybe they'll even see some troopships with guns and radar. So Louis goes off to the port with his brothers, his brothers who accept him as one of them, with whom he's associated in a business!

Best of all, Philippe has decided at the last minute that Édouard shouldn't go with them; the future seminarian has to be protected and, besides, he's much too young for this kind of *expedition* (Philippe always finds the words that make you dream). And so Louis will be able to make him green with envy when they come home and describe the troopships and the guns and . . .

"You wait here," says Philippe, who has brought the detachment to a halt in front of a wooden palisade. "You'll keep an eye on the wheelbarrow, that's very important. Without a wheelbarrow the whole business collapses. We need a sentinel; if you notice anything fishy, you whistle, understand?"

"But . . ."

But Philippe has already started to climb the fence, followed soon after by Léo. What's the good of protesting anyway? Philippe knows what he's doing, as usual. How could they jump over a palisade with a wheelbarrow? And if they leave it unattended they'll be robbed, guaranteed. Philippe is the leader and Louis is the youngest. Therefore he has to obey and to conscientiously play his part as sentinel (and isn't that a nice word?).

And so Louis stands there with no idea of what's going on across the fence, he stays there for minutes that feel like hours, imagining his brothers crawling under barbed wire, outsmarting armed guards, maybe even dogs that are trained to kill. He stays there counting the knots in the boards and wondering if he'll be able to whistle if he notices anything fishy.

"Are you there, Louis? Careful, look out!"

He barely has time to move away from the fence before a shower of boards crashes down.

"Stay there, we're going back to get some more!"

Three times boards will fall from the sky like that, and Louis will load them into the wheelbarrow, proud that he's no longer just a sentinel but a worker now, in charge of organizing materials, and even an engineer who must calculate the most efficient way to fit these irregular shapes into a wheelbarrow that's not completely rectangular itself.

"Perfect!" says Philippe when he see his work. "Now hurry up, we have to go!"

The three brothers say nothing on their way home or when they unload the boards in the shed, but they often laugh a strange muffled laugh in which triumph vies with incredulity: it's too easy, there's something wrong. . . .

But nothing is wrong. The expedition is a total success. There they are in the shed, gazing at the boards and wondering what they're going to do with them. At least, that's what Léo and Louis are wondering. Philippe has always known. He has an answer to every question even before it's asked. How is it that big brothers always know everything?

"Okay, we aren't finished," he says, looking at the piles of boards. "Now we tie them up into neat little bundles and you'll go door to door and sell them. Let's say five cents apiece. You'll tell them it's perfect for kindling and you'll see, it'll sell itself. The shed has to be cleared out by next Sunday at the latest. If you manage to sell it before then, we'll organize some nighttime expeditions."

"It'll never work!" replies Louis as soon as he realizes that it will be up to him and no one else to sell the boards. "Why me? Why not Léo? I can't go door to door, I always go red, I'm too embarrassed, you're always telling me that, I'll talk too fast and nobody will want to listen to me, I can put the boards away properly if you want, or saw them so they match or pull out the nails, ask me to do anything, Philippe, just don't ask me to sell them!"

There's nothing like fear to make us come up with a lot of good arguments in a hurry, and Louis would have found plenty more if Philippe hadn't cut in:

"Think for a minute, Louis; you wouldn't want me to leave my job at the factory to be a peddler, would you? And what'll happen when the river freezes, have you thought about that? The family needs my salary too badly to go without it. And Léo's more useful at the market. Anyway I don't think he'd make a good salesman."

"Neither would I! I'm not a salesman, I'm the very opposite of a salesman!"

"I know. And that's exactly why you'll succeed. How old are you now, fourteen? That's perfect! You're big enough but you still don't look altogether like a man. People won't be afraid to open their doors. And then it'll be up to you. The more you blush and stammer, the better it will be: you won't look like a peddler, you'll look like a serious child who sells wood at night to help his family. And I'm telling you it'll work, you'll see. You aren't going to ruin our whole business just because you're scared, are you? You have to measure up, Louis."

It's because I'm the opposite of a salesman that I'll succeed? What Philippe says is ridiculous, but the words have come from his big brother's mouth, so Louis yields. He has no choice. Unless he wants to seem like a coward, of course, admitting that he's afraid, very afraid, terribly afraid of giving three little knocks on a door and saying a few words, while his brothers have climbed over fences and faced up to a thousand dangers. . . . Big brothers know how to organize things so you don't have a choice.

• • •

That night Louis is very frightened when he lugs his boards a few blocks from home, where no one is liable to recognize him. He's completely terrified as he knocks on the first door, and anxiety makes his stomach tighten when that door opens slowly, very slowly and at the same time much too fast. He feels himself go red then, and he's terribly hot, despite the cool autumn wind. So much blood is rushing under the skin of his face that he's afraid there won't be a drop left in his heart. He's so scared that he doesn't dare look the customer in the eye. He holds his little package of wood in front of him and stammers whatever comes into his head.

The only thing the customer hears is "five cents," and she buys. She buys because she's full of compassion, because it's Sunday night and she's feeling generous or because she really does need some kindling to start her fire; it doesn't matter. She buys, that's all that matters for the moment, and Louis's career as a salesman has been launched. A second door opens and a second customer buys. A man in an undershirt, grumpy looking, yet he too takes some coins from his pocket. That's certainly a sign from heaven! In five minutes, Louis has made a profit of ten cents! After that it will get harder — some doors will close, others won't open even though Louis can guess there are people inside — but there'll always be someone to buy just as he's starting to give up hope, so that the total sales of Fillion et Frères will reach eighty-five cents that night. Eighty-five cents! Nearly a dollar!

Eighty-five cents that Philippe, accompanied by his two brothers, will give to their mother right away, spreading the money on the kitchen table with a broad gesture as if he were sowing seeds.

Annette gazes at the money, suspicious:

"This business of yours, is it honest at least?"

No one really dares to answer, but Philippe mutters something with a movement of his head that could in a pinch pass for a yes.

Annette looks thoughtfully at the coins her son has proudly spread on the kitchen table and she seems to hesitate. It strikes her as odd, this story about picking up boards at the port. (After all, fences are put up for a reason, aren't they? And why do her sons go to get them on Sunday morning, on the sly?) The mere thought that something in this world might be free is inconceivable to her, but she needs those few cents so badly that she drops them into the chipped sugar bowl where she puts her small change. She'll pray a little longer tonight, that's all.

"This will pay the milkman."

Louis hears the coins jingle in the sugar bowl and he feels condemned; he'll have to go on selling, again and again. Impossible to stop now that he's responsible for providing milk and butter for the whole family.

There will be many other nickels and pennies, soon transformed into dollars, and after the war into tens of thousands of dollars, when a cash register will replace the sugar bowl. Louis won't have to go from house to house any more, customers will beat a path to the door of his store, but always he'll be afraid when the time comes to talk to them, and always he'll feel the blood rise to his face.

My father was a good salesman. An excellent salesman. Who never stopped hating his work.

5

"The Little Cabin Boy"

Soon Fillion et Frères is suffering from growth problems. By moving at a trot, Philippe, Léo and Louis manage every Sunday to bring home from the Laurier wharf four and sometimes five loads of boards, and they'll spend the afternoon cutting them into even pieces and tying them in neat bundles. The rest of the week, though, Louis is on his own to dispose of the stock. As he has to go farther and farther to find new customers, it's hard for him to manage. He barely takes time to eat, he neglects his homework and comes home late. Much too late. It can't go on.

Philippe would gladly give him a hand but he works at the factory over sixty hours a week, usually on the night shift. Édouard is far too young for such a job and, after all, they aren't going to ask a future priest to withstand the city's many nocturnal temptations.

Which leaves Léo; but Léo is Léo. Oh, he's tried to sell a few bundles, but no sooner does a door open to him than he's forgotten what he's supposed to say. So while Louis can easily bring home over a dollar in just one night, Léo has to work an entire day to bring in no more than twenty cents. It's better than nothing but it's not much, and customers are too few and far between to squander them by trying to sell them the same merchandise twice. It's better for him to go on offering his services to the farmers at the Maisonneuve market during the day, even if it means working as Louis's assistant at night.

Louis is puzzled when Philippe suggests this new division of tasks (at fifteen he's to be his twenty-year-old big brother's boss?), but Philippe must know what he's doing. And, well, Léo is Léo. And Léo, not in the least offended, enthusiastically accepts the proposal; he likes to walk, he loves pushing the wheelbarrow and, since he's taller and heftier than Louis, he'll be able to transport much heavier loads, which will spare them pointless travelling back and forth; what's more, he'll be able to protect his little brother if anyone should attack him; all of this helps out the family, and that makes him happy.

It takes just a few weeks for the new routine to settle in, the roles to be defined and nearly cast in marble.

Philippe is the leader, the instigator, the organizer. No one disputes his authority, and the smallest suggestion from him is taken as gospel.

Léo is the man who can do everything, and he does everything with a smile. Of the four Fillion brothers, he's undeniably the one with the greatest gift for happiness, and that no doubt has a lot to do with the fact that not much is expected of him; his slightest contribution is received like an unexpected gift.

Despite himself, Louis is the salesman who travels the city streets every night, with Léo trailing behind. With pounding heart he rings doorbells, presents his wares, with a stammer and a hangdog look, and thanks his customers politely. He quickly realizes that his attitude is much more important than his sales pitch, and soon, without really being aware of it, he develops his character — the salesmen who's silent and even a little sad. Who could resist Buster Keaton going door to door?

All that still needs to be clarified is the status of Édouard. It's not easy to go into a business partnership with a future priest, especially one who's only twelve years old, and Philippe isn't too sure what to do with him. He doesn't want his little brother to feel rejected, but neither can he ask him to sell, much less work on Sunday. Édouard will be tolerated in the shed, but only on condition that he never works. He can watch his brothers and do the occasional small favour, that's all.

"And what if I play at tying knots? You can't stop me from playing, can you?"

Of course, seen from that angle . . . Philippe goes along with Édouard's proposal, though he adds an important amendment: in his mind you can only play at tying knots for a period of less than one hour. Beyond that, it is indisputably work, the proof being that bosses pay their employees on this basis. Therefore he asks Édouard to stop every fifty minutes and go to church and say a prayer to Saint Joseph. Since Joseph is the patron saint of carpenters, it's safe to assume, with no risk of sacrilege, that he'll also protect those who sell kindling.

Édouard obeys; he runs to kneel at the statue of Saint Joseph, speeds through the rosary and races back to the shed in a cloud of dust to "play" with his brothers.

"Aren't you overdoing it a little?" Philippe asks him. "I know the church is at the corner and I know you're a fast runner, but the whole rosary in ten minutes, really. . . ."

"It takes me a lot less time than that!" replies Édouard proudly. "Listen: *Hail-Mary-full-of-grace-the-Lord-is-with-you* . . ."

Incredulous, Philippe looks at his watch: Édouard says a *Hail Mary* in six seconds, an *Our Father* in seven and a *Glory be to the Father* in four. Only the *I believe in Almighty God* gives him trouble: twenty seconds.

"It's not my fault," he explains. "There's just one per rosary so I don't get much practice. But I'll get better, cross my heart. Listen: *I-believe-in-almighty-God-creator-of-heaven-and-earth-and-in-Jesus-Christ-His-only-son* . . ."

Philippe listens to him, flabbergasted; Édouard goes very fast but he enunciates so clearly that he doesn't skip a word or even a syllable. The prayers are valid then, there's nothing to object to. After all, Philippe can't ask Édouard to recite three whole rosaries. . . .

"That's okay, you can tie knots. But no more than an hour!"

Overcome with gratitude, Édouard goes back to his boards and plays as conscientiously as he can, tying knots.

• • •

Sometimes, to stave off boredom, the Fillion brothers will

strike up “On the Road to Berthier,” “Un Canadien errant” or “The Little Cabin Boy.”

Louis takes the part of baritone, if the word can be applied to a singer who has no particular register and not much talent as a singer but does what he can. Singing in harmony would be beyond his ability, but if he concentrates he can just manage to sing in tune, or almost. And so he’s assigned the principal melody.

Philippe would make a better baritone but he prefers to leave that part to his brother and to sing bass; that strikes him as more virile, more worthy of a leader. He sometimes sings off key but it doesn’t matter; with his chest inflated, shoulders back and chin pushed into his neck, he looks as happy as a village rooster singing “Silent Night” to the pope.

Léo is Léo. Singing off key is as natural to him as breathing and he’s got no sense of rhythm, but that doesn’t stop him from acting as conductor, using a plank as a baton, or from opening his mouth now and then to pretend he’s singing along with the others. No one would hold against him the sounds that sometimes escape him; they never know if they fit into the song and, if so, how. As it seems impossible to sing so badly off key, his brothers tell themselves that it may be something fundamentally new, which defies the laws of harmony.

Too happy just to be there, Édouard doesn’t dare to sing, at least not at first. When he ventures to do so though, they will all prick up their ears; the little brother is a fine soprano who soon allows himself some daring harmonies, sevenths and sometimes even ninths. Listening to him, they feel fortunate, calm, happy. From then on Philippe will stop asking him to go to church and pray every hour, and he'll let him tie as many knots as he wants.

By singing, Édouard has finally managed to dispel Philippe's religious scruples; if God is really sensitive to prayers, he tells himself, these are the ones He should listen to.

There's no doubt that Édouard will never be happier than on the day when he first feels he has acceded to the status of associate. Family businesses have their own logic, which can never be reduced to an organizational chart.

6

The Restless Soul

Those are wonderful Sundays, the Sundays when the Fillion brothers make bundles of boards in the shed. Yes, wonderful Sundays. Especially when the four brothers, touched by grace, sing "The Little Cabin Boy" in perfect harmony. It's been happening sometimes, ever since Léo finally found the octave in which he can venture a few notes. As long as he leaves the refrain to the others, this song suits him perfectly.

The Fillion brothers sing "The Little Cabin Boy" so well on those Sundays that they're silent afterwards, moved, as if they're giving themselves time to store this moment in their memories. There aren't many such moments in a lifetime.

• • •

I'm sure that's what my father thinks about half a century later, when he dozes in his chair, neglecting his crossword puzzle, and he hums to himself the song about the little cabin boy who sang on account of *his restless soul, words that the wind blew far and wide*.

7

UNWRITTEN LAWS

"Stoopid asse owle givit toumi guette awé wanna si deez?"

At least that's what Louis, who doesn't speak a word of English, thinks he's hearing from the mouth of Jimmy, the biggest of the Dorgan brothers.

There are four of them, too. Four Irish guys who live in the same neighbourhood and who also hang around the Laurier wharf on Sunday morning in search of something to bring home to their mother, or maybe simply for something to do. Four Irish guys who've been observing the Fillion brothers' goings-on for some weeks now, and who've quickly realized that, in logistical terms, their venture has one weak link: the wheelbarrow, the magical wheelbarrow that's filled up with wood every Sunday, is watched over by just one skinny little kid of fifteen — and a French Canadian to boot.

"Ouanna si deez?" Jimmy says again, letting Louis smell his leather glove.

"No sir!" replies Louis in his best English, while the second Dorgan brother plunks his big Irish paw on the wheelbarrow.

Louis doesn't know what to do. He has no intention of fighting four Irish guys, but he can't let them get away so easily either. If only he could negotiate or talk to them till his brothers come back; surely Philippe would send them running, Philippe who's not afraid of anything. . . . Should he yell so they'll come and rescue him?

And that's when the blows start raining down on Louis. First on his face and then, when he ends up on the ground, in his ribs. And on his legs and everywhere, and they're coming so thick and fast that he doesn't even know where it hurts the most.

"*Catholique! Catholique!*" he shouts then, remembering what his father said about the Irish. "*Catholique!*" he goes on shouting, hoping it sounds more or less the same in English.

And the blows do stop, as if by miracle, which proves that his father was right when he declared that the Irish are tough fighters but, even so, they aren't savages.

The Dorgans make off with the wheelbarrow while Louis is struggling to his feet. His clothes are torn and dirty, he has a black eye and he's covered with bruises and bumps, but he can move his arms and legs. And nothing's broken, except for his pride.

He's shaking, he's cold, he's scared but he stays there, not moving, because every move hurts. He'd have preferred to be killed and buried there, right away; he wasn't equal to the mission his brothers entrusted to him, he doesn't deserve to go on living.

"Mind your head, Louis!"

He'd like to tell them to stop, that it's not worth it, but he's too busy not crying to be able to talk. He protects himself then as best he can while the boards come raining down.

When he sees his brothers climb over the fence, the floodgates open and his tears, till now held back with difficulty, pour down his cheeks and fall on the ground, where they dig craters in the dust. Never has he been so ashamed.

Philippe doesn't need to have it spelled out. He can see that the wheelbarrow has disappeared and he just has to hear the name Dorgan between two sobs to guess the rest.

To console Louis, he explains that it's his fault and no one else's that this has happened; he was wrong to leave his little brother without protection, but the Irish guys made a much more serious mistake in disobeying an UNWRITTEN LAW.

Maybe Philippe knows that you have to talk to an injured person a lot, to console him or simply take his mind off what's happened. Or maybe it's to keep his own fear at bay that he talks non-stop. Whichever it is, he's transformed into a genuine windbag on the way home, proud to be contributing to his little brother's education by explaining these famous unwritten laws. (At the same time he contributes to the education of Léo, who's following one step behind and doesn't miss a word.)

See, a great many unwritten laws have been transmitted

from man to man for generations, and they're often far more important than all the laws passed in Parliament. For instance, everybody knows that a hockey player who sees his goalie being roughed up has to come to his defence right away, regardless of what it costs him. You must never shove a goalie, not even accidentally, just as you can't shoot the puck at him after the whistle blows, those are good examples of the rules that everybody knows even though they aren't written down anywhere. Same thing in baseball: A pitcher who intentionally hits a batter should expect to get his face smashed in when he leaves the stadium — or even before, if possible. Which brings us to a basic feature of unwritten laws: Anyone who contravenes them must expect to pay the price and, since no judges or lawyers are involved, it's dealt with right away, man to man, without wasting time.

Such laws exist in every sphere of life. You don't hit a man wearing glasses is a well-known example, but there are plenty of others: In a fight, girls can bite and pull hair; men, though, can only use their fists. You don't steal your buddy's girlfriend, to say nothing of your brother's. Having exhausted his repertoire of unwritten laws, after much reflection Philippe adds a final one of his own, which fits the present circumstances perfectly: When somebody's been a bastard to you, you aren't a bastard if you're an even bigger bastard to him, it's just normal.

In the event that his brothers haven't extracted the entire wealth of lessons from this last law, Philippe immediately draws up a corollary: You don't attack Philippe Fillion's brother with impunity, especially four against one and particularly if you're a bunch of dirty Irish sons of bitches. Tonight we'll be ten against four, and we'll see what's what!

• • •

The punitive expedition charged with getting the wheelbarrow back, avenging Louis and establishing solid jurisprudence on the matter of unwritten laws is made up not of ten individuals as Philippe hoped, but of five brave soldiers. The numerical advantage is ensured, then, but not by much. Should they risk it anyway? The enemy is dangerous, undoubtedly he anticipates a counterattack and is waiting for them on his own turf, but Philippe insists on going there this very night. For him it's a question of principle, a matter of honour even. And no doubt, too, he's afraid there would be even fewer combatants the next day, when another unwritten law would apply: When you're fighting the Irish, many are those who throw in the towel.

And so the battalion consists of Philippe and Léo, the two Masson brothers, Roland and Gérald, who never miss a chance to cross swords with Anglos, no matter what variety, and finally Maurice Dagenais, who isn't very strong and whom nobody can stand, only they want to give him a chance to prove himself. Maurice has always boasted that he's never lost a fight, because he has such an advantage over his potential opponents that he's practically unbeatable: his face is covered with so many pimples and pustules that no one would ever dare hit him. This has nothing to do with any law, written or not; he's simply too repulsive for anyone to touch. The strangest thing is that he brags about it, which always amazes Philippe, but in certain circumstances a leader can't be fussy.

Louis offers his services half-heartedly just as the battalion starts out, but Philippe magnanimously turns him down; in a war, you can't expect the wounded to fight. Wait for us in the shed, little brother, this won't take long.

And it doesn't. Half an hour later, the troops — at least what's left of them — are back at the base.

Léo's face is so badly swollen that he has trouble opening his eyes. He was definitely one of the toughest of the group, but apparently he didn't really understand what was expected of him. His only contribution to the fight was to take the blows. He kept several Irish guys busy, at least there was that. According to his testimony, which was often broken off as he spat out blood, the opponents were very numerous, seven or eight at least, and they were definitely waiting for them.

Aside from a few scratches, Philippe's face is nearly untouched, but he walks with difficulty, limping, and he'll have trouble sleeping for several months: it takes ribs a long time to knit. He maintains that there were a good dozen Irish guys who took them by surprise, the cowards, jumping on them before they even got to their street.

It seems that the Masson brothers had beaten up some of them, but abandoned the fight when some Irish guys — whom no one had ever seen around, as it happens, you have to be a real coward to call on strangers — took out their knives. As for Maurice Dagenais, he took to his heels when the hostilities began, thereby preserving his reputation for invincibility. Philippe took care of big Jimmy personally, and he'd have easily laid him out if he himself hadn't been attacked from behind at the same moment.

"But that's not serious," he concluded. "True, we didn't get the wheelbarrow back, but we won't need it now. With winter coming, the river will soon be frozen. No more boats, so no more wood. And then won't the Dorgans look sharp with a useless wheelbarrow! Besides, there are lots better things to do in life than sell firewood. . . . It's true we ate some knuckle sandwiches but that's nothing to be ashamed of. There were ten times as many of them and they know a lot more about fighting than we do. They've got nothing to brag about anyway; they're brought up on smacks in the chops, so they know how to take it; afterwards they practise by beating their wives. . . . The important thing is, we didn't retreat. The important thing is, we wanted to avenge Louis, which we did, and we weren't afraid and that's something to be proud of!"

Louis listens to his brother puff himself up with importance as he finds arguments to transform defeat into victory, and he too is very proud, hugely proud, to have such brothers. What Philippe and Léo have just done for him, he won't be able to pay back as long as he lives.

He doesn't know yet what form it will take, exactly, but he knows there will be other, many other Fillion et Frères, and that their business will always be more than just a company.

• • •

Winter came early, that year, so quickly that some ships were caught in the ice on the river and had to wait till spring to head for the open sea. Tough luck for the Dorgan brothers, who found themselves with a wheelbarrow they had no use for.

Winter came early and it started in the kitchen, when the

Fillion brothers came to ask their mother for bandages and Mercurochrome on the night of their campaign against the Irish guys.

"I knew it wouldn't work. I told you so but you never listen to me. That's what happens when you get involved in crooked business. You should be ashamed of yourselves. When I think that you wanted to drag Édouard into that. . . . The bandages are in the medicine chest. You'll have to figure something out. And who do you think is going to wash your clothes, will you tell me that?"

Then she starts banging things around in the kitchen, and Louis has the very strong impression that she is shifting her pots and pans from one cupboard to another just to make a noise and for no other reason. As if she needs a new punctuation mark, a little stronger than a simple sigh.

8

The Little Mickey

Louis leaves school at sixteen, with a commercial diploma, and he's taken on right away by Monsieur Lunn, a Jewish man who has just opened a furniture store on Ontario Street not far from Wellie's. Lunn doesn't pay a big salary but Louis's expenses aren't very high either, as his boss points out: he doesn't have to buy streetcar tickets, he can go home for lunch, and anyway he's still an apprentice. You're going to learn about business, young fellow, you're going to learn what business really is. . . .

But Lunn doesn't need to justify himself at such length. Louis respects authority. As far as he's concerned, a salary doesn't have to be negotiated: first you go out of your way to deserve it, then you accept it gratefully and that's that. Give me columns of numbers, Monsieur Lunn, and I'll show you what I can do. Adding is what I like best, but I can also file invoices or stuff calendars into envelopes if that needs doing, I can even sweep the floor, wash the windows, empty the ashtrays — anything at all, Monsieur Lunn.

Louis would have liked to be assigned to office work exclusively, but he'll soon be promoted to salesman, to his misfortune. And thanks to Monsieur Lunn he'll learn a lot, but that's not what I want to talk about just now.

What strikes me as more important is that when he starts working, Louis still hasn't resigned himself to leaving school. Words, books, the smell of ink, a pencil sharpened with a penknife — he misses those things and he'd like to go on studying by himself, in the greatest secrecy.

When he comes home from work at night, and on Sunday morning after Mass, he takes refuge in the upper part of the shed, climbing up a wobbly ladder. He clears a path through the cardboard boxes, bottles of lamp oil and cans of paint, then sits on the old mattress folded double that's used as a sofa, takes a look at the orange crate that functions as a table, at the ashtray and the bare lightbulb, and he takes a deep breath and he feels good, he feels terrific — it's hard to imagine what a luxury solitude could be in those days.

Often he'll read a few articles in *The Gazette* to help himself learn English. From now on he wants to understand when someone says "*wanna see deez.*"

Then he picks up a notebook — or more likely a pad, the kind that will go in your pants pocket — and he writes. What? I haven't the faintest idea; though my father sometimes talked to me about his writing, he never made clear just what it was. The only thing I'm sure of is that it wasn't a diary; Philippe, who had good instincts and an appetite for investigation, undoubtedly would have found out. And because he was convinced that his Big Brother's Moral Duty required him to track down anything resembling bad thoughts, bad tendencies or bad company — and if he found any, denounce them to one parent or the other, his mother in other words . . . In a big family you can never trust the oldest sibling, never. If Louis kept a diary it was in a secret language known only to him. Could he have written poems or personal reflections? The beginnings of adventure novels inspired by Jack London? But it doesn't really matter. It's the act that counts. The act of writing, of bending over the paper and withdrawing into yourself the way you do at night when you kneel at the foot of your bed to pray. The act of making your pen glide across the paper to capture moments of silence. And to stop writing now and then, the better to appreciate the rays of sunlight that push through the boards in the spring and work their way through the smallest chinks. Stop writing the better to hear the hum of solitude. Or, now that I think of it, maybe he was composing prayers.

"I knew you'd be here: look at what I've brought."

Composing prayers, yes: prayers to the Good Lord and to the Blessed Virgin, but also to Lucifer when Léo comes to join him, bringing liquor and cigarettes, the Devil's finest inventions. Warmth for the belly and warmth for the heart. Something to heat up his *restless soul.*

Louis can't forbid his brother access to his secret lair; Léo wouldn't understand his need for solitude and he'd suffer from the rejection. Nor can he suggest that he read, much less write; Léo is Léo. And so he puts away his books and notepads, he drinks and smokes with Léo and they talk about this and that. About hockey and baseball, wrestling and boxing, or about the relative merits of streetcars and trolley buses, anything at all, talk for the sake of talking, because it does you good.

Léo often describes his working day in detail, especially now that he has a real job thanks to Philippe, who used his influence to have his brother taken on at the cigarette factory. He has a real job as a sweeper and sweeping is very important in a cigarette factory, imagine if dust-bunnies got into the tobacco that people smoke, they could burn their moustaches, but it's also important for the workers' safety and it's true that he's not as well paid as the others but he doesn't mind, because the other workers have to stay in the same place whereas he can walk around wherever he wants, which means that everybody knows him and even if he doesn't get paid as much as the others he's still got a real job, so real that the boss pays him with a cheque, a real cheque that he has to deposit in the bank — he also receives a carton of cigarettes a week, but that's not a salary, it's a gift from the company — and when he goes to the bank he withdraws nearly all his money to give to his mother but he does keep a little for himself, it's supposed to be for the streetcar but he'd rather walk, and that explains why he's able to buy himself a little mickey and all he wants to do is share it with his brother.

What Léo calls his "little mickey" is forty percent alcohol.

When you want some heat in your belly it's alcohol you need, not perfume.

Pure alcohol that you drink from the bottle, with your brother. And sample slowly, in little sips. It burns, it even hurts a little, but it feels so good, so warm. It makes you talk loud at first, and often you laugh for no reason, but after that you talk less and less because you get so tangled up in the words, and then you don't talk at all, because it gets too complicated. Finally you fall silent and let yourself think in a different way. And it's then, when you've got to a point beyond words, that it becomes interesting. You're drifting, you're reeling, but your way of seeing the world is altered, your thoughts are woven together in a different way and it becomes another sort of prayer. Yes, a sort of prayer: you imagine the Virgin Mary, her bright blue robe that lights up the sea, the stars that come and settle on her shoulders. . . .

"What are you two doing?"

The problem, when you think in a different way, is that the words never come back as quickly as they left. There are just as many as usual, more even, but it's as if they don't turn up in the same order in your head as in your mouth, if you see what I'm trying to say. And then answering a question becomes terribly difficult. . . . What are we two doing? Let's proceed in order: the guy whose voice it is, is Philippe. Philippe, who seems to have pads on his feet, like cats, so we didn't hear him come in. Colonel Philippe, General Philippe, the professor and the priest, the Archangel Gabriel and the captain of the ship, at once father and mother — in a word, big brother — suddenly appears at the top of the ladder. Never has Philippe looked so much like the eldest. He's close by, very close by, yet his voice is far away, as if it's coming from beyond the grave, from another reality. And he points his finger accusingly, repeating his question: What are you two doing?

What are we doing, Léo? We're drinking cigarettes and smoking a mickey on Sunday, there must be at least ten sins all mixed up there together, at least ten, and what will happen next has already been written: the Archangel Philippe is going to go directly to the priest and the priest will denounce them from the pulpit next Sunday. At High Mass, in front of the whole parish. He will ask God to be ruthless with them, and He, furious, will open the trap door under their seat. Gripping their pew, Louis and Léo will try to escape from the flames of hell, but too late: the trap door will close on them and nothing will be left in the church but a terrible smell of sulphur and burning flesh. . . .

Philippe goes back down without saying another word, while Louis and Léo look at each other, absolutely terrified and still silent.

He comes up shortly after with a tin of turpentine which he sets down on the orange crate next to the little mickey. He lights a Sweet Cap and savours it slowly, blowing smoke rings and keeping his eyes on the tin. Then he goes down again and, still oddly silent, comes back up with a glass. He pours himself a finger of turpentine, sniffs it like a connoisseur, as if it were a great wine, and downs it in a gulp. A thin smile lights up his face and his two brothers breathe a little easier; they won't be denounced. But what's come over Philippe, drinking turpentine?

He pours himself another finger and gulps it down like the first, totally impassive, without wincing.

Then he fills his glass to the brim. It's a big glass that holds at least six ounces of liquid, six ounces of *pure turpentine*, that's written on the tin, he fills his glass, sets it down on the orange crate, then looks the glass in the eye, so to speak, as if there were a contest between them to be finished: *It'll be you or me, there's one too many in this town and that one is either a man or a glass of turpentine.*

"Put out your cigarettes, it's dangerous."

Philippe waits for his brothers to comply, then brings the glass to his lips and slowly but surely, sip by sip, drains it without stopping to catch his breath. He swallows, then winces slightly as he sets the glass down on the orange crate. His expression is quickly transformed into a strange grimace, a horrible grimace, that's transformed in turn into a huge guffaw:

"I just wanted to see the look on your faces. Don't worry, it's not turpentine, it's just liquor made from potatoes! I put it in the tin so the old man wouldn't dip into my stock. . . . It packs a punch, this potato liquor. Have a shot, you'll see."

He fills his glass again and the three brothers share it. Léo and Louis are so stunned that they feel simultaneously totally drunk and completely sober. Such clear spells appear sometimes when you've had a lot to drink, and that's precisely the condition Louis and Léo are in as they listen to Philippe talk to them as if he were a brother like the others, and not a big brother. He talks to them about this potato liquor that Wellie makes and sells for next to nothing, he talks to them too about everything he's afraid of — even the women who chase after him — he talks to them as if they were his best friends, and they all feel like bawling when Philippe tells them that he misses Fillion et Frères but they shouldn't worry, their company will soon be reborn from its ashes, he doesn't know how yet but it'll come, he thinks about it day and night, and then those goddamn Irish guys will see what's what. . . .

Philippe falls silent and downs another swig, and this time it makes him wince; then he doesn't say anything more. He too is thinking in a different way. He looks at the orange crate but it seems as if he's not really seeing it. Instead, he's staring at the mysterious point in space that is always in front of us, wherever we are, where visions form.

Louis and Léo don't say anything either. They won't remember a thing the next morning, won't even know if this conversation really took place, but for now they're overcome with admiration for Philippe, who really does know all the ways of being an unforgettable big brother.

Louis will go often to the upper part of the shed after that. But it won't often be to read, much less to write.

• • •

Once upon a time there was a young man who passed through the forest at night and was afraid, terribly afraid, so afraid that he couldn't say so out loud or even shout it. But maybe he could have written it down, who knows?

9

The Jew

Tall and lithe, with square shoulders and the hands of a piano player, Lunn is a good-looking man. Elegant, thirtyish, he's always dressed impeccably in a black suit, grey waistcoat, silver cufflinks and tie-pin and Italian patent leather shoes. His glossy black hair is combed back, and his complexion is so smooth that all you see is his eyes, which are also black but a very soft black, if that's possible, a velvety black, let's say. As a dandy he'd be perfect. But as a furniture salesman, especially in the Hochelaga neighbourhood, he's a little out of place, not to say doubly an outsider.

Louis doesn't know him to have a wife or a girlfriend and he never will know anything about his private life, if he has one. Lunn appears to live just for his business, which seems perfectly normal to Louis: every race has its bachelors, and there's no reason why the Jews should be an exception.

Lunn comes from a wealthy family, that's even more apparent from his manners than from his clothes. He must be on the outs with them, though: Louis has been working in his store for nearly five years but he's never met his boss's parents or his brothers and sisters. They're all alive, however, and they all have something to do with the garment industry. Why did this Lunn choose furniture then and why has he established his business in Hochelaga instead of the west end of town, or even New York or Chicago like so many of his co-religionists? And why do Jews, who are supposed to encourage one another by buying from Jewish stores, never come to this one? Louis will never know; he listens, he observes, but he never asks questions, which is only fitting behaviour with a boss.

And it's by observing Lunn that he learns most of what he'll ever know about selling.

No doubt Lunn has something to prove to his father or his mother or even to his God, but the fact is, he wants to succeed — and fast. When a customer walks into the store, Lunn jumps on him and jabbers away in all the languages he knows, learning a new one on the spot if necessary. It's as if he wants to hypnotize the customer, or rather to stun him. So anxious is he to conclude the transaction that he'll start bringing down his price before the potential buyer even opens his mouth. Then the customer will come up with any pretext to flee, to Lunn's amazement. And should it happen that a customer gets drawn into the bargaining game, he's never satisfied with the discount he gets. No sooner is the table, the lamp or the easy chair in his house than he wonders if he's been taken for a ride. Two minutes later he concludes that he has, goddamn Jews, they're all the same, next time I'll go to Dupuis Frères.

Louis, who often hears this kind of remark, is afraid that his boss is heading for bankruptcy, especially because Lunn seems more and more nervous, which only makes matters worse: he rushes at every customer who has the misfortune to open his door, even at anyone who lingers in front of the window for more than thirty seconds.

As long as he's given enough time, Louis thinks, every human being will manage to convince himself with no outside help. From the businessman's point of view, that law offers a twofold advantage: the customer who has persuaded himself that he ought to buy something will be certain of his choice for much longer and, should it happen that he's disappointed with his purchase, he'll be annoyed with himself, not with the salesman.

Louis is not a man of systems or theories, and he feels this much more than he thinks it. He listens to his feelings, that's all. And to his survival instinct, which yells at him to act — now — if he wants to hold onto his job.

"Let me give it a try, Monsieur Lunn. Next customer that comes in, let me look after him, just to see."

Lunn is wary: this puny gloomy Gus isn't going to show me how to do business, French Canadians don't have it in their blood and nobody will make me believe you can learn selling at school. . . .

"School's got nothing to do with it, Monsieur Lunn. You stock good furniture and your prices are hard to beat. It's just

. . . it's just that the customers don't get time to notice. Maybe people like to bargain in biblical lands, but they don't here."

Okay, let's see what he can do, thinks Lunn. Then nobody can say that I haven't tried everything.

"Go to your office, Monsieur Lunn, and promise you won't come out till I bring you the bill to sign."

Never before has Louis displayed such self-confidence, and he's surprised himself. And he'll never do such a thing again during his entire life as a salesman, which will be a very long one. But today he's absolutely certain that the customer who has just opened the door is going to buy the chesterfield in the window, he could swear to it, he *knows* it. It's a question not of magic or prescience but of stepping outside himself, in a sense; this customer is someone he doesn't know, he's caught only a glimpse of him through the window, but Louis feels as if he's known him forever, as if he knows him better than he knows himself. This will be not a contest between a customer and a salesman, but an inner dialogue.

The customer steps up uncertainly, while Lunn has trouble resisting the temptation to pounce on him. He takes refuge in his office instead, to Louis's great relief.

The customer is a shy type, Louis sensed that from his way of walking as well as from the way he pushed open the door. He feels at ease with this kind of man; he's just as shy himself, if not more so, and since there's no point in going against his nature, he doesn't try to hide it, quite the contrary. The customer senses it, which emboldens him; instead of only looking at the feet of the furniture or, even worse, at the toes of his shoes, he goes directly to the magnificent chesterfield Lunn has put in the window, setting it off with an attractive lamp, a carpet, a standing ashtray and a coffee table with a book lying on it. That's all it takes for the customer to imagine himself sitting on this sofa with his fiancée or surrounded by his children. He's playing horsy with them while they wait for supper, or nonchalantly patting his dog's head as he leafs through his newspaper after a hard day's work. . . . Louis doesn't need to say anything; he can see what the customer is imagining.

The man walks slowly around the sofa, he runs his fingertips over the fabric and ventures to test the springs by pressing one of the cushions as hard as he can, or nearly. It's solid, you can feel it. And it's precisely because you can feel it that Louis doesn't say a word.

He stands there at a respectful distance and looks at the chesterfield through the customer's eyes. A magnificent piece of furniture, true, and Lunn has lit it in such a way that it looks even softer and more solid than it really is. No, that's not it, Louis thinks, the art of display is no more a lie than is the art of makeup: women aren't lying when they wear makeup, they're only showing just how beautiful and desirable they can be. In the same way, Lunn suggests to the customer certain colour combinations and lighting effects that he himself can replicate at home, thereby making the most of his purchase. . . . (Salesmen can convince themselves as well as their customers. You just have to give them enough time.)

No one knows the precise nature of the strange force that causes two human beings to attract or repel one another, but everyone knows that such forces are as obscure as they are irrepressible, and that you can avoid a heap of problems by respecting them. The same is true for relations between people and objects, so much so that it's sometimes hard to say if it's the people who chose the things, or the reverse. There we have a sofa and a customer getting used to one another, seducing one another, choosing one another. Let nature have her way. Talking to the customer while he's checking out the sofa or sitting on it would only break the spell. It's equally pointless to present arguments in favour of buying it; you only have to look at him to know that he'll come up with his own arguments, which will be excellent.

If it's sometimes necessary to reassure him at the opportune moment, you have to tell him exactly what he wants to hear, but no more.

"It's solid," says the man half-heartedly.

"Very solid," Louis replies, spontaneously adopting the same tone but a touch more confident. "The structure is oak. The best there is."

"My wife would like it, I think."

"Who wouldn't? You should bring her in and show her."

"I was thinking of surprising her. . . ."

"A piece of furniture like that is an investment, it's for life. It's worth taking your time. Maybe she'll want to pick the colour? You know how women are. . . ."

"You're right. It has to be to her liking. I'll be back tonight."

"Good idea. Let's say seven o'clock, after supper?"

"Seven, yes, that's perfect. Thank you, Monsieur . . ."

"Fillion. Louis Fillion. . . . See you later."

And Louis shows the customer to the door.

"You're nuts, you're out of your mind!" exclaims Lunn, who

emerges from his office, waving his arms, as soon as the customer has left. "He wanted that chesterfield, you could read it on his face, he wanted it more than *you* would want Mae West if she was standing in front of you! All you had to do was get him to sign, but you let him go!"

"He'll be back, Monsieur Lunn. He'll be back tonight, take my word. At seven o'clock."

"How do you know that?"

"I gave him an appointment. For him an appointment is very important. And he's a man of his word, I know that. Leave it to me, you'll see."

• • •

Lunn and Louis have their eyes glued to the door when at five to seven, the customer arrives with his wife — or rather, behind his wife, a rather imposing woman who doesn't yet seem satisfied with the space she occupies. So that her presence will never be forgotten, she attacks all the senses at once: hearing, by talking as loudly as she can, non-stop; touch, by fingering everything she sees and by brushing up against every man; sight, by dressing in the gaudiest way imaginable — her hat, which is the size of a sombrero, mimics a basket of fruit; smell, by perfuming herself so extravagantly that Lunn would be justified in forcing her to buy the chesterfield after she's sat on it. That just leaves taste, which she isn't able to assault that day. At least, not in the literal sense.

This walking tornado and her little husband buy not just the sofa but also a lamp, an easy chair, a coffee table and a standing ashtray, all as mismatched as possible.

When Louis shows Lunn the bill, his boss is stunned; the customers have bought it all for the ticket price, with no argument or complaint. They haven't asked for the slightest discount, yet they seem happy! He'll never understand these French Canadians, who seem to enjoy buying but are ignorant of the joys of business.

• • •

Louis understands the soul of the French-Canadian customer instinctively. You have to let him come into the store, look at the merchandise, go around the easy chair, sit down, get up to look at it again. Once he's pictured the easy chair in his living room, half the work is done. Now he just needs to be reassured. There's a black stain on the heart of the French Canadian: he feels guilty for buying — or rather, for spending. You have to pick up a rag and get rid of that stain by rubbing gently, very gently.

You're right. It's a good buy. A smart buy. An investment. Everybody's buying them and those who choose another brand regret it. The structure is solid oak. They could have used another wood, after all, you can't see it! But they used oak, the hardest of the hardwoods. So think about the rest! The fabrics are treated with special products, it's as if each fibre has been soaked in varnish. A piece of furniture like that will last a lifetime. The springs are all galvanized steel and they've been checked individually. It's made right here in Victoriaville, by our own people. Now, some would rather buy American furniture, or even European. Instead of paying for something comfortable they pay for shipping. And imagine what happens if a piece breaks. . . . It's a good buy, an intelligent buy. Your children will be so happy. . . . Think it over, take your time and come back and see us with your wife. . . .

Above all, never talk about the price. The customer wants a dream, security or, in a pinch, a solid, comfortable easy chair, not a price. When you buy a car, Monsieur Lunn, you dream about travelling down country roads with a beautiful blonde at your side, not about gassing up, much less fixing a flat! Customers want a chair to relax in, not to pay for! The price is always the lowest possible, that goes without saying, and you mention it only half-heartedly, at the last moment, as you're writing up the bill.

Lunn doesn't understand these remarks, they mean nothing to him, but he accepts the obvious: it works, and it continues to work, day after day, week after week, month after month. He'll do the accounting, then, and the decoration of the store, even if it means satisfying his passion for bargaining with his suppliers, and he'll leave customer relations to Louis. To do otherwise would be suicidal, not to say criminal, and it's criminal to run a business badly if it can turn a profit, no matter how small. At least he can congratulate himself for being perceptive enough to hire this guy; he looks so thin and sad you feel sorry for him, but what a salesman! He doesn't just sell, he sells at top price and the customers come back. . . . What more could you ask?

• • •

Louis is pleased with the turn of events, but only in a sense. He's happy for Lunn and for his store, he's relieved at having saved his own job and he's even fairly satisfied that his skills as a salesman have been recognized. He'd have preferred it if the Good Lord had given him another talent — any other talent, actually — but at least He gave him one string for his bow, and a solid one. You can't chide Him for that.

And so he goes on selling, though he never really enjoys it; for him, making a sale has never been the equivalent of scoring a goal or hitting a home run. Business isn't a sport, it's work. You do your best at it because it's your duty, or your destiny. Louis adapts, he reasons with himself, he accepts. And he soon discovers something else to worry about: now Lunn depends on him.

10

Fillion et Frères, Take Two

"There we go, I've got it," says Philippe as he drops an Eaton's catalogue onto the kitchen table. "What we're going to do is *that!*"

Louis and Léo approach and all three fix their gaze on the catalogue, which is open to the furniture for babies.

That is two high-chairs. The first, more economical model is available for two dollars and forty-five cents.

"Two bucks and a half! For that money we can get enough wood for twenty chairs! And they'll be a hell of a lot better quality than their luxury model. Look at that! Four dollars and twenty-five cents! Four bucks and a quarter for a wooden chair! When you think there are people willing to go to the west end of town and get waited on in English to be robbed of four bucks and a quarter! Don't you think we could do better? We need wood, tools, varnish and that's all. The rest is work, and work is something we know."

They're so fascinated by the catalogue that even their father, who never shows interest in anything, finally gets out of his rocking chair:

"Can I take a look?"

Their mother is dying to stick her nose in as well but she restrains herself, preferring to heave a long sigh that could no doubt be translated as: *It'll never work, this business of yours, any more than the others, it's childish, it doesn't make the least bit of sense, honestly, you ought to be content with what you've got, that's what I do and do you hear me complaining? No, you most certainly do not!*

But since they're still bending over the catalogue and nobody's listening to her, she shrugs and goes back to the sink, where she washes the cutlery with as much noise as possible till her daughters finally understand that it's time to help with the dishes.

Annette's not altogether wrong to have doubts about her Philippe. She knows his speeches, his long pompous sentences, his comparisons that you can't make head or tail of. *Burning wood is a waste, that's what savages do. The more you transform it, the more you can sell it for. We're going to be like the Americans!* Sure, Philippe, sure! And what did the Americans do to get rich? Did they coop themselves up in the shed and get liquored up on gin?

Oh, Annette's right in a way. This isn't the first time her Philippe has come into the kitchen like this, waving his arms, with his plans and his calculations and his Eaton's catalogue. First there was that business with the breadboards. To hear him, they only needed the whole family to get involved and they'd soon have been millionaires; they'd have bought land so they could cut their own wood, then they'd have built factories and paper mills and the world would have been their oyster. After Philippe had made enough speeches, he shut himself inside the shed with Louis and Léo. A dozen breadboards, a shot of gin. Six breadboards, two shots of rye. Another board, three shots of cognac. Then they sing, as many false notes as they can, and they forget about the breadboards, in any case they don't sell but, what the hell, we'll try something else.

Six months later he began again, this time with magazine racks. After that came little stepladders so women could store their pots and pans on the top shelves, then doll houses for little girls, folding card tables and I don't know what else. One magazine rack, a shot of gin. One stepladder so the women can store their pots and pans on the top shelves, two shots of rye. One folding card table and why don't we try it out, just to see? Go find a deck of cards, Léo; I'll get some potato liquor from Wellie. . . .

That's what men are like. Children. Can't stop making crazy plans. Except to take a drink, of course. And there too they don't know when to stop. I suppose it's in their blood. That's what happens when you let yourself have children with a ne'er-do-well.

"But that's all right, Mama. True, it doesn't always work out the way we'd like, and no, we haven't become millionaires as fast as we thought, but we still sold a bunch of breadboards and some stepladders too, and it gave us something to do, it didn't cost anybody anything, and we aren't like those Irish thieves, we pay for our boards and use our profits to buy tools, anyway all three of us are working, we give you our whole pay, so what's the problem, why are you always complaining?"

"First of all, that's not true, I never complain. You ought to be ashamed of yourself, talking to your mother like that. And then, you buy your tools but mostly what you buy comes in bottles. And start wiping your feet before you tell me what to do, my boy; every time you come in from the shed your shoes are covered with sawdust. Obviously you aren't the one who cleans up!"

And while Philippe looks at his shoes, she turns her back. She always wins. It's hopeless, is what it is. But one of these days. . . .

The day arrives when the Fillion brothers start making high-chairs. All the planets, all the stars, all the heavenly bodies are in alignment, so this time it's bound to work. First of all, there's war in the air and prosperity is back and the Vickers plant is hiring to capacity. People have the wherewithal to buy furniture and the Fillion brothers have become skilful by dint of producing breadboards, stepladders for the top shelves and card tables. Their high-chairs are not only practical and economical, they're ten times as attractive as the ones at Eaton's. At a unit price of two dollars they're a genuine bargain, too, especially since customers are offered a wide range of colours, and free delivery.

Add to that the fact that Lunn's business is flourishing now, and the owner can't refuse a thing to his chief salesman, who saved him from bankruptcy. There's always a high-chair in his window, and he agrees to take a mere twenty-cent profit.

Even Léo has found his place; he's still a little slow, of course, as he is in everything, but he has an undeniable talent for applying varnish and also for making deliveries, provided you write the address on a scrap of paper and draw him a little map. As the price is always two dollars even, it's not too hard for him to make change.

Business is going so well that Étienne has finally extricated himself from his rocking chair to give his boys a hand. His fingers are rusty, of course, but he soon gets his reflexes back. Nobody has to teach him how to use a trying plane or a router. There's a smell of sawdust and varnish and turpentine again, and Étienne's happy.

All day Sunday, and often on weeknights too, the men work. Oh, they'll toss back a few slugs of gin when their workday is over, but generally they hardly have time to drink. Even Annette has to admit, they rarely sing off key now.

It goes on that way through 1938 and into 1939, so that Philippe quits his job at the cigarette factory to devote himself full-time to making high-chairs, then embarks on dressers and cribs for babies. Léo too leaves his job, and Lunn has to give Louis a raise every month for fear that he'll be tempted to leave.

In the summer of 1939, the Fillion brothers start making lawn furniture modelled on the famous Adirondack chairs. Soon, it's absolute madness: they barely have time to take them out in the lane to let the paint dry before they're sold, still for the standard price of two dollars, which has practically become their trademark. The chairs take more wood than high-chairs do, but they're much easier to build.

Philippe seems possessed; he works like a maniac, sweeping his family along in his wake, and there's no end to his plans: he'll develop a slightly smaller Adirondack chair with rockers, because men are working again and they're entitled to some rest even if they live on the second floor and have smaller balconies, and they'll need a footstool on rockers too, otherwise it's uncomfortable, and with the wood that's left they should start making stepladders for the top shelves again, and they're going to buy a truck with FILLION ET FRÈRES in big white letters on a blue background, and there's no more room here, we'll build a warehouse and we're also going to hire the Fillion sisters, maybe even some Fillion cousins, and all the members of our race who can put their hearts in their work, and we'll export our chairs to Boston and New York and — why not — to Florida. . . .

In 1940, Fillion et Frères is doing so well that even Annette can't deny it. She won't go so far as to make coffee for her men; she has her pride. But she doesn't scold them quite as much when they come inside covered with sawdust, and she holds herself very erect when she comes out of Mass, and she lingers a little longer on the church steps. When she's absolutely certain that none of her children can hear her, she tells Madame Turcotte's sister — the one who married an Irishman and who's always parading around in white dresses that make her look twice as fat, at her age, honestly — that she's very proud of her boys, really very proud, she's always been sure they'd succeed and just imagine, soon they'll be buying a truck. . . .

The second version of Fillion et Frères had got off to such a good start that nothing could stop it. Except Hitler, of course. Why couldn't he mind his own business?

11

WARS ARE COMPLICATED

"There's a lunatic on the other side of the ocean. A lunatic called Hitler. His armies have invaded Austria, Poland and even France. He bombs England day and night, he burns schools and hospitals, he kills women and children and are we supposed to stand idly by, are we supposed to let him have his way and tell him, congratulations, Mr. Hitler, keep up the good work? And come across the ocean, while you're at it! We'll welcome you with open arms, Mr. Hitler! Come on, guys, we can't just let him do as he wants, we have to fight! Now, it's true the French abandoned us, but that's no reason for us to be bigger cowards than they are! We'll show them they were wrong, we'll prove that our few acres of snow may be cold, but that makes for men who are tough. And so what if we fight under the English flag? Let's deal with the Germans first; we'll see about the English afterwards. If we don't have the courage to fight Hitler, we won't be any braver when the war is over. If some people would rather hide out in the woods or mutilate themselves or even get married, that's their business. I, Philippe Fillion, will go and fight, and I'll fight till the bitter end, and I'll even sign up with the Irish army if I have to!"

He knows how to come up with good arguments. And there's so much fire in his eyes that nobody can resist him. The Canadian army records confirm it: of all the boys on his street who were the age to go and fight, not one ducked out. Not a one. And this isn't the Anglo West Island, this is Hochelaga!

Philippe is so sold on the rightness of his cause that he waits at the factory gates to argue with the workers, and he hounds them all the way to the taverns to convince them. He neglects his other duties, including making Adirondack chairs; there's a war on, guys, this is no time to be sitting down! Put him across from any normal man, even the most mule-headed conscientious objector, and he'll make him change his mind in less than an hour. In front of his mother, however, his arguments fall flat. Philippe stammers and stares sheepishly at his toes.

"You aren't going to fight in the old countries, it's out of the question! It's their war, let them sort things out. Enough of your nonsense! And what about me? It makes me sick when you say things like that! My back is giving me so much trouble, my boy, you can't imagine. . . ."

"But Mama, Hitler . . ."

"Hitler is no skin off my nose, as long as he stays in Germany."

"But that's just it, he *isn't* staying in Germany. . . ."

"I'm not talking about him now. I'm talking about what's going to happen to me. I'm talking about your family. What will you do about your family? Your father? Your brothers? If you only knew how you're making me suffer, my boy. . . ."

The country is at war and she's complaining about a backache. Talk about Hitler and she replies family. She chooses the battlefield, always. There's a reason why she wins every time.

And it gets frustrating, Philippe thinks as he stares at his toes. Give her your whole salary and she sighs. Work day and night to establish a business and she complains about sawdust. You could give her the Holy Grail and she'd sneer at it: *What am I supposed to do with this bowl, there's no room in my cupboards.* . . . And if I brought you Hitler's head on a silver platter, Mother, what would you say? Maybe that would impress you. Would you maybe stop complaining for an hour or two?

Philippe never got an answer to the questions he never dared ask his mother. He left the house on November 12, 1942, and he never came home.

Six months later, in the spring of 1943, Louis followed him. He'd have liked to sign up at the same time as his brother and enlist in the same battalion, but Annette had managed to talk him out of that; if you're both going, at least don't go on the same boat.

"Go ahead, if it's so important to you. Leave me all alone with a good-for-nothing husband and a bunch of girls. Go on, what am I supposed to do? Go and fight and leave me all alone with my suffering, you always do what you want anyway."

"But there's Édouard, Mama . . ."

"It takes more than prayers to run a household, my boy."

"And Léo's going to stay with you. . . ."

"And where does that get me? He's not a bad boy, I don't mean that, but Léo is Léo; he'll never set the world on fire!"

And Léo, who hasn't missed a word of this conversation, still asks himself fifty-five years later why his mother was unhappy because he'd never be an arsonist.

Above all, he asks himself why the army didn't want him. He wished he could enlist too, God knows, but it seemed as if the generals invented a new aptitude test every day, for the fun of watching him flunk it. And still he went back to the recruiting office, and still he failed, and still he couldn't get over it.

"It's true I don't think fast, but give me orders that aren't too complicated and I'll follow them as well as the next guy! How does knowing how to read help you launch grenades, will you tell me? And if you think that throwing grenades is too complicated, I can always dig holes, in a war you always need holes and somebody has to dig them and you don't need Greek and Latin to do it! Why go chasing after people that don't want to fight when you won't hire people that do? I want to go, I want to do whatever I can for my country, I want to be useful. . . . Why are wars so complicated?"

A lot of tears were shed in the Fillion family when Philippe and Louis left. But no one was more deeply unhappy than Léo.

12

Shoe-Polishing Cannons

The officer who fills out all the forms at the recruiting centre decrees that Louis has a good knowledge of English and consequently he'll go into the navy. Had he been asked if he knew how to swim, Louis would have understood, but English? Do people who speak that language float better than others? Louis never knew; a signature, two stamps and bang, the die is cast. He's shipped off to Halifax, where he undergoes two weeks of intensive training (port means *bâbord*, starboard means *tribord*, the bow is *en avant*, the stern *en arrière*, now do *cinquante* push-ups), then they set sail on something that floats and that might resemble a destroyer if it were equipped with cannons or torpedo launchers — in short if it could destroy anything — and Louis is on his way to the old countries.

No sooner has he stepped onto the ship than the captain rounds up his men on the deck and explains to them the facts of life: the ships are built in Canada but they won't be armed until they get to England — it has something to do with contracts, the Department of War, Industry and Strategy, in short something complicated, anyway someone somewhere decided that it was better to export unarmed ships than to import cannons — no doubt it's much less risky for the cannons. Once the ship has been outfitted with English cannons, it will come back to Halifax to escort other unarmed ships, and so on till we win the war. It's the first voyage, then, that will be the most dangerous; if we meet a submarine, all we'll be able to do, men, is pray very hard.

And so the sailors understand, while the ship is quietly leaving port, why their training has been so brief: they're being asked to be not soldiers but make-believe soldiers on a make-believe warship. They've been taken on as extras. And the first duty of these extras is to build their own set:

"There are liable to be Germans in the sky and others underwater," the captain goes on. "We can't give them the spectacle of an unarmed ship. We've got a hold full of lumber and I want you to turn that lumber into guns, torpedoes, radar — anything along those lines. We'll be putting in in Newfoundland tomorrow night. By the time we get there I want a warship. On the double!"

During part of the war, then, Louis was sawing boards, planing, nailing and painting, exactly as he'd have been doing at Fillion et Frères. The only difference was that he was now building not chairs but stage sets. And that he felt lonely and bereft on this hostile sea, especially when the soldiers sang songs he didn't know.

• • •

The ship that sailed from Newfoundland looked like a genuine destroyer covered with a nearly incredible quantity of cannons, turrets and torpedoes. The extras had created a magnificent warship from scratch, much more terrifying than a real one, except for one detail: the top brass hadn't foreseen that the salt air would be as abrasive as sandpaper and that it would strip the paint off a cannon in less than two days. While the wooden cannons could still create an illusion at night, by day they looked like what they were: wooden cannons. The captain got the brilliant idea of using shoe polish. That's right, shoe polish. Black, needless to say.

"You want to know what I did in the war?" asked my father when he was at that point in the story. "I shoe-polished cannons. Every morning we were assigned to polish the cannons. And let me tell you, it takes a long time to polish one."

"Is that all? You didn't kill any Germans?"

"I didn't even see one. Mornings I spent with my cannons. After that I was on duty on deck. I'd look at the sea for hours, watching for periscopes or bubbles or wake, anything that would indicate the presence of a submarine. We didn't even have radar! I imagine that if we'd seen a submarine we'd have had to fire a rifle at it. . . . It was so cold we felt as if we were breathing icicles. But we had to stay on deck, watching the sea in case it blew any bubbles. . . ."

"And you never saw a submarine?"

"No. Never saw any torpedoes either. It was a mine that sank us. We were near the English coast, luckily, so we had hardly any casualties. I woke up in the hospital, I spent two weeks there; then I came home, they gave me a medal because of my wound and life went on. All I saw of England was a hospital. Now let's be quiet; the third period's about to start."

But my father never watched the third period; he always fell asleep long before the end of the game. Except during the Stanley Cup playoffs, of course. Or when I was bombarding him with questions, at the age when I'd have so loved to have a hero for a father. Then he'd hide behind his newspaper and try to change the subject, as if participating in the war was no more worth talking about than taking the bus to the dentist. His account was shorter every time, even absurdly so, and it always concluded in the same way:

"What did I do in the war? I shoe-polished cannons, that's what I did."

It was a long time before I understood that his behaviour wasn't intended to denigrate himself, much less to keep the spotlight on the role played by Philippe, the family's only real hero. Rather, he was afraid of the silence that would follow when he was absent-mindedly watching the contest between the Canadiens and the Maple Leafs, or pretending to be asleep while he was thinking about what came next: when he returned to Canada, his father would be dead, his big brother missing. He would have all the responsibilities of the head of a family without ever having the title. It would be a heavy burden for shoulders that weren't all that broad.

• • •

"It was at night, off the Newfoundland coast, I was watching the sea. . . ."

He took us by surprise that evening when he brought up the war. For no particular reason, just like that, spontaneously, without our asking — we hadn't asked him anything for a long time, in fact.

We're at Uncle Léo's cottage, around a campfire. I'm sixteen or seventeen, an age when I no longer need my father to be a hero, when on the contrary I go to great lengths to see only his flaws. Among others, that of babbling on and on till I stop listening to him. But a summer night, a campfire, some cold beer and cigarettes — that will soften the most intolerant teenager and leave him open to something besides himself.

"It was at night, off the Newfoundland coast. Our third night out, I think. There was a full moon. I was looking at the sea, which was perfectly calm. That's very rare, apparently. I mean for it to be *perfectly* calm: not a wave, not a wrinkle, nothing. Smooth as a skating rink. A broad grey surface lit by moonlight. You'd have thought the sea was made of steel, like our ship. A big steel plate as far as the eye could see. There were three or four of us watching this sight, and it was so unusual that we didn't say a word. Most of the time all we could do was be afraid. But that night it was so beautiful that we forgot to be afraid."

My father falls silent, takes a sip of the beer Uncle Léo's just brought him, picks up a brand to light his cigarette, takes a puff, then another. . . . We're hanging on his lips, we're waiting for some spectacular revelation, the appearance of a submarine or a sea monster, anything at all, you can't leave a story in the lurch like that. . . .

"And then what happened?" a cousin ventures to ask.

"Nothing," replies my father, amazed at the question. "Not a thing. It was so beautiful that I wasn't even afraid, that's all. Even though I never understood why poets are so fascinated by the sea. Me, I never liked it: it's cold, it's grey, it doesn't smell good and you never know what's going to come out of it."

We changed the subject then, but I've always felt a strange uneasiness when I think back to that episode of the campfire. The kind of uneasiness you experience when — to go along with the group, to seem intelligent or just to simplify your life — you pretend you've understood.

13

The Old Man

Étienne deserved to die in bed, taken by surprise in his sleep, but he died on the street, coming out of a tavern. Léo was assigned to pick him up and bring him home for the last time while Édouard took care of the formalities.

Annette felt sorry for herself for a few weeks: what will become of me now, he was so young, does it make any sense leaving me all alone at my age, he was so this, he was so that, he was such a good husband. . . . And then she must have told herself that there are limits to indecency, and she suddenly stopped talking about him. After that she went on as if he'd never existed, which in fact wasn't far from the truth.

Louis and Édouard never talked about their father either, except on rare occasions, particularly when their opinions differed. I sometimes caught a snatch of these remarks around a campfire at Léo's cottage, or on Friday nights when they hung around the store on the pretext of doing the books — like all the Fillion children, I had a guaranteed summer job in the delivery department of the family store.

Their father had been born old. He'd always had rough, wrinkled skin, a stoop, a drooping head, and his gait had always been slow, uncertain, apprehensive. He couldn't ever have been young, he couldn't ever have been pliant. Moreover, he'd never had a first name: he was just father, the old man.

The old man was rather small, even by the standards of the time, but no one would have dared to attack him. Even the toughest, the most forthright were afraid of him. He was the kind of brawny man who knew instinctively how to handle broken bottles and longshoremen's hooks in a fight. The kind of man who wouldn't stand by and let things happen, who'd struggle like a bass on a hook. The kind of man who smelled of tobacco, alcohol, sweat and damp wool, who would have liked to work twenty hours a day, who would have spent his life taking the lids off jam jars if he'd been asked, and after all it wasn't his fault if a bunch of nervous nellies in New York had decided one day that they no longer needed him.

He was old, stooped, stiff and silent, but he liked to sing "The Little Cabin Boy" with his sons and often he was too moved to finish the song.

He liked to give his blessing on New Year's Day. He was very proud then, very dignified, and every time he knew how to concoct in a few words, new remarks for you, and they always rang true.

He liked cats, autumn days, rainbows, the smell of wood, and he couldn't stay in one place when the Canadiens brought the Stanley Cup home from Detroit or better yet, from Toronto.

He liked talking politics with the men at Wellie's. He knew everything there was to know about telegraphing votes or graveyards voting, about wars and depressions, about Grits and Tories, and he knew just what he needed to know about the peoples of the earth — he who'd never travelled outside his province.

He left his sons not silver or blazons or coats of arms, but some very good tools in the shed and some judicious advice on how to use them. And a tremendous silence, a tremendous and very hard silence made of tempered steel, an armoured silence that is resistant to time. A silence so immense they could take shelter in it.

And that's all I know about this grandfather I never met. I heard it all from my father or from Uncle Édouard. While Léo never said anything, he'd nod his head every time, as if to confirm it.

Only once did I hear him put in his two cents' worth. Once again it was around a campfire, at his cottage, one Saint-Jean-Baptiste Day that hadn't been baptized with water. . . . My father talked about Étienne, then there was a long silence and after that the conversation took a metaphysical turn. That happened sometimes when the summer sky was filled with stars.

Louis had explained to Léo that, according to Hindu beliefs, our soul doesn't go directly to heaven after death but lives on in the skin of a cat, a dog, a bird, or even inside the carapace of an insect, and that this is called reincarnation. Léo had thought this notion of a travelling soul was very funny: they're wrong, that's for sure, those pagans sure have some weird ideas. . . . According to other beliefs, my father had gone on — he didn't know in what country exactly, but it didn't matter — not only does the soul live inside the body, it sometimes overflows it and that's the explanation for the saints' haloes: their souls are so big that they protrude a little, like the ghost images you see on television. Léo liked that idea, which was more compatible with Christian thinking, but he preferred to stick to what he'd always believed — namely, that the soul is quite small, that it's close to the heart, that it's light and transparent and that it's expelled by the lungs along with a person's last breath.

My father had gone on, saying that Jews, Christians, Muslims, Hindus, Indians — in short, everybody — agreed that there is a soul in each of our bodies, and in fact that's what is so strange: why should each of us have his own personal soul? A soul for each one of us. It's like the elections: one man, one vote. And what if a number of us shared the same soul? There would still be some unique souls, of course, because after all some people are exceptional, but what about the others? I say that because when Papa died, I felt that he wasn't the only one to die. It was as if . . . as if he'd been the last of the Mohicans. See what I mean, Léo? As if he'd been the last inhabitant of a soul that had been used a lot, that had travelled a lot. . . . I didn't see his soul depart, of course, I was still in England, but that's how I imagined it: a soul that was rough, tough, upright, the last representative of a race of souls. . . . See what I mean, Léo?

Léo didn't answer, but he looked annoyed. Instead of replying, he gulped some beer and drew nervously on his cigarette, he who was usually so calm. Maybe it was a little hard for him to follow, maybe he was shocked by these sacrilegious ideas, but maybe too he was thinking. . . .

"There's another possibility," he finally said much later, when everyone was looking at the stars.

"Another possibility about what, Léo?"

"About the soul. Why couldn't we have more than one soul? Something like dandelion seeds that take off one by one as we get older. And when there was nothing left but the heart, it would mean we were ready to go. What do you think about that, Louis?"

"Could be, I guess. . . ."

And then the men said nothing more. They merely smiled, very gently, as they looked at the fire. Maybe they went on thinking about their father's soul, and maybe too about the soul of Philippe, who had disappeared in the sky over Germany. Those are things that happen when people think differently: you can go back in time and fly in a plane that disappeared long ago — or you can imagine that the soul has a heart.

14

The Three Wise Men

While Louis is looking at the sea, Philippe is peering at the sky from a glass turret fastened to the end of a bomber; he's a tail gunner. Of all the positions a gunner can be assigned, it's the most dangerous. Philippe is all alone in his glass bubble suspended in the sky, with no steel to protect him, and since the radio is broken down half the time, he knows nothing of what's going on up front. If the Messerschmitts attack head-on, he'll be dead before he knows what's happened; and if they arrive from the rear, he'll be the only one to see them — and most likely the first to be killed. His companions wouldn't realize it until they were back at the base — assuming they could get there without him.

Their mission is to fly over German cities, to relieve the bay of several tons of bombs and return to the base as safe and sound as possible. The next day they'll start again, and the day after that, for as long as it takes to bring Hitler to his knees — or till they've completed their thirtieth mission, thereby earning the right to go home.

Philippe is alone in his turret and he's often even more alone at night, in the dormitory where everybody speaks English. But he doesn't feel isolated; he writes. Every week, it's sacred, he sends letters to his family, never forgetting one of his brothers or sisters. They read and reread the letters till they've learned them by heart, then they repeat them in all the factories, offices and schools in Hochelaga and even in the Collège de l'Assomption. Never has a serial been followed more attentively, despite the irregular deliveries, and never has Philippe had a praise-singer more zealous than his mother, who opens all his letters no matter whom they're addressed to; he's her son, after all, she's entitled to know what's happening to him, and you just try stopping me.

She reads the letters aloud first, to get the words into her mouth, then she phones the whole family, even her in-laws, so everyone will know how big a hero her son, her own son, is. When the family phone book is exhausted she rushes off to church on the pretext of going to pray, where she informs the entire parish about her son, her own son, who is bravely fighting the Germans over there on the other side of the ocean.

Philippe knows nothing about any of this — he'd no doubt have been the most surprised of them all — but he continues to write every week, talking about whatever comes into his head, in order or disorder, as if nothing on earth were more important than writing page after page.

He says that he's got used to the idea of death, that it doesn't bother him, that he doesn't even think of it now when he settles in behind his Browning machine-gun. All he wants to do is shoot down Messerschmitts and drop bombs onto Nazi heads. He knows that his plane bombs cities, he knows that very likely some civilians die under the clouds of smoke, but the Nazis started the war, so that's tough. When somebody's been a bastard to you, you aren't being a bastard if you're an even bigger bastard to them, it's just normal.

He writes that what he fears most when he's inside his turret is being caught in the cross-beam of the German searchlights. They're everywhere on the coasts of France. If two beams intersect on your plane you've had it. The Germans know how to take aim. They're a people who like precision. But if the Germans are precise, the Allies have good reflexes: the pilot has to go into a dive as fast as possible, so fast that the entire crew gets nosebleeds and burst eardrums, but it's the only way. At least you're alive, you'll get a few days' rest in the hospital and then you can start bombing again.

Even worse than the searchlights are the storms: you don't know if the rumbling all around you is caused by shells or thunder, and you soon find yourself bombarded by so many flashes that you'd like to unload your machine-guns on the clouds. It's enough to drive a man crazy. The worst, says Philippe, is being afraid for no reason.

When he feels the bays opening to drop the bombs, he says that he too feels delivered, like a woman who's just given birth. Even the plane seems free, nearly happy; suddenly lighter, it seems to be bouncing in the sky.

Men give up hope sometimes, Philippe writes, and they go so far as to doubt the existence of God. Nothing makes sense any more. Nothing but dropping bombs onto Germany till nothing's left of it but a big hole. And surviving. Surviving till the thirtieth mission so you can finally go home. And then. . . . And then they can't even imagine what will happen; nothing can be as it was before. It's better to think about what's happening now, or to polish your boots twelve times in a row, if that keeps you from thinking. Or to write page after page.

To write that the luck of the draw in this war has given him an Irish guy as navigator. He knew it when the man opened his wallet to buy him a beer. Among the shillings and the pounds sterling, Philippe spotted an image of the Blessed Virgin. The Irish guy hid it at once, blushing, but Philippe showed him the rosary he always carried in his pocket and they bought each other a few rounds that night. He may be Irish, says Philippe, but he's a heck of a good guy and I'm proud to be fighting at his side, especially because I've discovered another important difference between the Irish and the English: the Irish can sing — and you know, they're pretty damn good.

He also says that he thinks about all sorts of things when he's alone in his turret, at the other end of his Lancaster, lost in the German night. He thinks about the lawn chairs and about all the houses that will have to be rebuilt after the war, and he tells himself this will make work for all the Fillion brothers on earth; he even imagines plans for easily built houses to fill the most urgent needs, and sends sketches so his brothers can get used to the idea: why shouldn't we build houses, after we've built furniture? He says that he thinks about his father and mother, about his brothers and sisters, he asks how everything's going at home, if they've heard from Louis, if he's killed any Germans. He also thinks about Jesus and the Virgin Mary, he believes that as long as he's got a rosary on him, nothing can go wrong, and finally he says that a uncanny memory comes back to him, more and more precisely, after every one of his missions: he was twelve or thirteen, no more, and he'd spent many long hours in the shed carving figures for the crèche; he'd gone to a lot of trouble with the Three Wise Men, who had very rich costumes with intricate folds and bejewelled turbans. He remembers that these figures were part of the family crèche for years and then they disappeared; does anyone know, by chance, what's become of them?

But neither his mother nor any other member of the family has ever known that Philippe carved these Wise Men — or anything else, for that matter. In the Fillion family, the figures in the crèche were always made of plaster and the Jesus was wax. Still, they turn the house upside down to look, but without success. To everyone's surprise, Annette then decrees that her Philippe may be a little disturbed from something in the air in the old countries, or from eating English food, or simply because the war has mixed him up, but still, you must never go against a man who's fighting a war, so if he wants the Three Wise Men, very well, we'll invent some for him.

So she writes her son to tell him that she's found his Wise Men, as well as all the other figures, in fact, that they're in good shape and she'll keep them safe till he comes home.

Then she reads the letter to all her children, in a strangely solemn voice, and she asks them to swear that they'll never give away her secret. They're all dumbstruck; not only is their mother lying, she's so proud of it that she brags to everybody, including Édouard and the priest, who can't find anything wrong with it.

Never have her children seen her so proud, or even so alive, as on the day when she puts on her Sunday best to take the letter to the post office. She seems happy and light, as if she's just unloaded a cargo of bombs, and she still looks bright and fresh when she comes home and goes about her usual tasks, not sighing but humming.

Annette's letter does arrive at the military base at Tholthorpe, in Yorkshire, but it comes back unopened. Philippe disappeared over Hamburg on July 24, 1943, during the Gunmore operation. It was his twenty-third mission. He was twenty-seven years old.

15

Fish

On the day when Philippe's personal possessions arrived at the house, Annette had a good cry, then launched into a massive cleaning of the kitchen cupboards. She emptied them all, even the highest shelves, which she could reach without difficulty now thanks to Philippe's stepladder — there's no denying it, the boy had an imagination and he was hard-working too. While she was at it she washed knick-knacks whose existence she'd long since forgotten, then put everything away but in different places. For three whole days she tried every possible arrangement, even putting the cups and glasses in the most inaccessible cupboard, above the refrigerator, and the heaviest pots and pans above the stove, so she'd risk knocking herself out whenever she wanted one. After those three days of trial and error she went back to the first arrangement; they were still the same dishes, after all, and the same utensils and the same memories.

After that she put her excess energy into shifting Philippe's portrait, his official soldier's photo, all over the house. First she hung it on a wall in the living room, but it stayed there no more than a week; the gilt frame was too small on the enormous wall and her son was too far away to look at properly. She tried the other living-room walls, at different heights, but that wasn't any more successful; the room was too dark, no one ever went there anyway, I'm not going to leave him all alone in the dark after he died so far from home. . . . Philippe spent some time in the hallway, but if you walked past him every day you never stopped to look at him, and besides, you were liable to snag your winter coat on him, we'll have to put him somewhere else, this is no good; the bedrooms wouldn't be any better; don't even think of the bathroom, so that leaves the kitchen; it has to be the kitchen, we've got no choice, we may get grease and steam on the glass but we'll just wash it more often and that's it, we're hanging it in the kitchen and that's that, look, right here by the telephone, get me the hammer, Léo, instead of standing there with your arms hanging down, watching me work.

The rest of the Fillion family listened abstractedly to Annette: everyone knew that, after flying all over Europe, Philippe would end up here in the kitchen, next to the telephone, and that he'd stay here forever. The more time passed, the more Annette's world was confined to this kitchen, more precisely to the part of the wall where the phone hung. She would stand there for hours, chatting with her sisters or her cousins.

I still remember how my father teased her when we went to visit our grandmother and she'd fidget in her chair, eyes glued to the phone: "Wait till we're gone, Mama, before you call your sisters and tell them we came to see you!"

Annette would shrug, offended, and pretend she was listening to us, while she went on staring at the telephone. . . .

• • •

When I was a child I was always looking at Philippe's photo in its gilt frame with a braided palm behind it. How he intimidated me, this mysterious uncle who had lived a war movie *for real*, and how proud I was on the day I could tell my parents that at last I was taller than Philippe.

All my brothers and all my boy cousins without exception had the same reaction, around the age of thirteen or fourteen, when they realized that they'd outstripped Philippe. All wrapped up in our pride, it took a good while to notice that our grandmother had quite naturally hung the photo at eye level — her eye level. And because she was very short, it was her gaze that we'd outstripped. Philippe never had that chance.

• • •

On the day when Philippe's personal possessions arrived at the house, Louis went and prayed. A little. Then he went and drank. A lot. Because when you drink a lot, really a lot, there's always a moment, a very brief moment but still a worthwhile one, when nothing hurts any more.

• • •

That same day, Léo also went to church, but not for long. He loved the Good Lord but prayers were much too long to enter his memory completely. Then he went to the tavern to have a drink with Louis, but lasted only for five or six beers; he didn't feel like sitting there watching the bubbles rise to the surface and break.

Instead he went to the shed, where he found in his father's old things some fishing line, hooks, a bucket and a piece of wood from which he made himself a fishing rod. He rummaged in the fridge for some leftovers — a little salt pork, a little bread, a little corn — and went straight to the river, climbed over the fence that blocked access to the Laurier wharf and went fishing in the grey waters of the port of Montreal, where no one ever fished. He baited his hook any old way, with whatever came to hand, for he'd never gone fishing in his life, never even seen somebody fish — my father emphasized this whenever he told the story, that he baited his hook with whatever came to hand — corn, bread, salt pork — and came home with his bucket full of pike and perch. No one had ever shown him how to fish, ever.

When he came home his brothers and sisters asked all kinds of questions: how did you do that, where did you learn? As he didn't know the answer himself, he shrugged and invoked the Holy Ghost.

After that day, Annette treated Léo with a little more respect: it just goes to show, you never know what to expect in this life. Even a simpleton like Léo can surprise us, that was what she said on the phone. Annette always loved her children, but too late. And when she said anything good about them, it was always to somebody else.

• • •

When Léo still had his cottage, he'd take a lot more fish from the lake than it could ever contain, and there'd always be more the following summer, for him at any rate; when all the professional fishermen came home empty-handed, Léo could catch a grey trout in full sunlight, in mid-July, using a raisin for bait.

Just a few years ago you could often see him head out on a Sunday in winter, when the ice was solid, and go as far as the islands off Boucherville. An olive barrel to which he'd fastened leather straps served as his knapsack, in which he'd transport a small chainsaw for cutting holes in the ice, his box of secret bait and a little mickey for warming up. And every time, he'd bring home magnificent pike and even, when he was *really* lucky, sturgeon three feet long. Makes you want to believe in the Holy Ghost.

16

Enough Fooling Around

"Enough fooling around. Your father's dead, Philippe is missing, it's time you took on your responsibilities, my boy."

Annette walks from the table to the counter, from the counter to the pantry and from the pantry to the table, each time moving a utensil or a plate according to a logic that escapes Louis. Sometimes she'll take a potato masher out of the drawer, walk around the kitchen and then put it back in the drawer, as if her sole purpose were to stir up the air. Louis isn't really listening to his mother's speech, which he knows by heart: now she'll talk about Léo, and after that, his sisters. . . .

"Your brother Léo's as good as gold, but you know as well as I do, he's never going to set the world on fire. Léo is Léo.

And then there are your sisters; you seem to forget about them. . . ."

"My sisters don't need me all that badly: Margot's married, Juliette's working, Hélène and Thérèse are both engaged. . . ."

"Don't make me waste my breath. Philippe wouldn't have frittered his time away like you. . . ."

Philippe would have started a business and hired the whole family and he'd have paid everybody a good salary and he'd have given his mother a big fat allowance and everyone would have been proud of us. . . .

"And everyone would have been proud of us. Of course, you have to have your heart in the right place. Philippe. . . ."

"Listen, Mama, Philippe is Philippe and Philippe is dead and. . . ."

"Philippe isn't dead. He's missing."

"All right, missing. But Philippe is Philippe and I'm me. And I'm working for Lunn and I'd be the most heartless man in the world if I let him down after all he's done for me: he gave me my first chance, he made me sales manager — do you realize what that means, being a sales manager at twenty-four! And on top of that he gives me a share of the profit, though I haven't invested a cent in his business, and he hired Léo for deliveries. He can't get along without me. True, his store isn't called Fillion et Frères, but the rest is the same, isn't it? Everybody's working, we give you a, allowance, you've got nothing to complain about."

"I'm not complaining. Have you ever heard me complain? And don't use that tone of voice with me, my boy. What you have to understand, what you *would* understand if you listened to me, is that . . . is just that: your store isn't called Fillion et Frères."

"But what difference does the name make if everybody's working?"

"Don't play dumb with me. You know perfectly well what I mean."

"No, I don't know. Lunn has always treated me fairly. More than fairly. He's honest, he keeps his word, he's generous."

"And he's a Jew."

"So?"

"He's a Jew, that's all. That says everything. Do I have to draw you a picture?"

Just then, Édouard appears in the kitchen doorway.

Édouard, who is in his last year at the seminary and will soon be ordained as a priest; Édouard, who should be at the seminary studying his breviary to prepare for his priest's exams; Édouard, who comes into the kitchen as white as a sheet, eyes bulging, who drops his suitcases as soon as he's inside and drags himself with difficulty to the table. He has just enough time to collapse on a chair before he bursts out sobbing.

"I can't do it," he manages to stammer between sobs. "I'll never be a priest, it's all over."

Annette stirs up the air in the room a few times, out of habit; then she too collapses onto a chair, not moving, not speaking, not even sighing. Édouard sobs for so long, his hiccups sound so painful, his distress is so poignant that she could never seem as unhappy as her son. It takes talent to recognize talent in others; instead of risking a pale imitation, Annette chooses to relinquish the match.

• • •

The three brothers meet at the tavern that evening. Édouard doesn't stop crying and drinking, drinking and crying and crying again, the way men cry when they drink.

He tells his brothers that his mother wouldn't understand, it would be too painful for her, so he chose to blame his faltering faith and the Latin exams that were so hard, but the truth is much uglier, so ugly it just goes to show you that the Devil respects nothing, not even a seminary, and you can't imagine the sins that are committed there, and you can ask him to do a lot, but not *that*.

Louis and Léo don't know if they should ask questions or if they should understand without having it spelled out, or even if Édouard really wants to talk. So they fill their glasses and drink in silence till words lose their meaning, till they forget.

And it was on that night that Louis, just before he forgot everything, swore that he would bring back Fillion et Frères: Édouard needs you, Louis my boy. You have to do it.

17

L'ÉMÉRILLON

"Number twelve," says Louis to the beadle. "Twelve like the twelve months of the year."

"Twelve like the twelve apostles," replies the beadle.

He's a dry little man, gloomy and craggy, the kind of man who, even if he shaved three times a day, would still look like a cactus. Louis sees him at Mass every Sunday, but he has a hard time recognizing him on the night in question, with his jacket and tie and his conspiratorial look.

"The passengers on the *Émérillon* are expecting you," adds the beadle, as mysterious as ever.

He leads Louis to the office of the *curé*, who has donned his mauve chasuble to welcome him.

"Kindly close your eyes, Monsieur Fillion."

Louis feels someone blindfolding him. The fabric is very soft — velvet, most likely — and totally opaque.

"That's fine. Now, put your hand on my arm, Monsieur Fillion."

Louis obeys, thinking that this is the first time the *curé* has called him "Monsieur" — and not just once but twice. It gives him a strange feeling, at once reassured and intimidated. Blind, he travels endless corridors, descends a set of stairs, then walks down some more corridors. The farther he goes, the more he feels as if his soul has been put into a body that's too big for him, so big that he can't make out borders, as if he were dissolving into the darkness. He walks on and on until the *curé* whispers to him to stay there and wait. Is he still in the presbytery? He doesn't know all the nooks and crannies in this huge building, of course, but he never would have thought it could contain so many corridors.

"You can take off your blindfold now."

The voice is deep and nasal. It's not the voice of the *curé* but it's a religious voice nonetheless, one you could well imagine striking up a Kyrie. Louis opens his eyes and sees nothing but darkness. The room he's in is so dark that he can't even guess at its size.

"Faith alone can guide us in this world of gloom," says the voice. "The faith of Jacques Cartier, who crossed the hostile ocean on his frail *Émérillon* to found New France. And the faith of Champlain, and the faith of de Maisonneuve, and of the blessed Canadian martyrs. . . . Do you have faith, Monsieur Fillion? The true Christian faith?"

"Yes, I have faith. The true Christian faith. . . ."

"Walk, then, walk to me."

Louis steps forward cautiously, sliding his feet along the floor, hands held out in front of him, groping his way. After a few steps he touches a heavy velvet drapery; pushing it aside, he finds himself in a room that is nearly as dark as the first, but lighted by a number of candles that seem, in contrast, like so many suns. There's a lectern surrounded by mauve banners edged in gold, embroidered with Greek crosses, and a dozen straight chairs occupied by the same number of men, among whom Louis recognizes *Monsieur le curé* as well as some of the leading citizens of the parish: the manager of the Caisse Populaire, a restaurant owner, even the owner of a furniture factory in the east end of Montreal that Lunn sometimes does business with. There's no doubt about it, he has knocked on the right door.

A man in civilian clothes but arrayed in a mauve surplice shakes his hand and invites him to be seated.

"We're pleased to have you with us, companion."

It's the voice from before, the voice that could strike up a Kyrie. The man points to a chair, then disappears behind a drapery. Louis sits in the place indicated and ventures a few furtive glances, the way you would in a streetcar. All the "companions" are in suits and ties and they seem as anxious as he is. They keep their heads down, only venturing to glance discreetly at the new arrivals. There are two more after Louis, who already feels like an old hand and sympathizes with their shyness.

And then silence again, and waiting, interminable. Wait, wait some more. . . . It must be a test, thinks Louis; not sure how to occupy his mind, he recites a rosary. He has started the fourth decade when trumpet music resounds, so loud that the gathering nearly succumbs to a collective heart attack. Where can it be coming from? No record player could produce sound of such quality. Could an orchestra be hidden behind a curtain?

As if to answer his question, four men appear, goose-stepping, their trumpets held against their hearts. They stop at the lectern, play another few notes of regal music, then stand at attention while the man with the Kyrie voice appears behind the lectern. His face, lit only by candle flames, is so pale, so phosphorescent, that he could be a ghost — if you can imagine a ghost wearing thick horn-rimmed glasses.

Over his suit and tie and his mauve surplice the man now wears a red sash with gold fringes. On his chest hangs a Greek cross. But he can't be Orthodox, Louis thinks. *Monsieur le curé* would never let him into his presbytery. So he must be some kind of Catholic.

"We want leaders!" he roars at length, and the entire assembly jumps again. "Leaders for the revolution that will be ours, that will further the interests of the French-Canadian people!"

The man knows how to use silences to let people better appreciate his voice, which is authoritarian, energetic yet always contained, as if it comes from a tremendous inner river that is hard for him to hold back.

"And this revolution that will be ours will be practical, effective, calm and kindly, because it calls for only men who are pure, fundamentally Catholic and French. It is the revolution of liberated Spain, of organized Portugal, of Pétain's

France. And the first step in this revolution is to buy from our own people. We will train heads of companies, while we await the great leader who will help us at last to cross the Rubicon of our fears. While awaiting this great step, we will march slowly but proudly, while we tell the entire world that nothing can frighten the people of our race. Drink, companions, drink what *Monsieur le curé* offers you; it symbolizes the storms that we will surely have to confront, but that will break on the hull of our invincible *Émérillon*."

The *curé* then holds out a cup of bitterness to each of the men, and each takes a sip without grimacing — these are men well acquainted with bitterness.

Next they kneel in front of the man with the glasses, who dubs them — with a real sword that he drops heavily onto their shoulders — and finally teaches them, among other secrets, the famous handshake reserved for members of the Order of Jacques Cartier, better know to its detractors as La Patente.

• • •

It was under protest that my father became a member of the Order of Jacques Cartier. He had nothing against the spreading of the Catholic faith, quite the contrary — on condition, however, that he wasn't the one to do it. Nor did he have anything against the economic promotion of French Canadians, and buying from our own people; the policy of *achat chez nous* struck him as a fundamental application of common sense, particularly if his fellow-citizens applied it by coming to his store. But he didn't like secrets or doing things on the sly, much less expressions of admiration for Pétain's France; it was tantamount to saying that his fellow countrymen had fought in vain and that Philippe's death meant nothing.

While he always paid his dues religiously, he never achieved a rank above Commander. Having little interest in intrigues or the great ideological questions, he was content to support the "*Société du bon parler français*" in its promotion of the proper use of the French language, to subscribe to *Le Devoir* and to write to the mayor now and then, asking him to give French names to city streets.

For the rest, he was discreet.

He never liked La Patente very much, but he needed one of those little groups that society provides for the timid, called an organization. Above all, he needed a secret handshake and contacts that would allow him to engage in the only political activity he'd ever taken to heart: seeing to the interests of his family, whatever that family might be.

Beginning on the day after his initiation, he would exchange a secret handshake with the bank manager, with whom he'd speak at length about the economic advancement of French Canadians and the virtues of *achat chez nous*. He would pass quickly over his almost total lack of capital but enlarge upon his experience as sales manager, and finally he'd talk about his brothers, whose hearts are in the right place, like those of all the members of his race, and with whom he wants to open a furniture store called Fillion et Frères, a name that highlights the French-Canadian family, and they're going to succeed, guaranteed — provided, of course, that they have the support of a French-Canadian bank.

The banker, Maximilien Hotte, wore horn-rimmed glasses, had a voice that could sing the Kyrie and was the fourth Grand Chancellor of the Order of Jacques Cartier.

All things considered, it was a good thing that La Patente existed; how could Louis have found the words to convince a Scottish banker? As well as providing his financing, the Order of Jacques Cartier would bring him customers — to whom he would grant a secret discount — and would help him enjoy significant discounts from his suppliers. That made it worthwhile putting up with endless speeches, come home at dawn and submit to Annette's interrogations.

"Would you mind telling me where you've been? And what's the big idea of getting dressed up for Mass on a Saturday night?"

It's impossible not to reply to his mother. And equally impossible to tell her the truth. Among the many promises he made to join the Order of Jacques Cartier, Louis undertook never to disclose his commitment to a woman, not even his wife or his mother. Women have many fine qualities, the Grand Chancellor said, but it's in their nature that they can't keep a secret. If your wife asks questions about our meetings, you have to explain, very calmly, that she has nothing to fear from what's going on and that it's her duty as a Catholic wife to trust her husband. Obviously, he added at once, rare are those among us who are lucky enough to have such virtuous wives. As curiosity is also part of female nature, and as a woman is often ready to use any means to achieve her ends when her curiosity is piqued, it's best to be realistic: if your wife asks questions, lie.

What's true for wives is undoubtedly equally true for mothers, thinks Louis, as he racks his brains to come up with a decent lie.

"Tell me the truth: you've got a girlfriend, is that it? Are you going to abandon me too?"

"No, not at all. . . . I . . . I was at church, for the Nocturnal Adoration."

"The Nocturnal Adoration? What's that?"

"A prayer movement. We get together in church at night, men only, and we pray to the Blessed Sacrament. If you don't believe me, ask the *curé*."

Louis is proud of himself; the *curé* certainly won't betray him. He'll also use the opportunity to urge him to really come to the Nocturnal Adoration — a matter of covering up his lie after the fact but, well, a man's got to do what a man's got to do.

Annette doesn't know where to turn: it's too late to call *Monsieur le curé*, and too late to call one of her sisters. She paces for a few moments, then gets into her rocking chair and says her rosary furiously.

No doubt she deliberately placed her rocker in the corner of the kitchen where the floor creaks. She always goes to bed very late when this kind of crisis occurs, and her sighs and her creaking can be heard all way to the back of the house; it gets under your skin and penetrates your bones.

18

MONSIEUR MAN

The first Fillion et Frères store doesn't look in the least like what it will become in the fifties and sixties, when, from expansion to expansion, the brothers added two storeys and knocked down a number of walls, after annexing some adjacent premises. At first the business occupied only the ground floor, and there was room to display one bedroom set and two living-room sets and nothing more. There was a huge warehouse out back, though, that was soon converted into a showroom. The show window was narrower and not so high and they didn't have the big neon sign that went around the corner of the street. . . . The only thing that hasn't changed with the years, in fact, is the address, the famous address on Saint-Hubert Street for which the Fillion brothers would be congratulated so often later on: what stroke of genius made you sense that this part of town would develop as much as it has?

It wasn't foresight, Louis would reply with a shrug, even less market research; it was simply a stroke of luck: the building belonged to French Canadians, that particular corner seemed promising, there were already some businesses on Saint-Hubert Street, the banker agreed, all it took was a few handshakes. . . .

If he'd continued his remark instead of concluding it with an evasive shrug, he'd have mentioned another element that was a major factor in his decision: simple decency had made him go as far from Ontario Street as possible, so he wouldn't be competing with Lunn.

This precaution would soon prove pointless, however. No sooner had Louis resigned than Lunn again started cutting prices, harassing customers right on the street and putting garish posters in his window, so you could hardly see the furniture. His business looked like a poor people's store, and that would soon force him to close; no one likes shopping with the poor. The garish posters would be replaced by newspaper showing ads for Fillion et Frères on Saint-Hubert Street, the furniture store for the French-Canadian family.

Louis wouldn't see Lunn again until the sixties, when Fillion et Frères was at the height of its fame.

Lunn walks into the store, holding out his arms to Louis; he gives him a long embrace, congratulates him with many slaps on the back, talks to him about new horizons in the clothing field and about his many plans, all of them amazing;

in particular, he's dreaming about a big store with clothing sold at prices so low that people will line up for them, he'll open branches in the four corners of the city, he may even move in across the street, why not, the neighbourhood seems promising and you're doing well from what I can see, a hell of a fine-looking store, Louis, really, my friend, you've got a good head for business, I always knew it. . . .

As long as he's talking about his plans while he strolls through the store, Lunn is as lithe and elegant as Fred Astaire, with Bing Crosby's voice. Unfathomable, elusive, he always seems to be somewhere other than where you're looking. But as soon as he stops for a few seconds in front of an easy chair that has caught his expert eye, as soon as he stops laughing at nothing and catches his breath, you can see that his suit is worn thin, his shoes are shabby, his face is too pale and his hair too black. And that skin, so smooth. . . . It's as if he pasted on a mask long ago and has never taken it off, forgetting that he's even wearing it.

Every time such a silence settles in, Louis comes close to suggesting that Lunn come and work with him. But how could he dare offer a job to a man who repeats *ad nauseam* that he's going to be a millionaire if even one of his plans works out? A man who has been his boss and who went on to make him an associate? Maybe Louis should have made the offer anyway, if only so that Lunn could turn it down.

There never was a clothing store across from Fillion et Frères, of course, and Louis never saw his former boss and associate again, at least not in the flesh. The ghost of Lunn will often haunt him, though, when he settles into his easy chair, alone in the middle of the night, and lets his memories drift. Each time, he'll tell himself that he couldn't have done anything else, that he did the right thing, treated him properly, but it's not enough; why does that bitterness persist deep in his memories? So then he'll tell himself once again that he couldn't have done anything else, that he did the right thing, treated his former boss properly — the kind of reflections that keep you going in circles for hours, that inevitably conclude with a "Such is life."

• • •

When I was a small child, whenever I heard people talking about this Monsieur Lunn, what I heard was "Monsieur L'Homme," Monsieur Man, and I'd wonder what a human being could have done to the Good Lord to deserve such a name. One day I asked my father, who of course couldn't imagine why I heard the name that way; he explained that his former boss's family came from Poland or Russia or some such place with unpronounceable names, and that one of his ancestors had probably been given a new name by some official in the Immigration Department, as often happens.

I pretended that I'd had an answer to my question, even if it only diverted the mystery: what would make an obscure official decide that this particular man should stand in for all the others?

It wasn't till I saw the name written out many years later that I realized my mistake. A rather venial error, in fact, that I never really tried to correct. I write Lunn, but for me that man will always be Monsieur L'Homme.

• • •

July 1944. Édouard and Louis are painting the walls while Léo puts the finishing touches to the fine wooden sign that will adorn the front of the store until the early 1950s: *Fillion et Frères*, in red letters on a beige background, with the parallel curving capital Fs set apart, their arabesques linked and answering one another like an echo. Léo never knew it, but he was an artist.

The three brothers sometimes have an urge to sing "The Little Cabin Boy," but they hold back; singing without Philippe still seems indecent. All they'd hear would be his silence. It will take them many years before they venture to do it and, every time, the song will break their hearts.

Édouard tries to tell some funny stories he's heard at the tavern, without much success. His head aches so badly that it's hard for him to pretend to be happy. Mornings have always been hard for Uncle Édouard. Afternoons too, for that matter, when he invariably leaves the job on the pretext of going to buy plaster or nails or nothing at all. On the way to the hardware store there's always a place that sells beer, and Édouard doesn't mind stopping there to wet his whistle. Sometimes he'll come back late at night to rejoin his brothers, or more often the next morning, feeling guiltier than ever and asking them to forgive him, and he swears he won't do it again, it's the smell of paint that goes to his head. . . . His brothers forgive him, of course, the way they always do. If you can't forgive your brother, whom can you forgive?

Louis is in no mood to sing or even talk, with his head full of credits and debits to be balanced. Besides, how could anyone sing in this empty space, so empty that there's no room for anything except fear?

Léo doesn't sing either; he'd never dare set the tone, and he's never done more than one thing at a time, in any case; for the moment, he's painting.

And then, the Fillion brothers have never sung except when they were absolutely alone, and look, here comes Béa to give them a hand.

Béatrice, Léo's fiancée, whom no one has ever called anything but Béa.

Béa like a vision, like music, like springtime. Red cheeks, sparkling teeth, long brown hair done up in an elaborate coil — Dear Lord, where does it fall to when she lets it down! — just plump enough, with rather short legs, the kind of girl the early settlers of Canada would have picked out at first glance on the wharf where the *Filles du Roy* were disembarking, a sturdy girl who would cultivate the soil without complaining and who'd produce fine, healthy, vigorous children. Not only is Béa healthy, she's beautiful too; and not only is she healthy and beautiful, she laughs all the time, so you can't help falling in love with her the first time you see her — and forever.

Which is what happened to Léo. He wanted to get married. So he went dancing and he met Béa. And since Léo was Léo and Béa was Béa, they decided to get married, and that's that.

Béa howls with laughter, beautifully, whenever Léo opens his mouth, and she goes into ecstasies over the slightest thing he does; she can't get over the fact that she's found a fiancé who is so handsome and so nice. He may not be the smartest man on earth, but there are already more than enough people who can set the world on fire. And it's true that he doesn't talk much, but she can very easily talk for two. And when her Léo does decide to speak up, what he says is so amusing, so different, so funny!

That Léo is funny is something everyone already knew, Louis thinks. But amusing? No one had ever really noticed that. Béa's beauty, yes, Louis noticed that, a little too much, in fact, and he'll sneak a glance at her while he's applying his paint, he'll look at Béa covering her hair with a scarf, at the same time revealing the nape of her neck and the soft fuzz that grows there. . . . Béa, who hums while she's scrubbing the floor, who hums while she's scraping paint off the window with a razor blade; Béa, who is quite simply happy, who was born like that and sees no reason why she should change; Béa, who works and works and never complains and is always laughing.

• • •

"Isn't that window too small? It's way too dark for a store! People won't see anything! And look, there's a spot. You've never been a very good painter, Édouard. . . . Of course, they don't teach that in a seminary. . . . And you'll have to change those tiles, green tiles look terrible, you never see that colour any more, it's been out of style for ages. . . . Is that a sign you're making, Léo? A wooden sign? Don't you think it looks cheap? I would've made the second F smaller than the first one, but I suppose it might work. All right, I think I've seen everything there is to see. . . . Doesn't take long to visit an empty store. . . . If you ask me, you could've waited till you had some furniture before you invited us. . . . How can you stand to breathe the smell of paint all day long? I can't take any more of it. . . . I think I've seen quite enough. . . . Are you coming, Margot?"

That was Annette, who'd come for a quick look at the premises with Margot, her eldest daughter. Margot, who married a man so rich that he owns a convertible, a man so enthralled by his Margot that he lets her drive it. Annette doesn't like seeing her daughter drive a car, especially not a convertible; it looks vulgar. But as she also hates taking the streetcar, she doesn't fuss too much. Which doesn't mean that anyone can stop her from speaking her mind about the store: it's too far from her house, she wouldn't be surprised if the customers are all foreigners who can't even speak French, but that's your business, after all, nobody ever asks for my opinion.

• • •

And Annette barely glances at Béa and barely says a reluctant goodbye on her way out. Annette has always looked askance at her daughters-in-law, particularly Béa. "You want to get married, Léo? I can't stop you, it's your business. But let me tell you one thing, Léo: women are always good-humoured at first. Then comes marriage and that's another kettle of fish. First thing you know you've got children, and that's when the suffering begins. Your Béa will be like the others, you'll see. I'm telling you for your own good, so you'll know what to expect. . . ."

As for Béa, she'll never have the slightest problem with Annette:

"Is your mother always like that? She's quite a character! And so funny!"

• • •

When Annette is a very, very old woman, Béa will be the only one of her daughters-in-law who comes to see her regularly in the old folks' home. Every time, Béa will try to catch her unawares, but without success.

"I'll tell you, Madame Fillion, it's no fun, is it?"

"It's a lot worse than you think, my girl! A lot worse! If you only knew!"

• • •

Louis goes outside with Margot and his mother, opens the door of the convertible, watches them leave and stays outside for a few moments to have a smoke.

He needs fresh air. He needs to breathe deeply. Because of the paint smell inside. And Béa. He has to get married too — and fast. . . .

19

Queen Margot, the Little Mite and the Rest

A responsible man has to set himself up first. Only after that does he get married, otherwise he'll have nothing but trouble. There's no better recipe for ruining your own life and the lives of others than letting your emotions overflow, giving free rein to your natural inclinations; that only leads to illegitimate children, unwed mothers and poverty, which is not exactly the kind of life you'd wish for those you love.

While he waits to set himself up, the responsible man has a duty to control himself, which forces him to keep a respectful distance from women so he can devote the bulk of his time to studying the laws, written and unwritten, that govern the universe of men, which are already complicated enough.

Louis was a responsible man, an eminently responsible

man, who didn't marry till the age of twenty-five, when his business was well established. He'd never known a woman before, nor was he really interested in their world. At twenty-five he still felt that they spoke a foreign language, and lived in a parallel universe that had little to do with his own, and that the strangest of these strange creatures were without a doubt his own sisters. And of his sisters it was most assuredly Margot who was the biggest puzzle.

While the other Fillion sisters were fairly slim and rather pretty, Margot had always been fat and ugly. Puffed up everywhere except where she should have been, hairy, with a crooked nose and a flat voice — in short a walking horror show, and — oh yes — slightly bowlegged. But even though she was as ugly as the seven deadly sins, she herself never seemed to have noticed.

It was always an amazing sight to see her leave the house on Sunday morning. Instead of dressing in dark tones and trying to blend into the walls and sidewalks, she wore garish flowered dresses and extravagant hats trimmed with plastic flowers or grapes. Her lips were slick with flaming lipstick and she always wore sickening perfume that you could smell long after she'd turned the corner. Perched on her high heels, as discreet as a fire engine, she strutted to the church where she would sit in a front pew with all her lights blazing. As she knew the ritual of the Mass and the little ways of all the priests by heart, she always managed to stand, sit and kneel a quarter of a second before everyone else, so that she had the impression — quite well-founded as it happens — that it was she who ruled the parish with an iron hand. If the priest was dragging his heels a little, she'd speed up the tempo. The priest would invariably adopt her rhythm, and the nine-thirty Mass, which everyone called the Margot Mass, always ended five minutes before the hour.

After that, she'd go home and take her place at the kitchen table like a queen, to pronounce judgements that everyone accepted as infallible decrees: the choir had been off key, the priest had made a mistake in his sermon, I ask you, does it make any sense to study at a classical college and then say Mass the way he did, honestly, besides, his soutane was wrinkled, that's what happens when you sit all the time, somebody will have to tell him one of these days, and it looks as if that somebody's going to be me, again. . . .

Margot talked so loudly that everyone, girl or boy, fell silent to listen, or at least to let her carry on. Even Philippe, when he was still there. Even Annette, who merely nodded at her daughter's remarks, as if each time she was hearing the voice of wisdom.

When Margot had finished her negative review, she'd take off her long openwork gloves with very slow movements, as if she were a beauty queen, and admire her nails while she waited for her servant to bring her lunch. If Annette was distracted, Margot would clink her cup against its saucer till her mother woke up and poured her coffee. Margot would register her displeasure with a faint sigh, then wolf down five slices of bread and butter in ten seconds and hold forth again without let-up till nightfall. Sundays belonged to her. The other days too, for that matter; Margot was the queen of the universe, which had been created for the sole purpose of satisfying her desires.

Margot was so convinced that she was a divine creature who by some error had ended up in a world populated by hideous monsters that she'd managed to persuade her whole family of this — its female members, at any rate. If one of her sisters wanted to know something about creams or powders or perfumes, it was Margot she would consult. Her reputation as an expert had spread throughout the parish, so that for a while she'd considered opening a beauty parlour. Her suitors, though, wouldn't leave her enough time.

Yes, Margot had suitors, and quite a few. She even got married, not just once but four times.

Her first Romeo (which was actually his name) was a good-looking, well-built man with a square jaw and wavy hair. He'd inherited his father's jewellery store and made it prosper, and all his profits seemed to go to covering his wife with jewels, pendants and charms. It must have cost a fortune; there was a lot of Margot to cover. But the result was impossible to ignore: Margot's appearance was so distinctive, and she produced such undulations when she walked that her jewels continued to jingle long after she'd stopped moving.

That first marriage lasted ten years and didn't produce any children. When Romeo died, he left Margot an inheritance so substantial that it could have provided an income for the rest of her days. But she wasn't a woman to stay on her own very long. And so there was a second Romeo (for the Fillion brothers, all of Margot's husbands were called Romeo), who worked in fur, then a third, who owned a Dairy Queen and spent his winters in Florida, and finally the fourth, a Chrysler dealer.

All these Romeos seemed to be built along the same lines:

strong, beefy men with a booming laugh, the kind who crush your fingers when they shake your hand and couldn't smile without showing all their teeth; prosperous businessmen who owned big eight-cylinder cars, often convertibles; each one more enthralled by Margot than the one before, as if they'd all been victims of a collective hallucination.

Margot kept her husbands on a tight rein, and they seemed to love it. They were her devoted escorts, her footmen. At family parties it was almost comical to see them hold her plate while she served herself from the buffet, and light her cigarettes and warm up the car when she decided to leave. All four died in the prime of life, perfectly happy, all of heart attacks.

Convinced that she brought her husbands bad luck, Margot decided to stop marrying, but that didn't prevent her from being surrounded by suitors — especially in the winter, which she spent in Florida.

Twenty-five years later, Louis still didn't understand it.

• • •

"Don't you think it's funny?" Louis asks Léo one day, when Margot has just left the store.

"What?" asks Léo after his usual slight delay; whatever question you pose, it always seems as if he has to translate it into a foreign language, then retranslate it into French before he replies.

"Margot. Your sister. You can't deny, she's not exactly Brigitte Bardot. Some fat women are attractive, but she . . . Her extra weight is in the strangest places, I've never seen anything like it. And it hasn't stopped her from marrying four times. Four husbands who were always at her beck and call, who seemed as happy as kings and who died, one after the other, of heart attacks. . . . And she's never had children. What did she have to offer them?"

Louis and Léo watch Margot get into the big Chrysler Imperial she inherited from her last husband. The car sinks down, then bobs back up two or three times, as if a particularly hefty mechanic wanted to test the suspension. Their sister has just replaced all her furniture, once again. With her, it's simple. She strolls through the store saying, I want this, I want that, regardless of the price, and she doesn't care if she's mixing Colonial and Spanish, avocado and harvest gold. Generally, one of her husbands followed behind, blissfully happy, cheque-book in hand. But Margot hasn't got a husband now and she'll never have one again. She loves men too much to make them die. That doesn't stop her replacing all her furniture, from cellar to attic, every two or three years. Each time, she fans out hundred-dollar bills on the counter, bills that have been marinating in her purse for a long time and now reek of perfume; and since she wets her fat thumb to count them, the bills all have lipstick stains. She's so used to controlling the whole universe, thinks Louis, that she even prints her own money.

"Don't you wonder about it?" Louis asks, turning towards Léo, who's still looking out at the street, even though Margot's Chrysler has been gone a long time.

"What?" Léo repeats, as if he's just dropped down from a cloud.

"Margot. Her husbands. What could she have done for them?"

"I've known that for a while now. It's not complicated."

"You know! How did you find out?"

"I asked the husbands. That's what you have to do, apparently, when you want an answer: you ask. People tell us whatever they want, that's their right, but at least you've asked. When you get answers, you aren't quite as dumb when you go to bed that night. And if you haven't got answers, you may be no further ahead but at least you haven't lost any ground, that's what I tell myself. So I went to see her Romeos, one by one, to find out what they saw in Margot. To find out if they were blind or what."

"All four? You did that with all four husbands?"

"No, not all four. Just the first three. I may not be quick, but I always understand if I hear the same thing three times."

"Understand what? What did they tell you?"

"Who?"

"The husbands. . . ."

"Ah, I see, the husbands. . . ."

And Léo's off in the clouds again, which happens often when he's in mid-conversation or at the wheel of his delivery truck: he's got just one mattress to deliver, just one address to go to, two blocks from the store, but it's too much for him. He'll start up, drive around, come back to the store still holding the bill. "What's up, Léo? Didn't you give the customer the bill? There's nothing difficult about it: you give him the white copy and you keep the yellow one. . . ."

"I was thinking I'd forgotten something. . . ."

"What about the mattress? I hope you at least delivered it."

"Mattress? What mattress?"

Léo is Léo: on one of his cloudy days, everything's too complicated. You just have to get used to it.

"Léo? Léo?"

"What? Sorry, I guess I was in the clouds."

"Yes you were, a little. . . . We were talking about husbands. . . ."

"What husbands?"

"Margot's husbands. I get the impression you're pulling my leg, Léo. . . . What was it that Margo did for her husbands? Come on, Léo, out with it, for God's sake!"

"Oh, right, that! Well, the reason they were so happy was that she did special things to them."

"Special things? What special things?"

"I have to get back to work. We can talk all we want but meanwhile the job doesn't do itself. . . ."

"Léo. . . ."

Though Louis is a model of patience, he'd sometimes like to grab his brother by the lapel and shake him, just to put his neurons back where they belong. He stands facing Léo, preventing him from going to the back of the store, and asks his question again, two inches from his nose (maybe he hears better through his nostrils than through his ears, you never know).

"What are those special things she did to them?"

"No idea. I got you this time, didn't I?"

"You mean. . . . You didn't go and see the husbands?"

"Of course not. You can't do that, for Pete's sake. I may not be quick, but if you ask me, Louis, you're pretty naive."

And Léo displays that half-smile he always wears when he's

pleased with himself, the strange smile I've never seen on any other face, which can be translated more or less as "I may not look very smart but try and prove it, just to see."

• • •

First Léo, the eldest. Immediately after him, Philippe, the hero. Born in the same year. Then two girls, both at one-year intervals: Queen Margot and Juliette, whom I'm saving for dessert. Louis is the middle child. After him came Hélène, Édouard, Thérèse and finally Rita, who died when she was barely two years old. Consumption, as they said back then. Tuberculosis. My father would tell me that he still dreamed about her nearly every year, around Easter. He'd hear her coughing and coughing, again and again. In his dream, he would wake up then but he wouldn't hear her; she was dead. Then he'd wake up a second time, as if he were waking from two sleeps that were superimposed. The next morning, we'd find him in his armchair in the basement; he hadn't been brave enough to get back into bed, for fear of dreaming the same dream again, endlessly.

• • •

Hélène and Thérèse were born two years apart, but they could have been twins. Always together, always dressed the same, they had constructed inside their female universe one that was even smaller and more feminine, in which they were perpetual princesses. While still very young they liked frills and lace, powders and perfumes, five-cent romance novels and fashion magazines. They were always shut away in their bedroom so we never saw them. Only their perpetual babble gave away their presence. They only left the bedroom to parade around at church or to put on plays or fashion shows in the laneway.

The two sisters managed to marry without really leaving one another: both wed rather wealthy men who took them to live in the same neighbourhood, on the other side of the mountain. The abodes of both were vast and dark, with wood panelling, stained glass and a piano in the living room. There they continued to live the lives of princesses, as if nothing had changed, spending their time consulting fashion and interior decorating magazines, going to the same clothing and furniture stores and giving each other permanents.

They had children I never really knew and then they peacefully grew old, still with nothing to do but go to the stores to see if there was any basis to the rumour that Peter Pan collars were coming back in style or, if it was too gloomy outside, play bridge with women friends and drink sugared wine.

When I was a child, we'd sometimes visit the two aunts on Sunday. I hated their houses, which blend together in my memory, in fact; no matter which aunt we were visiting, the two were always together to entertain us. It felt like being in church on Good Friday. Whether their husbands were there or not, they were always absent. The aunts would pour the sweet wine into crystal glasses and then right away they'd start gabbing, until my father fell asleep in his armchair, to the dismay of my mother, who would upbraid him all the way home: as far as you're concerned there's nobody but your brothers. . . .

We didn't visit those aunts very often, fortunately, and even less frequently did they come to visit us. They did show up regularly at Fillion et Frères, though, alone or with their bridge club friends, and they'd move around the store as if they owned it, looking down on the merchandise: it's not the quality we're used to, but we have to encourage the family, after all. . . .

When my father had assured them that he'd sold them the piece of furniture at cost — and God knows how he hated that kind of bargaining, especially in front of strangers — they'd ask for free delivery, it's the least you can do, and they wanted it tomorrow morning, but not before ten o'clock or after eleven because we've got an appointment for a pedicure, or was it at the hairdresser, yes, that's it, Thérèse, don't you remember. So it's agreed, Louis? You'll tell Léo to deliver it tomorrow morning. Let's hope he doesn't get lost along the way. . . . By the way, why don't you hire someone else for once? It shouldn't be hard to find a reliable delivery man, should it?

Louis never said what he thought of them. You don't speak ill about your own sisters, it's not done. But sometimes even he would heave an exasperated sigh.

• • •

Léo, Philippe, Margot, Juliette, Louis, Hélène, Édouard, Thérèse and Rita. Nine children. A normal family for the time. It keeps the parents away from you, besides giving you some interesting individuals of the opposite sex to observe. Each little boy can even choose a favourite sister. Every era has its own forms of luxury.

But do we really choose? Louis always had the impression that, to economize, the Good Lord had given him a piece of

Juliette's soul, no doubt deciding that hers was too big for just one person. It was a tremendous soul, a soul you could live in. A great soul, like a castle where he was the steward and Juliette occupied the top floor.

Juliette was born on the fourteenth of February and Louis on the sixteenth, one year later. The two birthdays were celebrated on the fifteenth; that way, no one was forgotten and they saved on the cake. Louis didn't mind; he adored his sister and was perfectly happy to share everything with her, including and in particular the one day of the year when he should have been a little more important than usual. Juliette didn't mind either; if it costs the family less, she would say, it's fine with me. At the age of just six or seven, she was glad when her family could save money. Genuinely glad. Sincerely. Her soul was the uppermost one at the top, in the highest room of the castle.

Margot had been quick to nickname her "the little mite," predicting that Juliette would never marry; no normal man would want a wife who was so small, so skinny, with such sad eyes. Annette had endorsed everything, both the nickname and the prediction, which explains why the family paid for private secretarial lessons for Juliette, so she'd always be able to provide for herself.

And yet, to the amazement of Annette and Margot, from the age of thirteen Juliette did not lack for suitors. It didn't surprise Louis. For him, Juliette wasn't skinny, she was delicate, and she had eyes as deep as an August night and a smile that could melt your heart. Why should he be the only one who was sensitive to her discreet and subtle beauty? But

Margot hadn't asked for his opinion, of course. Where aesthetics were concerned, boys weren't supposed to have anything to say.

"No accounting for taste," Margot had concluded when it became obvious that there would be crowds in the shadow of Juliette's balcony. "It's amazing how many men are afraid of real women."

Juliette though had kindly rejected all advances, trying never to hurt anyone. If her suitors were insistent, too insistent, she would finally admit that her heart was already spoken for. And the sheepish young men would leave with their bouquets and their poems.

Of course, the rumour quickly reached the ears of her brothers and sisters, who weren't going to let go of such a piece of news that easily: so our sister Juliette, our own Juliette, our little mite has a sweetheart and we don't know? Let's get to the bottom of this.

Interrogated to the point of nausea, harassed as one can be by brothers and sisters trying to extract a secret, Juliette would finally admit that her sweetheart's name was Julien, that he was very handsome and that that was all they were going to know, even if they tortured her.

But brothers and sisters who have a little imagination couldn't care less about torture, as long as they have other resources: they can search every nook and cranny in the suspect's room, for instance, and turn up drafts of Juliette's love letters to Julien. They didn't find a trace of a reply from Julien, though, not even in the form of confetti or ashes. They watched the mailman for months, and went out to meet him before he climbed the stairs, but that didn't advance the investigation either: Julien never wrote to Juliette; or at least his letters didn't follow the usual route. A thorough inspection of Juliette's books and notepads had turned up numerous examples of two capital J's intertwined, and of "Juliette loves Julien" in hearts pierced by arrows, but nothing more.

Who on earth was this Julien? There were no cousins with that name, the only Julien in the parish was six and a half years old, there was no Julien among the high school teachers or even among the parish priests (girls sometimes have that sort of fixation, Margot assured them).

The investigation went on for six months; then the file was closed when Philippe, who had played the part of chief investigator, decreed that their sister had simply invented an imaginary boyfriend, that it was a kind of nonsense fairly common among girls — they're such romantics — which finally went away when they were in danger of becoming old maids; then they'd make do with whoever came along, and too bad for them.

If Philippe says so it must be true, the Fillion brothers concluded, and they moved on to something else. Margot, who was in charge of the brigade of female investigators, made the same observation to the other Fillion sisters, as well as to everyone, male and female alike, whether they asked for her opinion or not, it didn't matter. This marked the first time in Fillion family memory that Philippe and Margot had agreed on anything whatsoever. So it had to be the truth, the absolute, undeniable truth.

The file was closed then, to the great relief of Juliette, who could finally write "Juliette loves Julien" in the margins of her notepads in peace and didn't hesitate to do so.

Louis may have been even more relieved than his sister. He had cooperated in the investigation, rummaging in wastebaskets in search of fragments of letters, rubbing ashes against blank sheets of paper to make ghosts of writing appear there and questioning school friends who had brothers of Juliette's age, but he'd done it with a heavy heart, torn between his strange feelings for his sister and his fundamental duty of fraternal solidarity. How could he have refused to cooperate when it was Philippe who'd asked? But what a poor investigator is someone who doesn't want to discover the truth. . . .

No one had welcomed Philippe's conclusion more enthusiastically: if his favourite sister had to have a sweetheart, better an imaginary one. He could keep watching over her without saying so, and listening to her when she didn't say anything. In the world of the imagination everything is possible, everything is *still* possible.

• • •

After her secretarial studies, Juliette soon got a job with a law firm on Saint-Jacques Street. She gave all her money to Annette, keeping just enough for streetcar tickets, her secretary's outfits and scented notepaper for writing to her sweetheart. Juliette could now talk freely about her Julien; no one believed in him any more and no one paid any attention.

The cat was finally let out of the bag one Sunday night shortly after Édouard had left the seminary. Everyone was at the table, listening to Margot gossiping about certain women in the parish who didn't know how to dress, it was a disgrace, you don't have to let yourself go just because you're poor — that sort of thing. Juliette took advantage of the fact that her sister's indignation made her take a somewhat longer breath than usual, and clinked her cup with her knife the way people do at weddings to make the bride and groom kiss. It created a commotion: Juliette is going to speak? She's interrupting Margot? What's got into her?

Juliette looked at the bottom of her teacup, as if she were addressing herself directly to her destiny, and said in one breath, without looking anyone in the eye, that she wanted to become a nun, that she'd started taking the necessary steps, that probably no one would object to her taking over from Édouard; a nun's not worth as much as a priest, of course, but it's better than nothing; moreover, she was going to pray hard for Édouard, who was going through such terrible ordeals, perhaps the flame of his vocation would be rekindled, you never know; she wanted to become a nun, that had always been her most devout wish, if she hadn't brought it up before, it was because she thought the family needed her salary, but now that Édouard wasn't costing them anything, now that her brothers were working, she could finally marry Julien, I mean Jesus, and. . . .

After that her voice became very thin and no one heard anything more. She brought her napkin delicately to her lips, she tried to excuse herself, but the words were too small, her voice too tiny. She got up and went to her room. The whole family, stunned, kept their eyes glued to the closed door till it opened again:

"I'm going to church," announced Juliette, who seemed happy, radiant. "I'm going to pray."

The whole family watched her go and watched the door close behind her. They remained silent until Margot, after she'd swallowed the mouthful stuck in her throat, finally managed to speak.

"I think it's a good idea. I'm sure it's the best thing that could happen to the poor little mite. . . ."

Annette nodded in agreement and had nothing to add. For her, the religious vocation of a man, particularly if he was her son, was an extraordinary event that deserved to be celebrated with great pomp and ceremony. It provided fuel for hundreds of hours, at least, of telephone conversation. But a woman's vocation? That was so trite it seemed redundant. Yes, it was the best thing that could happen to the poor little mite, Margot was right, and maybe it could make up a little for Édouard's failure in the eyes of the Lord. That was exactly what she'd tell her sisters and her friends on the phone: "Yes, it's the best thing that could happen to her. And maybe the Lord will forgive us. . . ." Two sentences punctuated by a half-sigh, then she'd change the subject.

Hélène and Thérèse joined in to ask what happens when you become a nun: is there a special ceremony, is the family invited and, if so, what do you wear, surely you don't wear white like for a wedding, I suppose, but black, on the other hand. . . .

Louis said nothing. He'd known for a long time, even if Juliette hadn't said anything. He had just known. He had eaten in silence, wondering if Jesus knew how lucky he was. Louis thought, sometimes we make generalizations about men and women because generalizations are often true and it makes life simpler, but there are always exceptions, of course, and certain women, for instance, can think much further than plenty of men. After that, he didn't think anything more. He was just sad.

• • •

Juliette wanted to be not just a nun but a missionary. As soon as the war was over, she set sail for Japan; they've suffered so much, they have so much to be forgiven for, they're working so hard to try to get back on their feet. . . .

She would stay there till the 1960s and she'd be more and more disappointed with the life she lived there. She would have liked to care for victims of the war and offer her suffering to the Lord, but what she was asked to do was teach English in schools attended by the wealthiest Japanese. It was a little, she wrote to her family, as if she'd been asked to travel halfway across the planet to end up teaching in Outremont. She even suspected the Japanese, who were very polite, of being totally resistant to Jesus and Mary, only pretending to be interested in them. In retrospect, it must be admitted that Juliette wasn't mistaken. The Japanese may not have been famous yet for the quality of their industrial production, but they definitely had good business sense: they exported their cheap junk to Canada and they imported Juliette, who didn't cost them anything. Sometimes it takes more than prayers to work miracles.

Then Juliette arranged to be transferred to China, arriving

just before the Cultural Revolution. For four years the Fillion family didn't hear a word from her. No letters, no phone calls. Nothing. While the others all thought she was dead, Louis was reassuring: she's suffering but she isn't dead. He would know. Everyone respected his opinion; hadn't those two been born on the same day, or nearly?

• • •

And then one day they finally got a letter, from the Philippines. Juliette asked to be forgiven for her long silence, and explained that there had been serious trouble in China and they must pray a lot for the Chinese, but not for her, though she had suffered humiliations and hardships of all kinds; they were the finest prayers she had ever offered to Jesus.

She spent more than twenty years in the Philippines. After that she retired, if you can say such a thing about a nun, and spent the rest of her life on Gouin Boulevard, where her community had a rest home.

• • •

There are always places we go back to when life is hard, when things are going badly, when we're afraid. Our footsteps take us there without our even realizing. Sometimes it's only in our dreams, but we go back all the same, irresistibly.

As a small child, Louis loved to hide under the kitchen table. He liked to watch the adults' legs, he could see clouds of flour and breadcrumbs fall and he'd breathe deeply to sort out the smells. He would also pick up scraps of conversations, and sometimes he was amazed that the words no longer made sense when you heard them from underneath. Sometimes his mother knew he was there. Sometimes she pretended to forget. But sometimes she really did forget, and Louis knew it, he could sense the very moment when she forgot. He felt all alone then, it was painful, he was afraid, the words had less and less meaning, but at the same time he would savour this solitude that he could break whenever he wanted: he'd emerge from his lair quietly, on his hands and knees, and he'd meet the gaze of his father, who was sitting in his rocking chair. His father would give him a wink as if he were in on it, as if it was all just a game and everything was going to work out just fine.

And then there was the corner of the shed where he'd go to read as a teenager, and to warm up his insides and make furniture with his brothers as they sang "The Little Cabin Boy." Long after he was married, long after his mother had moved out, even after the shed had been demolished and the laneway was nothing at all like what it had been, Louis would take a detour to go that way. He'd walk past the house, that was all, without stopping, barely even slowing down. And it did him good.

Later on there would be Léo's cottage. The veranda. The two rocking chairs that they turned towards the tip of the lake on August nights when the clouds changed from white to pink and then to orange; when the firmament became dark blue, then black, and the stars came out, one by one. You could see them shine so clearly you'd have thought you could reach out and touch them.

And churches, always. Any church as long as it was somewhat old, any old church that was steeped in incense and prayers; modern churches are so empty, it's like being in a refrigerated warehouse. Louis always looked there for a statue of the Virgin, preferring those that depicted her as a mature woman rather than a pale-faced adolescent. He liked her subtle smiles, her blue and white robes with their artistic folds, the haloes and stars that surrounded her. They were just plaster statues mass-produced in Italian factories, he was well aware of that, but even so he sometimes felt that the Virgin inhabited every one of those statues, and that her smiles were meant only for him. While he liked churches, he preferred them empty, in the middle of the day when there were only a few old women, so inconspicuous they could have been ghosts. He could stay there as long as he wanted, and nothing obliged him to use those prefabricated prayers people learn by rote and repeat out of habit. But he liked churches even more in the depths of night, when they were attended only by men praying to the Blessed Sacrament, their arms outstretched. The ceremony was called the Nocturnal Adoration and while Louis had started practising it to tone down a lie, he'd gone back often, by choice. Churches are much more beautiful in the middle of the night, when they're surrounded by silence.

Finally, there was the convent on Gouin Boulevard, where he often went on Sunday towards the end of his life, to visit his sister. They didn't talk much, those two. They didn't need to.

There are always places we go back to when life is hard, when things are going badly, when we're afraid. Our footsteps take us there without our even realizing. Sometimes it's only in our dreams, but we go back all the same, irresistibly.

The kitchen table, the shed, the cottage, a church and an austere bedroom in a convent. A wink. A song. A patch of sky.

The Virgin's smile. And Juliette's eyes, a foretaste of paradise that makes you long for death.

• • •

"It's funny," Léo said to Louis one day; "of all your sisters, the one you get along with best is the one who talks the least. I don't think you'll ever be comfortable with women, Louis my pal . . ."

Léo's intentions were sometimes hard to grasp. This time, though, Louis could have sworn that it wasn't a joke.

20

The Blue Dress

Louis got married after Léo and after Édouard, even though he was three years younger — long after all the others, in fact: on his wedding day in 1945, he was twenty-five years old. While he had an acute sense of his responsibilities, he was also very shy with women; when you learn a foreign language late in life, it's always harder to pick up the accent. Still, it did happen that he went dancing a few times, that he felt a warm body against his, that he stroked hands, got dizzy from sweet perfumes, but he'd never gone any further. It was all good, of course, and disturbing, and the source of a sweet light-headedness, but at the same time it was too easy and, to be blunt, not enough. Even though Juliette was at the other end of the world, he felt closer to her than to the girls he waltzed with.

Maybe there was another Juliette somewhere, with whom he wouldn't be obliged to talk, to explain, to persuade, a woman with whom he'd feel good right away and forever, a woman who would make him happy just by being there. Was it so crazy for him to wait a while, just in case?

If anyone asked why he'd married so late, he would sometimes tell the story of the girl in the blue dress. He always recounted it the same way, as you do when you tell a story so often that it becomes fixed in its words, and in a belligerent way that wasn't like him.

It had all started in England, in the hospital, when he had as a companion in misfortune a man named Bonin — I've forgotten his first name. Bonin had been a make-believe soldier like Louis, but he hadn't been as lucky: since he was in the hold when his make-believe destroyer struck a mine, both his legs had been torn off. This Bonin was the best companion you could imagine, always telling funny stories and encouraging his buddies, even though they weren't as badly off as he was. Never a moan, never a complaint. I've heard plenty of men complain more about a simple toothache, Louis would say. A force of nature. A morale of steel. By day at least; at night sometimes, always in a very low voice, he might ask the nurse for a sedative.

"It's no big deal," he'd say, looking at the big empty space that took up half the bed. "I'll walk again, I guarantee. And take a look at this, guys, take a look and tell me if it makes life worth living!"

Then he'd take the photo of a young girl named Diane, let's say, from his wallet. His fiancée. The loveliest, the sweetest, the most sensitive fiancée in the world, and she was waiting for him in Montreal, and it didn't matter if he'd lost his legs because he was good with numbers and he'd take courses and become an accountant and he'd be so happy with his Diane because they were so much in love. . . .

Bonin couldn't read or write, said Louis, though he wouldn't have been surprised if the plan had succeeded. The guy had a will and a certain gift for numbers; in card games he was unbeatable.

They would marry as soon as the war was over, said Bonin, and they'd have a house and a car and children and a big dog; at night after work he'd sit out on the balcony with a cold beer and watch his children running on the grass with the dog — he even pointed out that the dog would be beige because there's no finer sight than a beige dog on the green grass — the oldest boy would be called Michel and the oldest girl Louise, after that they'd see...

It was so wonderful to hear him talk that the whole room would fall asleep and dream about a beige dog running across the grass, and a beautiful woman named Diane who smelled so good.

But Bonin never went back to Montreal. He died in England, where he was buried in a little graveyard behind the hospital — during the war people had other things to do than send bodies home. A white cross and that's that. Thanks for coming over.

Because Louis was going home to Montreal a few days later, it was he who took Bonin's personal belongings to his family. Practically nothing, in fact: his wallet and his military papers, his mess tin and his drinking flask, his deck of cards and his rosary.

Bonin's mother was a very kind person, Louis said, very generous, too; she welcomed him warmly and didn't want him to go. Have a little more fudge, she said between sobs, and come back any time, there'll always be a place at my table for you, Monsieur Fillion, if you're hungry or thirsty or even if you're just passing by and you feel like a visit, I'll always treat you like my son.

Louis often thought about that woman, who had left him grappling with a cruel dilemma. Her invitation was sincere, he was sure of that. She would have liked him to come back. But they'd have talked about her son and that would have upset her. What do you do in such a case? Louis let his own shyness decide, and he never went back. Later on he was sorry.

After visiting the mother he took the photo to Diane, along with a letter, her first and last love letter from her fiancé, who'd died in the war.

• • •

It's a Friday night in June, around seven o'clock. Louis rings the bell at Diane's parents' house on Adam Street. His mouth is dry, his hands are clammy and his heart is pounding as if Diane were his own fiancée. Indeed, he knows the contents of the love letter by heart; he's the one who wrote it.

He first spies Diane's figure through the frosted window, her long legs and her slender waist, so slender that. . . . No time to think about that, the door opens and now Louis can see Diane's face which is even more beautiful than in the photo, her silky hair with little curls that fall to her shoulders, he can smell her perfume. . . .

Eventually Louis finds the words he needs introduce himself, though he does stammer.

"Ah yes, it's you," Diane replies. "I . . . I was expecting you a little earlier. . . ."

Louis looks at his watch, puzzled; he's sure he said he'd be there around seven.

"I can come back some other day if you want. . . ."

"No, it's not that. It's just that . . . I won't be able to talk for very long. . . ."

"For heaven's sake, Diane, ask him in!" says a voice behind her. (Her mother, most likely.) "Ask him in," the voice repeats, "offer him a glass of ginger ale or something. . . ." (Definitely her mother.)

"Would you like to come in?" Diane asks eventually. "Would you like something, a glass of water, some ginger ale?"

But she opens the door barely a crack, and stands there, not giving him room to come in. In a hockey game, Louis thinks, the referee would give her two minutes for blocking.

"I don't want to disturb you," Louis replies. "I just wanted to give you this. . . ."

As Louis is handing Diane the photo and the love letter, he hears a horn behind him. A car has just pulled up. A big two-tone Buick with running boards and sunshade, a magnificent shiny new Buick. From it emerges a Brylcreemed Beau Brummel in a fedora. With a flick of his fingers he sends his cigarette flying into the sewer grate on the other side of the street. Then he makes his way towards Diane, slowly, rotating his shoulders.

Diane gives him a sparkling smile, a dazzling smile, immediately trying to tone it down by biting her lips, which does nothing but get lipstick on her teeth. All the rest happens in a tenth of the time it takes to write it. She tries to slip the letter into her purse but it's too small. So she drops the letter on a little table by the door, probably the table they put the mail on, and maybe even department store circulars. She knows what it is though, they talked about it on the telephone: a love letter from her fiancé who died in the war. A love letter that she drops carelessly onto the little table. She says, "Thanks for coming, it was very nice of you, very kind, really," then she skips down the three steps to the sidewalk and joins the owner of the Buick.

All that's left to Louis is an image of a very beautiful young woman flying over those three steps; it's like a dance step, very graceful, that makes her blue dress swirl and sends a mixture of all her perfumes into the air. A light dress that leaves her shoulders bare, that seems made as much of wind as of cloth. Inside that dress, a slight young woman made of wind and perfumes who runs to a man with the air of a fashion plate, who stands on tiptoe to kiss him — the movement is very pretty and gives a nice curve to her legs. She kisses him on the mouth, not too long though, just enough to entice him, lets him open the car door, smoothes her dress under her rear to sit down and then goes off without even waving to Louis, without even looking at him.

She knows exactly how to make every move, though; she could be an actress or a ballerina. So she could have waved.

Just waved her hand to Louis and, at the same time, to Bonin, on the other side of the ocean.

"Would you like some ginger ale?" asks the mother, who has come out on the balcony. "Or a little pick-me-up?"

"No, thank you," Louis replies.

And he goes away thinking about the blue dress, so light and so frivolous.

21

The Butterfly Tamer

"An excellent choice, yes. A classic model. Won't go out of style. Fabric like that doesn't wear out. Most important is what you can't see. Oak frame. Victoriaville. Our own people. Around there, they know the difference between an oak tree and a spruce. Quality has its price. But at the end of the day. . . ."

The decision has not yet been made by this middle-aged couple who are engaging in discreet and silent warfare. The woman wants this new furniture, but the man is resisting. If it were the man who wanted to buy, his wife would no doubt be the one to apply the brakes. Louis knows this isn't about furniture, quality, guarantee or oak frame, but he talks anyway, for the music of the words, to relieve the tension, to shift the problem. *Guarantee, your mind at rest, oak frame*. . . . He speaks softly, for the same reason you might put an alarm clock in a puppy's basket to remind him of his mother's heartbeat, *important purchase, investment, take your time* . . . *tick tock* . . . then he tiptoes away to look after another couple who've just come in.

The guy is hefty and crewcut but you mustn't go by appearances: he's the sluggish type. Since he doesn't have the blank gaze of the soldiers coming home from the old countries, we can deduce that he stayed here. So he worked seven days a week and he's scraped together a nice little nest egg which his fiancée is anxious to spend. Yes, his fiancée; if they were married, even if they were newlyweds, she wouldn't be clinging to his arm like that. A little bit of a thing, but she's the one who wears the pants. Her gaze lights on a piece of furniture and immediately hardens. Like a padlock snapping shut. You can practically hear the click. She's done the same with her fiancé: I want him, I slip my arm into his. Click. Her gaze has hardened on this French-style living-room furniture that's such a good seller, contrary to all expectations. With its bowed legs, the armchair looks like a bulldog. Not too inviting. But the royal blue fabric, which contrasts with the usual browns, is a success. Léo doesn't like this furniture either. He says it reminds him of those little French women in the fashion magazines: pretty but uncomfortable. It lacks stuffing. This furniture sells, though, and always to skinny women, God knows why. . . . The fiancé would probably prefer something massive and padded, but since she leads him around by the nose. . . . How can you intentionally buy uncomfortable living-room furniture? It's like buying shoes that are too small! Sell them the blue furniture, then. It's in the bag. Ask about the size of their living room, or of a den where you could put this very comfortable armchair for the gentleman. After all, he's the one who works and he's the one who pays. . . . No, no, it doesn't clash, those shades go very well together. . . .

Bonjour monsieur, bonjour madame, French furniture, high quality, no mistake, something elegant, yes, hard-wearing, you're right, maple frame, it's both solid and light. . . .

Go on talking softly, glancing now and then at couple number one, who are still engaged in trench warfare. The woman is sitting in the armchair. Sitting well into it, not just on the edge of the seat. She sinks into it, strokes the armrests and takes possession of her throne while the man is still looking at the label, one eyebrow higher than the other. He's still not tuned in. Wait a while longer.

When the decisive moment, the crucial moment, zero hour arrives, Louis knows. The customer's eyes stay open for a long time, then his lids flutter very quickly, as if he were waking up after having hypnotized himself. The most expressive even go so far as to nod their heads, as if to say yes to themselves, then their face muscles relax and their voices come from the belly instead of from the head. The customer smiles, relieved, and sometimes makes a joke that he laughs at a little too hard. Then you have to talk to him very quietly, reassuringly: *excellent purchase, you won't be sorry, tick tock, speedy delivery, yes, just sign here. . . .* A handshake to seal the pact and Louis Fillion of Fillion et Frères is proud to have contributed once again to the happiness of a French-Canadian family.

Now couple number one seems ripe. Louis knows. He

knows even if his back is turned, even if he can't see the customers, even if he's talking to someone else: when the decision is made there's an infinitesimal change in the overall electrical tension, as if a storm were brewing, and the air doesn't have the same taste, the same density. Madame has finally convinced her husband, who takes his turn in the armchair. His head rests against the back, his feet on the footstool, his neck relaxes, his legs feel heavy, he melts. *Top quality, flexible and solid, galvanized steel springs, you feel like a bird in down, delivery is so swift you won't even have to interrupt your nap, tick tock, tick tock. . . .*

Louis would rather sell to individuals than to couples. Men or women, there's not much difference: there are always the same tensions, the same resistance, even if they're expressed differently. First you have to be quiet and observe. Foreheads crease, eyebrows frown, hands caress to appreciate the fabric's softness, fingers glide over scrolls, bellies relax when the backside sinks into the softness of the upholstery. After that you have to talk quietly, for the tick tock but also to give the customer time to talk himself into it. If it's absolutely necessary, you can always come up with a final argument at the right moment, but on the express condition that it doesn't seem like an argument. Talk very softly, so the salesman's voice merges with the inner voice of the customer. That can't be taught, can't be learned. You can sense it, you just know.

With couples it's harder. You have to decode. The customer never speaks to the salesman, even when addressing him directly, but always to the spouse, as an intermediary. The salesman is his foil. Never contradict, much less take a position.

With couples, you often have to use crossed arguments: you speak to the husband out of deference to the power he thinks he possesses, but you choose arguments that will persuade the wife, and vice versa. Yes, Louis really does prefer individuals. They're not so tiring.

Another couple has just come in — there's no doubt about it, this is couples' day — and goes directly to the French living room. A glance at Édouard, who responds with a nod: he'll look after them. Édouard is a good salesman too. When he's sober, of course.

Though his voice is high when he sings, it's distinctly lower when he speaks and even more so when he wants to be convincing. There's still something religious in that voice, something unctuous, like fudge. He says, "Victorian ornament," and you'd swear that the words are bringing him an intense pleasure that he wants to prolong by rolling them around in his mouth as long as he can. He's so serious, so distinguished that the customers don't dare bargain with him: you don't bargain with a priest. And if they do take the risk, they're always surprised when he says that he'll have to talk to the boss; how can someone with a voice like that not be the boss?

Talk to the boss. . . . That's an old tactic that the Fillion brothers use whenever customers insist on bargaining. Édouard takes advantage of it to smoke a cigarette with Léo in the back of the store, while the customer stews in his own juice. "I'll speak to my associate," Louis will sometimes say, for a change, and he'll go and empty his bladder. It's when he comes back that things liven up. If the customer is alone, he'll readily accept being told, "Sorry, it's house policy. . . ." But if he's accompanied by his wife or his fiancée, he'll be granted free delivery, *just this once*, or a full, unlimited one-year guarantee on labour and parts. The customer will be appreciative, even if he's well aware that at Fillion et Frères the delivery is always free and the guarantee unlimited. At least he will have saved face.

Édouard looks after couple number three, while Louis gives couples one and two their invoices to sign. All goes well until customers four and five arrive, one after the other, followed shortly by the mailman, who usually stops for a chat but today has to settle for leaving the mail on a corner of the desk, and Léo, who's lost the address of the old lady whose mattress he's supposed to deliver. And then the phone rings, as you might expect: "I was in the store last week and I've changed my mind, I'd like a loveseat instead of a sofa but I won't bother with the standing ashtray, I hope this won't cause you too many problems, it's because of my husband, you see. . . ." "Don't worry, madame, I'll take care of it myself, what's your name again? . . ." Wedge the receiver between shoulder and ear, jot down the name and the order, glance at customer number five, who's getting impatient, consider hiring a secretary as soon as possible, and here comes customer number six and the phone rings as soon as he hangs up and Léo is standing there and doesn't know what to do with his mattress. . . .

There are days like that, when cigarettes burn away in the ashtray, when sandwiches with one bite taken from them dry out on their paper plates, when you feel as if you're weightlifting from answering the phone. Days when you don't see time passing, when you have to talk and talk and talk until a quarter after nine, when the last customer finally leaves the store. The door closes and the three tired brothers treat themselves to a last cigarette, savouring it in silence. But the day's not over yet; there are invoices to file, cheques to write. . . . Louis sits at the desk while his two brothers put their hats on.

"Night, Louis," says Léo, who's always anxious to go home to his Béa. "Don't stay too late; adding up numbers won't help you find a girlfriend."

"Night, Louis," adds Édouard before he goes off to join his Simone. "Careful with that handle on the adding machine, it might give you ideas. . . ."

Louis looks at the adding machine, which is made of cast iron and must weigh a ton, and he doesn't understand what kind of idea it might put in his head. He lets out a forced laugh to throw his brother off track, but he doesn't care for jokes like that, which he always gets too late, especially when it's Édouard who tells them: Édouard and his priest's voice, his Radio-Canada voice. . . . Édouard, who's always putting his foot in it, even in front of customers sometimes, who don't get the jokes either. But Édouard can't help it, since he left the priests and met his Simone it's all he thinks about.

• • •

Half-past nine on a Thursday night. Louis is in the store office, hunched over his invoices. The room is tiny and windowless and the only furniture is a wooden filing cabinet that's permanent home to an electric kettle — which is rarely used, in fact, the Fillions not being big coffee drinkers — a small corner table that holds the huge adding machine, a coat rack and a big desk covered with papers, as well as the telephone, the wooden calendar courtesy of the Banque Provinciale, an in-box and a strange "automatic" ashtray that looks like a top: you butt the cigarette against a metal plate, then you work the mechanism and the butt disappears inside the belly of the ashtray. It's strange that this marvellous object hasn't been more successful, though it promises no more smoke, no more odours. True, the mechanism sometimes jams when the receptacle is full, but that tells you it's time to empty it. And when it's empty, you catch yourself working it like this, for no reason, just for the pleasure of watching the metal plate spin.

Nine forty-five. Pensively, Louis butts a cigarette and works the mechanism a couple of times, then thinks about the wisecracks Édouard would deliver if he saw him doing this and goes back to his invoices, ashamed.

Ten p.m. He opens the top drawer of the filing cabinet very gently, so he won't break the jar of instant coffee or the chipped mugs, to say nothing of his little mickey carefully wrapped in the purple bag — a bonus from Seagram's. He doesn't know if it's the bitterness of the rye or its concentration that makes him grimace at the first swallow. Both, most likely. But it does so much good as it goes down. Bookkeeping is excellent for the head but very bad for the back. You need a pick-me-up. One swig straightens the backbone, makes you breathe more deeply, clears the voice, cleans you out. Nothing better for purifying the blood, as the doctor says. And it's so good for the morale, too; if it takes a lot of alcohol to dissolve your troubles, it takes very little to make good news ten times better. And there's as much good news now as there are soldiers coming home from the front, or jobs in the factories. The big wheel is going around now, as they used to say at Wellie's, and it's never gone around so well, turning with it the wheels of trucks and trains, the propellers of ships and planes, the gears and pulleys of factories, the ball bearings and dials, lathes and engines — and all of that puts money in the workers' pockets. Factories have sprung up all along the Saint-Lawrence, fine brand-new factories full of strapping young men with muscular arms and their hearts in the right place. They worked day and night in munitions factories, and now that the war is over, they're coming to Fillion et Frères to spend. Everything's running, everything's turning, it never stops, it's almost too good to be true. If only Philippe could see it. . . . Maybe he's got something to do with it. Maybe he has convinced the saints up there, even the Holy Ghost, that would be just like him. . . . Hi there, Philippe. This swig's for you. After this I'll go back to my invoices. I ought to do that right now? Okay, you're right.

Half past ten. All that glue on the stamps and envelopes leaves a funny taste in your mouth. The little mickey will take care of that. A swig to dissolve the glue, another for good luck and another for *la chance*, aren't we lucky to live in a bilingual country. You can buy a water-dispenser to put on your desk so you don't have to lick stamps and envelopes, but they aren't really convenient; either they get all gummed up with glue and it's all over your fingers, or the water evaporates and you've never got any when you need it. A secretary. That's what we need. Tomorrow. A secretary with nice legs, like Édouard's

Simone. It would be good for business. *Maybe for you too, old Louis*, says a voice inside, the one that sleeps so lightly that a couple of sips of liquor will waken it. *Look at what's happening to Édouard since he found his Simone; he's so anxious to go home he doesn't even think of stopping at a tavern. Simone packs him a lunch to avoid the temptations of noon. Result: he hardly drinks at all any more. He's put on a bit of weight, he seems cheerful, full of piss and vinegar. True, he sometimes takes too long to buy cigarettes and he'll come back with his mouth full of Life Savers, but at least he does come back. Whereas you. . . .*

Me? That's different: I'm always working. I just drink a little at night, after work, and I hold it a lot better than Édouard. I control myself. A man's entitled to relax. My father always said, it's mixtures that are dangerous. As long as white stays with white and dark with dark, there's no problem. It's because of the glue on the envelopes. . . . Because of the words, too. Talking all day, persuading, answering the phone, it dries the mouth. My father lived in a world of handsaws and trying-planes, a world of silence. Even when he was a foreman, he couldn't talk because of the noise from the machines. He'd walk around with his hands behind his back, working with his eyes. But he still got thirsty. It's work that does that. Selling is hard on the voice, it's hard on the throat, and it makes you tired in a strange way that sleep doesn't cure. A drink or two makes it better, though. This one's for you, Papa. And a cigarette along with it. I'm sending smoke to you in heaven, just in case smoking isn't allowed up there and you feel like a drag. I'll blow some smoke rings too, in case they're out of haloes. . . . It's mixtures that are dangerous. Liquor and defeat, liquor and problems — that can weigh you down, give you dark thoughts. But liquor and success, that gives you wings. And Fillion et Frères is a success, right? It's running, it's rolling, all is well, why shouldn't I have the right to celebrate, to congratulate my gullet? *All right, so liquor's not a problem, but what about women? You need a woman, Louis, not just a secretary to lick envelopes. You need a woman to look after you. Cécile. . . .*

Cécile. Cécile, who's often still out on her balcony at night when you don't come home too late. Who sits in her rocker every Sunday on that same balcony, when you come back from the ten-thirty Mass. . . .

"Cécile Desmarais? The daughter of Étienne Desmarais, the accountant who died in the war, at least that's what his widow wants people to think, but I'm not going to repeat nasty gossip, that's not my way, but the fact remains that since her husband's been gone, the widow arranges things so her daughter's always out on the front balcony on Sundays, have you noticed? I'm sure it's just a coincidence. . . ."

The voice of Margot, the voice of Annette, the voice of all those women who talk so much that finally, inevitably, their words force their way into the world of men. . . .

Cécile's often out on the balcony when I go by, but that's normal, she lives on the corner and it's summer. Everybody's on the balcony in summer. You have to walk past her place to catch the streetcar to go to church, so. . . .

She's always there, sitting in her rocking chair, hulling strawberries for her mother or saying her rosary or leafing through *Radio-Monde* on the sly — her mother doesn't like her doing that, she says looking at photos of movie stars puts bad thoughts in your head. . . . Always there, sitting on her balcony. Is there a plot, some kind of feminine machination cooked up by the two mothers, to have her there every Sunday morning after ten-thirty Mass? Could be. And it wouldn't be surprising if Margot were involved.

So? Even if it's true, you'd be going out with Cécile, not her mother, and certainly not with Margot. . . . And Cécile's quite pretty, isn't she? Plump, the way you like them, and healthy and she smells so good. . . . Of course, she has that sad little look, but actually it's the mixture that makes her so special, so mysterious. A happy body but a melancholy face. Between the rows of stitches, between the decades of the rosary, she sighs faintly and it isn't unpleasant to hear: it's very light, it floats on the air. Clouds. Butterflies. Have you noticed the way she can modulate her sighs to say that it's too hot or too cold, to protest when the streetcars turn the corner too abruptly and send up showers of sparks, to reply to her mother when she asks her to help fold the sheets, or to complain that nothing's happening? Cécile sighs to say that she's there, that she's weary. She sighs to say that she's bored and she'd like to mark the passage of time like Robinson Crusoe on his island, who cut notches in his tree. She sighs to say that though she's still very young — barely twenty — she despairs of ever finding someone who can distract her, make her laugh, make her happy. Twenty years old. Barely twenty years old. And she smells so good. . . . So good that even her sighs are perfumed; they light on your shoulder and they're with you all day long, like tame butterflies. Surely there's someone on earth who can show her that life is beautiful, that it's worth living. And why shouldn't it be you?

It's true that the business is doing well, wonderfully well. . . .

Wonderfully well, yes. If you can't make her happy no one can. Didn't you manage to make her smile the very first time you stayed on her balcony for a while one Sunday? And the next day didn't you achieve the feat of making her laugh when you said something silly to her? First a smile, then a laugh; why wouldn't you be able to make her happy? Why shouldn't you open a gigantic jam jar for her? Think of yourself a little, Louis, look how good Béa is for Léo, and Simone for Édouard. . . . Cécile and Louis, Louis and Cécile. . . .

Louis and Cécile. . . . When I talk to Philippe about it, when I talk to my father, they don't say anything.

They never say anything in any case.

That's true. But sometimes I get the impression that they're there to pat me on the shoulder, to encourage me. . . . When I talk about it to the living, to Léo and Édouard, it's as if they cough a little longer than usual, as if they look elsewhere, as if . . .

Did Léo ask your permission before he married Béa? And Édouard with his Simone? It's your business and no one else's, no one's going to decide for you. The truth, old Louis, the truth is that you're scared.

Scared?

• • •

Half-past eleven. Louis is still at his desk. The little mickey's in the wastebasket behind him. It's empty and that's just fine. Louis wants to stop drinking. Because he always has one drink too many, because he always knows that at the very moment he's downing it and because he downs it anyway. If Édouard has nearly managed to stop drinking, Louis ought to be able to. It will be his first gift to Cécile. His wedding gift.

"Sunday. Next Sunday. Next Sunday I'll stop at her place. If she's on the balcony, that's fine; if not I'll climb the stairs, I'll knock at her door. . . . Sunday. Next Sunday."

Eleven forty-five. The little mickey is in the wastebasket, the package of Sweet Caps has just joined it, the invoices are filed, the ledger is closed and Louis stays in his office a good while longer, spinning the ashtray.

22

A Nice Long Car Ride

All week Louis deliberately avoids going past Cécile's house, even if it means boarding the streetcar two stops away. He doesn't get in touch, doesn't phone, nothing; and the following Sunday he takes a long detour after Mass to avoid her street. It's not that he's afraid, no, much less that he wants to keep her on tenterhooks — strategies like that he leaves to the women — but he'd never dare turn up at her place with his heart and his hands empty. He needs an enormous present, one wrapped in steel.

It was worth the wait: the sun is even more radiant the following Sunday when Louis stops in front of Cécile's balcony at the wheel of his Dodge van, so sparkling that the windows, the bumpers and the gas tank cover, which he spent a good part of the night polishing, are spattered with light. No sooner has he finished his parking manoeuvre than all the children in the neighbourhood come to admire their reflections in the chrome, laughing at their distorted features or admiring the two parallel curving capital *F*s that Léo has painted on the sides. He took his time but he surpassed himself when he created those arabesques, that strange maze so intricate they all want to trace the letters with their fingers to figure out where they start and stop. Louis is proud to see his family's name on his truck — it was one of Philippe's fondest dreams. Whenever he looks at the two entwined *F*'s he feels several inches taller. Today, he needs that.

Slowly Louis shuts the car door, kicks a tire (in a car salesroom he's seen men do that, and he assumes it's what you're supposed to do to feel like the owner), straightens his hat and tie, goes up to the little wrought-iron fence and swings open the gate, then finally goes towards the balcony, with a self-satisfied look. But the farther he goes, the more self-conscious he feels in his suit — at that time they always seemed too big for him — and squeezed into his new shoes; Cécile is there, she's looking at him, he feels he's being scrutinized from head to toe, judged, weighed, appraised; luckily there's the van in the background, the van on which Cécile's gaze now lights, otherwise he'd have dissolved on the sidewalk.

Cécile is holding up her *Radio-Monde* but she hasn't been reading it for a while now. She's looking at this man getting out of his van, this tall skinny man whose image is confused for a moment with that of her favourite singer, Fernand Robidoux, whose photo she's been gazing at; Louis may not be a crooner but he's still a businessman, as her mother says over and over, a businessman who's coming towards her, who's coming for her. . . .

"Come look at this, Mama!" she calls to her mother through the screen door.

Madame Desmarais steps onto the balcony, still covered with flour — she always bakes pies on Sunday — just as Louis sets foot on the bottom stair. He doesn't dare to take another step. He doesn't know if he should take his hat off or leave it on; a man is supposed to take off his hat inside a house, he knows that, but what does he do on the front stoop? At what point is it appropriate to *start* taking off your hat? Since he doesn't know what to say, much less to whom he should say it, he stands there with one foot on the sidewalk and the other on the stair, off balance, hat in hand, and his legs are wobbly and his heart is racing as he starts talking at top speed. Since Madame Desmarais's eyes are glued to the van, he explains that it's not an automobile, of course, he can't afford that, he has to be practical, but it's not a truck either, actually it's a combination of the two, it will be handy for small deliveries but even so it can be used as a car, it's a long way from La Fontaine Street to Beaubien, sometimes he has to do the books and come home late, so now he won't have to wait for the streetcar and that will save him time while he's waiting to move, it's not new, no, it's a 1941 model but they haven't changed anything since then because of the war so you could say it's practically new, my brother Léo did the lettering, it's not an automobile, that's for sure, but there's still a good-sized front seat. . . . *(You don't have to talk so fast, Louis, catch your breath, let them admire the van, let them convince themselves. . . .)* Would you like to come for a ride?

Would they like that? It's about time he made up his mind, honestly, Madame Desmarais seems to be saying; she couldn't have been happier if he'd offered her a box of chocolate-covered cherries. In less than a minute she's gone inside, taken off her floury apron, changed her dress, sprayed on some perfume, checked the contents of her purse, shut the door behind her and finally emerged onto her front steps, ready to leave for the ends of the earth or, better yet, for Saint-Hubert Street.

"I can't wait to see that store of yours."

While Louis did suggest going for a spin, he never mentioned visiting the store, he'd swear to it, but Madame Desmarais's remark doesn't surprise him; for a long time now, his mother has been getting him used to tactics like this. And after all, it's not a bad idea; he'd thought about driving onto Mount Royal, but maybe he'll be more comfortable on his own turf. . . .

Cécile seems happy too, but Louis has trouble guessing what's on her mind. For the moment she seems preoccupied by her *Radio-Monde*: should she leave it on the balcony, fold it in half and stow it in her purse or put it away in her room? She chooses the third solution and soon comes out of the house with that slightly weary air that suits her so well.

Louis opens the door, lets the two women get in — Cécile first, then her mother, who's afraid of getting carsick and insists on sitting by the window — then takes his place in the driver's seat. He pulls on the choke and switches on the ignition and the engine turns like a windmill. Louis is dying to say, "Listen to that, it's just got six cylinders but a big six is better than a small eight," but he keeps silent. Women aren't interested in cars, they can't appreciate the sounds of engines. He's content to drive in silence, while Madame Desmarais takes charge of the conversation. She's the kind of woman who says whatever comes into her head, as if they'd forgotten to put a filter between her thoughts and her words, but who talks so fast that you never know if she really said what you think you heard. Just now she's commenting on the van:

"All those lights are so complicated, what are all those pedals for, I wish I'd had a car but my husband never would have let me drive, is there something wrong with that clock, good grief, it can't be three o'clock!"

"Clocks in cars usually don't work," replies Louis.

"So why do they put them in?"

Louis doesn't answer. He'd have to explain how a battery and an alternator work, and she probably wouldn't listen. Besides, it wasn't a real question, it was meant to show that she was smarter than the Dodge engineers. His mother has long since got him used to these phony questions, always twisting first her backside, then her torso as she formulates them, to show her indignation as much as her moral superiority. It's as if she straightens herself up while swaying, which is exactly what Madame Desmarais just did. Louis is reassured: he knows how this kind of woman functions, talking all the time, seeming to change the subject with every sentence but invariably knowing where she's going: "I've always thought Saint-Hubert Street was so beautiful, especially at night with the lights, too bad it's Sunday, we can't buy anything, I wonder if I shut the fridge door before I left, say, how much does that cost, a new fridge?"

He knows how Madame Desmarais functions, there's that. But what about Cécile? Why isn't she talking? Now, he has to admit it wouldn't be easy, given that her mother never stops. . . . Courtesy, that must be it. Or shyness. But what's important is that she is there, very close, so close he can sometimes sense her leg against his, and her shoulder, and her perfumes. . . . *This is no time to have an accident, Louis, concentrate on driving, try to shift smoothly, to brake gently, that's it. . . .*

Louis has always enjoyed driving, in silence, while the women gab and the children sleep or the oldest ones squabble. He likes the reassuring sound of the motor, he likes to think that he's the one who controls the machine, who dominates the steel and the power. He feels important, responsible. He knows how to shift smoothly, without grinding the gears. He can come to a stop on a hill and start up again without stalling, he's mastered the art of driving on ice and he can even back up with a trailer. He likes to drive in the rain at night and let himself be lulled by the back-and-forth motion of the windshield wipers. He knows how to clean a carburetor or spark plugs, how to fix a flat and even, if he has to, replace a burnt-out fuse with the foil from a cigarette package, or a broken fan belt with a woman's stocking. He knows everything he needs to know so the women can gab away peacefully and the children can sleep safely in the back seat. He's always liked to drive, and likes it particularly on that day, when Cécile is sitting next to him, and he has to rest his arm on the back of the seat behind her, to park the van in front of the store. The manoeuvre is perfectly executed, as usual, and Louis allows himself to leave his arm on the seatback a little longer than necessary. He'd leave it there even longer, maybe venture to brush Cécile's neck with his fingertips, but Madame Desmarais doesn't give him the time; no sooner has the motor stopped than she's out of the van and standing by the store. And she's so excited that Louis has to persuade her to let him by so he can unlock the door and turn off the burglar alarm. As soon as the way is clear, she swoops inside the store — a store just for her!

"Look at that gorgeous kitchen table, things are so nice when they're new, needless to say my husband never could have bought me that, he can't buy me anything any more, poor man, oh! look at the beautiful fridge, how much is it? Is this still the store over here? What a beautiful armchair! Can I try it? Mind you, I expected it'd be bigger; not as big as Dupuis of course, but bigger anyway, seems to me Margot told me that. . . . No, it was Madame Gingras, that was a slip of the tongue. . . . Ooh! Would you look at that chesterfield!"

If it's true that certain hockey players can turn on a dime, women are even quicker at changing the subject when they get tangled up in their lies, or just want to change the subject. But Louis's not in the mood to laugh at her; Madame Demarais keeps on babbling and she's already at the very back of the store, while Cécile hasn't even started to look around yet. She has stopped here right in front of this bedroom set, she stopped for so long that Louis has dared to approach her slowly from behind and to drop his hand onto her shoulder; she hasn't pushed it away, she's even encouraged him, and he thinks he actually felt her shiver, so he has placed his other hand on her other shoulder, a little closer to her neck, and he feels his own heart pounding harder and harder, and his whole body is seething and he'd surely explode if he hadn't heard Madame Desmarais, who has already finished her first inspection and is now coming back to start the second one: "Those fabrics are very nice but I wonder if they're washable, I imagine they show the dirt, I'd put on slipcovers, anyway I'm glad I've seen this store, and how much did you say for a new fridge?"

• • •

Louis was invited to the Desmarais' for supper that night, and then to sit out on the balcony. And it was there, on the balcony, that Louis and Cécile decided that the wedding would take place the following spring, that they'd rent an apartment close to the store but buy a house as soon as business permitted, and that Fillion et Frères would pay Madame Desmarais an allowance, since she was a widow and Cécile could have worked if she weren't getting married.

That night, for the first time in his life, Louis kissed a woman who wasn't his mother — a woman, period, in fact; he couldn't remember ever kissing his mother, or receiving any sign of affection from her.

He was twenty-four years old.

When his lips touched Cécile's, his heart was beating so hard that he nearly fainted. It was as if there were a boxer inside him, a boxer who was punching him from within, leaving him punch-drunk.

Meanwhile, Madame Desmarais was glued to the telephone, tirelessly repeating the same message to all her acquaintances, who would then repeat it to infinity, or at least the female part of infinity. "I thought he'd never decide, but it looks like he finally did it."

• • •

"The little Desmarais girl?" asks Annette, feigning surprise. "The little Desmarais girl from Bennett Street? I say the little girl, but that's just a manner of speaking, of course, since those Desmarais . . . You want to marry Cécile?"

"I'm twenty-four years old, nearly twenty-five. . . . You shouldn't be surprised, you knew I was seeing her. . . ."

"How was I supposed to know? Nobody ever tells me anything. . . ."

Annette can't help rubbing something when she lies, as if she's trying to erase her sin while she's committing it. If she were at least polishing the silverware, Louis would understand, but a stainless steel tea-kettle. . . . Mind you, her latest lie is a little obvious: when Louis came home from Cécile's place, Annette had barely hung up the phone. Simply from the way she hung up he knew that she knew.

"But never mind, I'm used to it. . . . Your father, Philippe, Léo. . . . Everybody goes away, everybody abandons me but it doesn't matter. . . . If you ask me, that's what being a mother means: we suffer when we bring children into the world, we suffer raising them, we suffer again when they leave us. . . . You're hurting me, my boy, you can't imagine how much you're hurting me. But never mind, I'm used to it. I'll offer my suffering to the Lord. I hope that you will be happy, at least. . . ."

I don't know if the Lord appreciated Annette's sacrifice, but I do know that it took Louis a long time to forget that *you*.

23

Niagara

No more war, no more bombs, boats, planes. Since nobody's sure what to do with the surplus tin, it's painted white and made into stoves and refrigerators, washers and dryers. At Fillion et Frères, major appliances come in the back door by the truckload and immediately leave by the front, so quickly that customers complain about drafts, especially in winter. The store is selling stoves, refrigerators and washing machines for the housewife's convenience, but they're also selling walnut-finish kitchen sets, baby beds and high-chairs, studio couches and dressers, along with rocking chairs and standing ashtrays for the comfort of the soldier home from the front, or the tired worker. Louis hires a secretary, salesmen, delivery men and even a handyman to unpack the crates, wash the window and clear the laneway, which is always clogged with cartons. He rarely talks with customers any more, and then mainly to handle difficult cases. He checks invoices, works the cash register, phones orders in to suppliers, greets sales reps and tries to get rid of them, explains to his own salesmen how they mustn't try too hard to sell, and answers the phone sometimes, on the second line, to reassure Simone, who's wondering if Édouard is back from lunch: "He mustn't eat on his own, Louis, do you understand, somebody has to be with him, otherwise the temptation's too strong." *Sure, Simone, sure, but if he goes for lunch with another salesman, it's no better: when salesmen start drinking.* . . . "I'll tell him to call you as soon as he gets back, Simone, I promise." He checks some more invoices, sends away some more sales reps and answers the phone again — the private line; this time it's Béa, who wants to tell Léo she loves him and she's thinking about him. "I'll tell him, Béa, I promise."

Cigarettes burn away in ashtrays, coffee gets cold and sandwiches dry out, but things are going well, so well that he has to work every day and every night: long after closing time there's still the bookkeeping and the mail, paperwork and forms. Business is good beyond their wildest dreams, and Louis isn't complaining. The only trouble is, it doesn't leave him much time for seeing people.

Luckily there are Sundays. Louis and Cécile often cross the Jacques-Cartier Bridge to stroll the streets of Longueuil and Saint-Lambert, where there are such beautiful houses surrounded by lawns; it would be good for the children, we could even have a dog. . . .

"Lawns are fine to look at through the window, but the upkeep's a lot of trouble; and if you get a dog you won't have any lawn at all, I know it's none of my business but. . . ." Madame Desmarais never fails to add her two cents' worth, if one can use the verb "add" of her: she talks all the time. But she likes long car rides so much, and she loves the countryside so much. Mustn't take her too far, though; if they sometimes venture as far as Saint-Bruno or Saint-Hilaire, they absolutely have to be back for five o'clock so she'll have time to cook supper.

After that will come the game of canasta or Parcheesi, the fudge and the spruce beer, then another game of canasta, and so on till ten o'clock, when it will be time for Louis to go home. Right now, though, it's five o'clock, Madame Desmarais is cooking and it's the moment Louis has waited and hoped for all week: the hour when Madame Desmarais is fixing supper, which is always served on the dot of six, and leaves them alone; the hour when he has his Cécile all to himself; the hour of downy skin and curls and perfumes; the hour of light touches and silences, of gentle gestures and sweet shudders. Sometimes they sit side by side on the living-room sofa. Sometimes too, temperature permitting — and their inner temperature always permits it — they stay on the front porch. Finally, Cécile gets up to fetch a shawl from her bedroom, let's say, and when she comes back she lingers behind Louis, behind his back, she stands and puts her hands on his shoulders, very gently, she puts her hands on his shoulders and he feels their warmth all through his body, she puts her hands on his shoulders and sometimes she gives him a light massage and she tells him, "You work so hard, you must be tired. . . ." Those are the moments Louis likes best, his favourite moments, moments of sheer bliss, and sometimes he almost feels like complaining so she'll go on and on, so he'll feel that warmth radiate and spread out in great waves. He protests a little, for form's sake, says that he doesn't work all that hard, that it's normal, then he falls silent; he has never imagined feeling so good, and just for that, just to have her rub his shoulders, he'd work two hundred hours a week if it were possible. Since he can't get up or turn towards her, since he can't return her tenderness or try to "go further" — which she wouldn't allow — he gives himself up, he gives in, surrenders. Sometimes he'll raise his shoulder a little and lower his head to imprison that soft, soft hand, to feel it against his cheek, but Cécile always manages to free herself. He loves this little game.

The first time she rubbed his shoulders like that, he talked to her about his childhood and gave away some of his secrets. Since then, whenever she puts her hands on him he starts again, or rather he goes on. He tells her how he felt when he saw Philippe and Léo jump over the fence at the Laurier wharf, tells her about his secret hiding-place in the shed where he read Jack London and imagined that he saw the Blessed Virgin when a ray of sunlight made its way between the boards.

If Cécile stops, he immediately falls silent. Then she'll come and sit beside him, he'll take her hand, and now it's her turn to talk about school, which she didn't like very much, about sentimental novels by Delly or Berthe Bernage that she reads on the sly and about her mother and how she doesn't want to be like her. No one knows what happened to her father, but some people suspect that he didn't go to war. If what they say is true, if he really did abandon her mother, well, Cécile can understand, a little. It's not because he's gone that her mother is so bitter, it was because of her bitterness that he went away. If I ever become like her — rancorous, never happy — if I ever become a complaining machine, tell me, Louis, I beg you, tell me.

"I promise," replies Louis, even if he doesn't really know what he's committing himself to or how it concerns him. He doesn't dislike Madame Desmarais. He thinks she's predictable and perfectly normal for a woman her age. And since Cécile has decided not to turn out like her, it's up to her to see to it, right? How could he help her with that? Women are so complicated.

He prefers to change the subject: it may be hard to take a honeymoon in the spring, since that's the big season for weddings, as well as the busy season for furniture. He wouldn't want to leave his employees responsible for the store for a whole week, and his brothers have lots of good qualities but. . . . But Léo is Léo, and Édouard isn't really reliable — Simone has trouble controlling him these days. . . . I know we'd talked about spring, but why not the fall? This fall, of course, not next, all the same. . . . It isn't the season for weddings, but in the fall it would be easier to take a little trip around Labour Day or Thanksgiving. . . . Trouble is, we couldn't go to Quebec City like we thought: apparently Stalin and Churchill are coming to town, the hotels will be full, so I was thinking maybe we could go to Niagara Falls, they say the falls are beautiful. . . .

Cécile would have preferred Quebec City in the spring, she

doesn't like the idea of marrying in the fall — people will talk — and she'd imagined that her honeymoon would last longer than one weekend, but she can't dispute Louis's arguments. In the furniture business, fall is a quiet season compared with spring — and, as he says, you're never sure about the future: how can they know if there's going to be another war, or if another depression's going to hit us?

Nor can she reproach him for thinking about his brothers before her: neither Léo nor Édouard had a honeymoon.

She would have preferred Quebec City in the spring and a slightly longer trip, but she won't complain, especially not today. So she goes along with it, says, "That's fine, you're right, I understand," but she sends a little sigh into the air, a tiny little sigh that Louis, who has become a good ornithologist from being around Annette, promptly identifies: *Resignation. Renunciation, female style. Nothing to worry about. You'll see, Cécile, you'll see, in a few years we'll be able to afford to go on trips. . . .*

24

PALISADES

"Tell me, Léo. . . . I . . . I'm not sure how to put this but . . . Remember when you and Philippe used to climb over the palisade at the Laurier wharf and I'd wait for you on the other side?"

"Yes, I remember," replies Léo as he pours a few drops from the little mickey into his chipped mug. "That was a long time ago. . . ."

"Not all that long. . . . Depends on your point of view. . . . But never mind. What I wanted to say was, there're times in life when some people have already crossed over a palisade while others have just waited for the boards to land on their heads. The ones who've gone to the other side know more than the ones who haven't jumped over the fence yet, of course. . . . See what I'm getting at?"

While Louis's eyes are still focused on his cigarette, as he shakes off the ash into the spinning ashtray — actually there are no more ashes, just the glow of this cigarette he's tapping nervously — Léo, leaning against the filing cabinet, swigs some rye and savours it, then knits his brow so he can think. This is liable to take a while, Louis reflects: I've got time to pour another drink. . . . Friday night, eleven o'clock. Édouard has just left so now they can take out the little mickey without too much risk, and it's great that Léo's the only one here. . . .

"Is it the honeymoon you're worried about?"

Does it show that much? wonders Louis as he butts his cigarette, lighting another one almost immediately. Is it written on my face? Or is it one of those days when, just for a change, Léo understands a little too quickly?

"Me too, I was worried. Actually, I didn't sleep for a week. . . . Looks to me like that's happening to you, Louis. . . . Want me to pour you a drink?"

Not only is he understanding quickly, he's anticipating Louis's questions! What luck to have a brother like him, sometimes. . . . Louis accepts the cup that Léo holds out, takes a first sip and immediately feels relieved: he was right to talk this over with Léo and not Édouard. Already he doesn't get half the latter's references, and it's doubly painful to feign comprehension just to save face. . . . And how could he have admitted to his little brother that he hasn't jumped over the fence yet, that, to tell the truth, he's actually still quite innocent. If Philippe had been there, of course, he could have asked him to explain the unwritten laws governing these areas. . . . Louis wouldn't have dared bring up the subject with his father, though. And certainly not with his mother. Absolutely unthinkable. In any case, he'd only have been given a "My poor boy, if you only knew," followed by a multitude of sighs. The priests? They'd have talked about lilies and purity, about pollen and respect. And he didn't need metaphors or morals, he needed some straight answers to his questions: How does it work? What do you have to do? Léo seems to be living a great love story with his Béa, and he's a simple man. So he'll give good advice. With him there'll be no circumlocutions, no oratorical precautions, it will be straightforward, with no fuss, first you do this, then you do that, and that's it. . . .

"Will this be your first time?" asks Léo, blushing a little and not daring to look his brother in the eye.

"Yes, my very first time. I mean. . . . I've kissed Cécile of course, I've even. . . ." *(Even what, exactly? The truth is, you've never done anything more, not a thing, so you're not going to start using vague words to suggest that you've had some experience, you're going to tell your brother the truth and, nothing but the truth. Léo won't betray you, you know that.)* "I . . . I've kissed Cécile but as for the rest. . . ."

"Yes, I understand. It was the same for us. We were like Mary and Joseph, we didn't really know where to start. . . ."

"Exactly. . . . So tell me: where *do* you start?"

"Look. . . ." replies Léo, who's getting redder and redder and isn't sure how to lean against the filing cabinet. "You've . . . you've done it with your hand, I imagine?"

"I . . ." *(The truth, Louis, nothing but the truth.)* "Yes, sure."

"Well, it's the same with a woman, except that the woman

replaces the hand; I mean, it's inside the woman that replaces the hand, if you see what I mean. The trouble is, the woman usually isn't ready right away. So you have to pet her, starting at the top. You have to always start at the top. It's more . . . more diplomatic, see. More refined. You tickle her neck, you kiss it, stuff like that, and you say sweet things, the kind of words women like to hear, you tell her she's beautiful, she smells good, whatever comes into your head, you tell her you want her. . . ."

"I get it, Léo. And then?"

"And then what?"

"Look, Léo, you aren't going to pull that one on me again . . . So, pet her, tell her sweet things. . . . Then what?"

"Oh, right! And then. . . . And then you go down, down. . . . You stop for a while where . . . umm . . . where there's something that isn't by itself. Do what you did for the neck, except do it twice and if she likes it she'll tell you to go on, otherwise you go down, down, be careful when you get to where it's ticklish, and then it's time to check the oil. The idea is, you put a finger in the . . . in the . . . Where the man goes. You put a finger in and check to see if it's wet. See, the kisses, the sweet words, they're like the choke. They get you up and running from a cold start . . . in a way . . . I don't know about you, but I could use a little refill. . . ."

You'll need it, thinks Louis, who has never seen his brother so red-faced. You too, Louis; you've never had such a dry throat. Admit that you're impressed by that brother of yours, talking in metaphors. . . .

"While you're checking the oil, you can . . . Right away if

you want, you can always use something smaller to do what you're going to do later with something bigger. Can't hurt."

"How long?"

"Oh, I couldn't say. A minute, two minutes. . . . Cécile ought to tell you if she likes it, and she'll also tell you when she's ready. So then you put your . . . your you-know-what in the . . . the . . . you move a little, not too fast, and you hold back till Cécile makes some funny noises. It'll surprise you the first time, but don't worry: that means she's happy. And then you let yourself go. And that's that, Louis. If you've got any other questions. . . ."

Louis has tons of other questions but he doesn't dare ask them. He has the impression that he's been torturing his brother, making him walk like this across a minefield, and Léo has pulled off quite a feat by avoiding all the words that make you sin just by saying them or even thinking of saying them. Léo is getting his normal colour back now, like a thermometer put in cold water: first his forehead, then his cheeks. . . .

"I'll try to manage. . . . Thanks, Léo."

"Don't worry about it. . . . It always seems complicated at first, but it's like going somewhere new. The first time you're always looking at your map, asking the way, getting lost, but once you've travelled the road you know it by heart and it just keeps getting easier. Good luck, Louis. You'll see, the Good Lord has set things up right."

• • •

It's been six months since Louis and Cécile came back from Niagara Falls and moved into their apartment on Drolet

Street, while they look for a real house. Six months that Louis has seemed tense and preoccupied when he gets to the store in the morning.

"Listen, Léo. . . . I'd like to talk to you about something. . . ."

From the sound of his brother's voice, Léo can guess what that something will be. He knew it was coming. It's Friday night, like the other time. The three brothers always stay around after closing on Friday, to review the week and collect their salaries. Édouard insists on being paid cash and he always leaves first, anxious to get home to his Simone — or so he tries to convince his brothers, without much success. If he does go home to her it's much later, and there's no guarantee he'll recognize her. And the next morning you'd better not count on him coming to work, at least not before noon: first he has to wake up, then he has to remember his name. . . .

So Édouard has left right after getting his pay, and Louis has taken advantage of his absence to get out the little mickey and pour his brother a drink without even asking if he wants one — as if he'd turn it down. The two brothers have talked about the problems of Édouard, who has never been able to control himself (incidentally, how is it that he hasn't yet found the little mickey's hiding-place? A thirsty man is a man of sound hunches...), then about how good business is and finally about their mother, who has asked for an increase in her allowance since life's so expensive, it's terrible . . . . Louis knows what he's doing as he fills Léo's glass faster than usual: Béa knows you'll be home late, Léo, you can have another little drink. . . .

"By the way, Léo, speaking of Béa, I want to tell you that

you . . . you helped me a lot that time when we talked about . . . about marriage, in fact I want to thank you again. . . . You said that at first you have to keep looking at the map and asking directions. . . . I wanted to ask you — if you don't mind talking about it, of course — I wanted to ask how it is for you and Béa, usually."

"Fine. Just fine. Why?"

That I already know, Léo, just from the look on your face, what I want to know is how it's fine, and I don't know how to ask you that. . . .

"The other time you told me about . . . about strange noises when she's happy. . . . Does that . . . does that happen every time?"

"Not every time, no. But often. Often enough, anyway. When it's not so good she tells me it doesn't matter, she likes it all the same. Her parents were born in the Gaspé. Both of them. Her father and her mother. They were young when they came to Montreal, but you could still say that Béa's a hundred percent pure Gaspesian. Did you know that?"

"No. . . . And why are you telling me, anyway? What does the Gaspé Peninsula have to do with anything?"

"The Gaspé Peninsula, nothing. But it's where Béa comes from, that's what's important."

"Why?"

"Apparently women from the Gaspé always like it. So people say. And I think it's true. Every time I'm in the mood, she is too. Sometimes I go to bed tired, I'm not even thinking about it, and I tell you, before long she wakes up my Canadien. . . . Why d'you want to know?"

"Oh, no reason. . . ."

"Is everything okay with Cécile?"

"Oh yes, everything's just fine."

Just fine except Cécile wasn't born in the Gaspé, shall we say. . . . But maybe Béa's an exception too, even for someone from the Gaspé. Maybe Cécile's right when she says it's exactly the way her mother told her, the way all mothers tell their daughters. Put up with it, my girl. Cécile, who greets a proposition with a sigh, who fulfils her conjugal duty without passion and ends it with a sigh, the same sigh, the very same sigh as at the beginning. . . .

"Would you rather not talk about it any more, Louis?"

"That's about it, yes. . . ."

"Have another little shot, then. . . ."

• • •

Louis will never talk about those things again. Not with anybody, not even Léo. He won't feel like it and he won't have the time. Soon there'll be Jocelyne, Christiane, Benoît, Louise, Yves, Marc-André. . . . Life moves so fast. It's scary.

25

CHROME

A Sunday morning in 1950. Madame Desmarais settles into the back seat with Jocelyne and Christiane, and Cécile sits in front with Benoît in her arms; he's just three months old — at the moment, Louise, Yves and Marc-André are just vague probabilities. Louis locks the door of the Drolet Street apartment, looks at the key for a moment — *won't be using you much longer, old key* — and proudly takes his place behind the wheel of his brand new De Soto. A De Soto De Luxe, royal blue, with wraparound bumpers, built-in sun visors and whitewall tires. Everything works incredibly well in this car, from the fluid-drive transmission to the dashboard clock, which keeps excellent time as long as he remembers to set it every morning, including the six aligned cylinders, which make the most beautiful music: it sounds powerful, reliable, solid, like a lion's roar.

"Don't drive too fast," says Cécile as soon as he's turned the ignition key. "The children will get carsick. . . ."

Louis doesn't like being given this kind of advice. He never drives too fast, especially when there are three babies on board, not to mention his mother-in-law. But Cécile always has to give her warning, as if she wants to prove to her mother that, while Louis may be driving, she controls the driver. He mutters something that sounds like a reply, then thinks about something else: it's a beautiful day, a wonderful day, he can feel the motor humming all the way to the gearshift, you move it from Park to Drive and the gears change by themselves, automatically. *Drive a De Soto and feel De Luxe*. Maybe he should write the company and suggest that as a slogan? And the seat, it's so comfortable. . . . It resembles vinyl, which is all the rage for dining-room sets these days. Everybody wants a chrome-legged table with a gleaming Arborite top, and chairs that have chrome legs too and vinyl seats that go *whhsshh* when you sit on them. Customers want vinyl and chrome, gleaming and clean, so that's what they get. The trick is to adapt. Leave appliances to the specialists and the department stores, for instance. You have to offer guarantees, hire repairmen, a pile of trouble. While a chrome kitchen table, before it breaks down. . . . And you don't change washing machines because there's a new model. A living-room suite, though. . . . There too, no more wood, not even veneer. Wood looks poor. So people lay carpet everywhere, they want padding and stuffing, as soon as they've got a little money they buy new furniture, as if to help them forget the war and the Depression, forget everything from *before*. That's what fashion is for. But we won't complain, if it lets us buy a royal blue De Soto and a house, a genuine new house that we've watched grow like a flower.

A new house, ten minutes from the Jacques-Cartier Bridge — the contractor didn't lie, it's ten minutes exactly. Here we are. Only yesterday there was nothing in these big fields but alfalfa, a ramshackle barn and a few cows, and that's all. We drove by it every Sunday, just to confirm that there was nothing there. But in the spring of 1950, the alfalfa didn't have time to grow. From one Sunday to the next, streets and avenues were laid out, fire hydrants and telephone poles planted and, finally, big holes were dug and filled with cement, where houses would go up. It's happening everywhere around Montreal, no matter which bridge you take to get there. Wherever there's a vacant lot, it's marked off with streets and sown with houses. Houses that spring up in the middle of a big playground, with air and trees, green lawns and blue skies, swings and rinks, dogs running around and children's laughter. Everywhere, houses are growing — houses that will have to be filled with tables and chairs, sofas and beds — for the time being, though, the important thing is *my* house, *our* house. It's a little far from the store, of course, I'd have preferred Pont-Viau, but Cécile insisted on Saint-Lambert. Doesn't matter, I'll be able to decompress, it's not such a chore to drive a De Soto De Luxe across the Jacques-Cartier Bridge; you bounce onto Île Sainte-Hélène the way a flat stone bounces off the water, to go to a greener land. It will be so good for the children. . . . "Everything all right back there, Madame Desmarais?"

"It's fine. I think your clock's slow, though . . . And new plastic has a strong smell. . . . Do you really think your house will be finished?"

"It's supposed to be. . . . This time, it's supposed to be completely finished. . . ."

Every Sunday, Louis brings the women and children to Saint-Lambert to watch their house grow. Too bad he can't go during the week when the workers are there. Is there any finer sight than a house frame rising into the sky? A few blows of the hammer and you've got walls and a roof, doors and windows. Before, there was nothing; now, there's the framework of a house. The men have carved out their space in the sky. And then the hammers fall silent and the Italians arrive with their plumb lines, their mortar and their bricks, which they lay slowly, one after the other, because you can't do it any other way; a long series of slow movements, very slow movements, the proper speed for the wall to go up before your eyes. And then the plumbers and electricians, the painters and handymen, and it's all done so fast that by the beginning of July the house is standing proudly against the blue sky, a beautiful brand-new house surrounded by a sea of mud.

"They aren't going to leave it like that, I hope!" says Cécile as soon as she's out of the car. "Is that supposed to be a sidewalk? Those old beams?"

Louis explains that it's normal, the contractor is hired to build a house, not a botanical garden, and the man who was supposed to pave the entrance got behind; as soon as he's finished, Louis himself will do the landscaping, with his brothers; but Cécile isn't really listening to him and she grumbles again when she nearly slips on the muddy beam. Madame Desmarais is not to be outdone — and who's ever heard of wearing high heels to visit a construction site? — as she repeats that what's important in a job is the finishing, what's the idea of leaving a mess like that, I hope it's better inside because if you ask me. . .

But once they're finally inside the house, they change their tune; oh, there are a few details to complain about — drops of paint on the windows, a closet that's not as deep as expected — but these big white immaculate rooms with no useless woodwork that would just gather dust, the light that streams in the big bow window in the living room, the brand-new kitchen cupboards. . . .

Louis has gone to the basement to check the electrical panel. He's already picturing a bedroom or two for the children, a rec room with a television set — apparently it'll be here soon, since they've already got it in the States — a La-Z-Boy where he'll be able to relax. . . .

Before he goes back upstairs he shuts his eyes, takes a deep breath of this basement air that stays cool even in the middle of July and slowly savours what Madame Desmarais said to her daughter as she was opening and closing the cupboards, never suspecting that her son-in-law would hear her down below — but in a new house you can hear everything: "All my life I've dreamed about having cupboards like these, and a bow window. . . . You've got lots to be happy about, my girl. . . ."

• • •

As soon as the asphalt is down in the driveway, Édouard, Léo and Louis, equipped with rakes and rollers, cords and levels, will landscape the two lots, Louis's and Léo's, because Léo has bought a house a few streets away from the same contractor. The three of them will spend three Sundays on it.

When anyone asked Léo and Louis which of them had influenced the other, they would shrug. Not only did they not know, the question was of no interest to them. They'd told themselves that it would be more practical to live in the same neighbourhood, that they'd be able to share some tools, it would cost less, the cousins would be able to play together. . . . Which of them got the idea first? Though they scratched their heads — and that's not just a manner of speaking, they both did that whenever they were asked this kind of question, even taking off their hats if necessary — they didn't remember.

Cécile, though, remembered perfectly well: it was Louis — actually she and Louis, the two of them, the couple they formed, who had chosen first Saint-Lambert, then the neighbourhood and finally the contractor. The problem was that Béa was convinced of the contrary, and not just a little. It was the one subject that could make her hit the roof, she who was usually so calm: Léo was quite capable of making his own decisions, it was an insult to think otherwise, they'd discovered this part of town ages ago, in fact a cousin of Béa's knew the contractor. . . . Ten, twenty, fifty years later, the two women would still stick to their guns. It was far from being their only disagreement, but it was the one that always seemed the most important, the most crucial. No one among the aunts and uncles and cousins ever knew why the two sisters-in-law went at each other over something so minor. As for Léo and Louis, they were adrift in an ocean of perplexity. Especially Léo. It was enough to broach the topic with him to see the water level rising in his eyes and there was nothing as sad as the sight of that man in tears. It was best to avoid the subject.

And so Léo and Louis — or was it Louis and Léo?— bought their houses at the same time, and no doubt they tried to persuade Édouard to do the same, but he preferred to wait a while — or was it Simone who applied the brakes? — though that didn't prevent him from giving his brothers a hand; whatever condition he was in, Édouard was always ready to bundle boards, paint, even level the ground. He'd even have run to the church every hour to speed through a rosary if his brothers had asked.

• • •

Louis, Léo and Édouard had never done any landscaping before, but you'd think they'd been removing stones, placing cement slabs for a patio, unrolling turf and planting trees all their lives — Louis will plant a weeping willow because they grow fast and children need shade as well as sun; Léo a clump of birches because he's always loved birch trees. At the end of summer the municipality will plant maples in front of all the houses, and thirty years later it will look very beautiful.

But for the time being, the three brothers are there, tired from the good work they've done, and looking in silence at the huge orange sun as it takes forever to set over the suburb.

In all the neighbours' yards, tired, worn-out men have stopped pounding nails, pouring cement and unrolling turf at the same time, and at the same time they're all treating themselves to a good cold beer.

Louis, Édouard, Léo. Dirty, muddy, exhausted. Their backs are killing them, their hands are covered with blisters. Édouard is leaning against the roll of turf, Louis and Léo are sitting on the steps. They drink a beer, then another, why not, there are plenty in the kitchen sink. Édouard, whose throat is dry from the dust, knocks them back as quickly as he used to recite Hail Marys. Go get yourself another one, Édouard, you've earned it, but watch out all the same, we need you at the store tomorrow. . . .

At the third beer, Édouard ventures to sing a few notes, very softly. Hardly more than a murmur to express the pain of the little cabin boy who used to sing at night on the main mast of the corvette. Louis clears his throat — damn cigarettes — and he in turn ventures a murmur. When he's found the key — it doesn't happen automatically after all these years, he finally sings the words: *Over and over the restless soul*, and then Léo joins in, not so much singing as reciting, *words that the wind blew far and wide*.

26

Because Happiness Beckons across the Waves

Louis, Léo and Édouard sing "Le petit mousse" while the sun takes forever to set over the suburb. Louis, Léo and Édouard sing "The Little Cabin Boy," then they fall silent, all three of them at the same time, halfway through the fourth verse.

Thus sang the little cabin boy
High on the mast, to the billowing main;
And all through the night his soft, soft voice
Rose over the water, a sad refrain.

It's at that moment, that precise moment, that they hear, all three of them at the same time, Philippe's voice joining in with theirs. They stop singing, they stop drinking and talking, and they stand there for a very long time, all three of them, looking at the clouds.

27

Accountant's Day

Though accountants are reputed to be boring, that's certainly not the fault of Monsieur Vinet, who spends the first Monday of every month at Fillion et Frères. He's short and bald except for two or three endless hairs that he insists on plastering to his skull from ear to ear, which make him look as if he's wearing permanent headphones. He is round everywhere, from his belly to his face; even his eyebrows and mouth, always split with a big smile, are perfect semicircles. If he's not smiling it's because he is roaring with laughter, laughter so contagious that he's easily forgiven for his most hackneyed gags, his weakest jokes; there's nothing funnier than the sight of him laughing. He's also a happy practitioner of the art of imitating weird sounds, specializing in flushing toilets, various chimes, cats in heat — more than one tomcat has been fooled — or his undisputed masterpiece, the sound of tearing cloth. Before executing this one, he always waits till a man bends over to tie a shoelace or pick up a pencil; when his victim straightens up and runs his hand over his rear end to check the seams in his pants, he bursts out in a booming laugh, proud of his accomplishment; his laughter feeds itself, and Monsieur Vinet doesn't stop till he's on the verge of apoplexy. Poor Léo must have been taken in at least twenty times.

When the Fillion brothers saw him parking his enormous automobile — he always bought the longest, widest models — they were already laughing in anticipation. Monsieur Vinet would ring the bell and the show would begin; one of his favourite sketches was a domestic scene between Monsieur and Madame Doorbell, in which he played the female part. He got them every time. Then he'd take off his hat very slowly, as if he were afraid that a bird or rabbit was going to escape from it — he'd take the opportunity to flatten his three hairs surreptitiously — and deliver a couple of risqué jokes before settling into the office where he'd spend the day filing invoices, filling out government forms or doing who knows what. When they'd finally forgotten he was there, he'd do his imitation of a ringing telephone, a dogfight or a police siren, and startle everyone, and then he'd break out laughing again, laughing till the tears came, till he had to hold his belly in both hands, till he was out of breath. Next he would turn pale again and go back to being an accountant with his books, but undoubtedly some part of his brain was concocting new gags while he was adding up numbers.

At the end of the day the three brothers would gather around him for the monthly financial report, which usually took no more than ten minutes: expenses were so-and-so, income was such-and-such, which gave a profit of X. While the figure sometimes seemed impressive, not much was left once the taxes had been deducted, along with Madame Fillion's allowance, the funds to be invested and the reserves set aside in the event of hard times — Monsieur Vinet was a cautious man. The three Fillion brothers were usually happy with their strictly identical weekly salaries. If there was a profit left, they'd divide that too into three equal shares, but using different methods. Édouard's share — like his salary for that matter — had for some time been paid in the form of a cheque made out to Simone, who would pick it up the next morning. Édouard had signed a letter to that effect before a witness; even if he pleaded with his brothers on his knees, or threatened the accountant with the worst forms of cruelty, no one was allowed to pay him any amount whatsoever. Monsieur Vinet wasn't even authorized to give Édouard the cheque to be handed over to Simone; he could have traded it for liquid cash. Very liquid.

Léo too was paid by cheque, a cheque made out to Béa, but for a totally different reason: too often he simply forgot his money, or even lost it altogether. Béa too preferred to pick it up herself.

Louis left his salary and his profit in the hands of Monsieur Vinet, who looked after his personal accounting: he paid his taxes, sent an allowance cheque to Madame Desmarais and deposited in a bank account the money Cécile would need to look after the needs of the family. It corresponded roughly to an average salary — sometimes high average, when business was good, and sometimes average average. "*You're a business-man in just one respect,*" Cécile would say, "*and that's the hours you work. Aside from that, we scrape by like everybody else. Worse even: other women at least get a chance see their husbands, while you, you're always working. . . .*"

"*Aren't you exaggerating a little, Cécile? You're forgetting that the store supports both our mothers, we get a good price on furniture and a company car. . . .*"

"*And what about your sisters, do they pay your mother an allowance? Hélène and Thérèse could certainly afford to, couldn't they? And what about Margot, does she pay your mother an allowance?*"

"*No, I don't think so. . . . We've always had an agreement that . . .*"

"*That Fillion et Frères would support your mother, I know. And the result is, your sisters get their furniture for half price and they don't give your mother a cent. They get just the good side of the deal, besides having rich husbands. And who gets the short end of the stick? Me, that's who! Fillion et Frères supports everybody except me! The only thing that matters is your family! I always come last! And that's the truth!*"

"*That's not fair, Cécile: you're forgetting that I pay your mother an allowance. I don't have to do that. . . .*"

"*Do you mean you're going to take it away?*"

"*I didn't say that!*"

"*But you're thinking it, I know you're thinking it!*"

"Come down off your cloud, Louis!"

Léo stands there waving his arms as if he were wiping an imaginary windshield, and Louis wakes up: don't spoil Accountant's Day with these reminiscences of quarrels, especially when Monsieur Vinet is closing the ledger. Once the accounting is done they can move on to serious matters: playing cards.

Léo takes some beers from the fridge in the back of the store and hands them out to everyone except Monsieur Vinet, to whom he offers a ginger ale. Monsieur Vinet has never drunk anything but ginger ale with nothing in it. He maintains that it has as many bubbles as beer does, and that it has the same effect — on the belly anyway. The men play blackjack and poker, but only for fun: the stakes are always symbolic and the games themselves are just a pretext. The moment will always come when Monsieur Vinet imitates the sound of tearing cloth as Léo is getting up to fetch more beer, or Édouard and Monsieur Vinet will embark on a dirty joke contest and they'll forget the cards, they'll forget everything, and they'll leave the store around midnight, totally exhausted, cheekbones aching and abdominal muscles as sore as if they'd spent the evening at the gym. At Fillion et Frères, they call this doing the books.

At least, that's the way it was most of the time.

There were other times when it was not so joyous.

For instance, an evening in the mid-fifties when Monsieur Vinet takes Louis aside to tell him about a recurrent problem: the store's cash doesn't balance. Sometimes there are ten dollars missing, sometimes twenty, rarely more, but it happens very often, especially when the end of the week comes around, and it never happens when Édouard is off or on vacation. "I'm not telling you anything you don't know, Louis. You've known for a long time. Everybody does. It's getting serious. You have to act, as soon as possible, for everybody's good."

It's true that everybody knows, starting with Louis: Édouard has never found out where the little mickey is hidden, but he blithely dips into the cash when it's time to satisfy his tyrannical needs. The secretary has often told Louis, who has actually caught his brother red-handed. Édouard claimed that it was just a loan he'd repay as soon as possible, and Louis pretended to believe him. But the loans were never repaid, of course, and Édouard would leave work at three in the afternoon and come back two or three hours later, his mouth full of Life Savers. Sometimes he would say he'd had a business lunch with an important buyer who wanted to furnish a hotel, or a man with a tavern who needed five hundred chairs. . . . The unsteadier his gait, the bigger his lies. Louis didn't know if Édouard was really trying to sell furniture to tavern owners, but he knew he was providing them with the means to buy it. Just as he knew that Fillion et Frères couldn't support an employee who took two salaries and brought in nothing.

Sometimes Édouard would drop out of sight for two or three days. No one knew where he was, not even Simone. When he came home, he'd dissolve into tears, shamefaced, and swear they wouldn't catch him doing it again, he wouldn't drink another drop, or only now and then, moderately. . . . It's a terrible thing, it's getting worse day by day, we have to do something. But what?

Louis had talked to Léo about it. Directly, without hiding anything. Léo had replied that for sure they had to do something, but he didn't know what, and then he had scratched his head sadly and Louis had seen the water level rising in his eyes. "*You* do something; I don't know what," he'd managed to get out, before he returned to the back of the store. It was too big a problem for Léo, and talking about it would just upset him.

Louis had also written a long letter to Juliette, asking for advice. She had advised him to pray, to pray a lot, assuring him that she'd join her own prayers to his and that by dint of praying the solution would appear one day, it would seem to come out of nowhere, it would take surprising paths, but it would come, of that Juliette was certain. . . .

Louis reread the letter three times and felt soothed by it, but it hadn't been very helpful. He'd have liked something more, let's say, pragmatic. Nonetheless, he'd gone back to the Nocturnal Adoration, praying for a long time to the Virgin and Jesus and Saint Joseph, patron saint of those who sold firewood, and even to Philippe and Étienne, who made up the celestial section of Fillion et Frères. This had brought him a few good moments of meditation and silence, but no solution.

Then he'd talked to his mother. Without too much hope, but you never know: some mothers give good advice, apparently — the ones in movies and novels, at any rate.

"That's impossible. Édouard went to the seminary. He was practically a priest. I know he has a drinking problem but he didn't take money from the till. You're making that up."

"But I'm telling you, I saw him. So did the secretary. And the accountant knows. . . ."

"Your secretary? That old maid, Mademoiselle Thibeault? Seems to me she used to have her eye on Édouard. . . . I wouldn't be surprised if she made the whole thing up out of jealousy. Who's the other one? Vinet? You mean you take him seriously? For pity's sake, he's trying to pull a fast one. . . . By the way, did I tell you I got a postcard from Margot, from Florida? Wait, let me go and get it. . . ."

His mother's way of changing the subject had always exasperated Louis, and did so even more on that day.

Finally he'd talked about it to Cécile. Unfortunately.

"I've been telling you that for ages, but you never listen to me. Édouard is a good-for-nothing. You ought to fire him. Take this opportunity to get rid of him. You've already got Léo, who isn't good for much. . . . You're throwing money out the window, Louis. . . . Behave like a man, for once."

"Is a man supposed to kick out his brother when he doesn't bring in any money?"

"He may be your brother but he's a drunk. A bottomless barrel. A drunk and a thief."

"Look, Édouard's sick and I don't think being on the street would help him. Have you thought about Simone, have you thought about his children?"

"And you, have you thought about me, have you thought about your children? I know the name of his sickness: it's called Fillionitis. Sell a hutch, a shot of Scotch. . . ." (When she's annoyed she bustles around the kitchen, *she's like Annette, exactly like Annette*, and then she attacks on another front, *like Annette, exactly like Annette*.) "Anyway, why are you telling me if you've already made up your mind? Your brothers come before me, as usual. Make up your own mind; after all, you're the one wanted to be a *businessman*. . . ."

If she'd been able to whistle the word like a tea-kettle she'd have done it, but she contents herself with flinging a handful of utensils into the sink and splashing soapy water on the cupboards, and she turns up the volume of the radio in case the message wasn't clear enough: give me some air, Louis, get out of my kitchen.

Louis goes outside for a smoke and he walks for a long time, a very long time, before finally coming in to bed very late, long after Cécile. When he slips between the sheets, she pretends she's asleep.

There was no slamming of doors or breaking of dishes, but this exchange has certainly been their worst domestic fight. Hard. Deep. That leaves indelible traces. Louis can't get to sleep. He stares at the ceiling, where the same questions keep turning around and around. Why that sarcastic emphasis on the word "businessman"? Louis has often heard Madame Desmarais employ the term but he's never used it himself. Rather, he sees himself as a merchant, because that's the simplest way to define what he does, which is buying and selling. Besides, he never *decided* to become a businessman, it was life that pushed him in that direction, and it was life that pushed Édouard to drink. No one can know why he drinks so much, you mustn't judge people, and you certainly mustn't put them out on the street when they need help. . . . "You ought to fire him. Take this opportunity to get rid of him." *She wants me to kick out my brother. My own brother. When he's sick. When he needs help. And even if I wanted to, I couldn't: the store is as much his as mine. . . .*

The next morning they find Louis in the basement, asleep in his La-Z-Boy, surrounded by empty bottles.

• • •

"You can't do anything for him, Louis; he's your brother, and besides, the store is as much his as yours. You can't do anything for him and it's not your fault. But if you want to leave it to me, if you'll give me a free hand, I think I can find the right words. . . . There's a good reason why I only drink ginger ale. . . ."

"I can't tell you what a help you are, Roland, my friend. . . ."

"I'm not making any promises, but I'll try."

Monsieur Vinet. Roland Vinet. An accountant. A mere accountant whom some people see as a clown. A mere accountant who puts his hand on Louis's shoulder, oh, just barely, just long enough to console him a little, to relieve him of part of his tension, to express his friendship. An accountant who goes on to take Édouard into the office and give him some straight talk.

There won't be a card game that night. They talk, that's all. They talk for a long time, and you have to believe that Monsieur Vinet has found the words he needed, because on his way out of the office Édouard announces to his brothers and associates that he's going to take a two-week . . . vacation, let's say, because he wants to get himself back in shape.

No one knows where he went exactly, or what was done to him. Words, shots, pills? They don't know. What they do know is that he came back a different man.

At first he was a frightening sight, he'd lost so much weight and looked so dazed. “You know, Louis,” he said, “I’ve always felt guilty at being the only one who wasn’t beat up by the Dorgan brothers. But now I have been.”

Maybe that’s their therapy, Louis thinks: stop drinking or we turn you over to the Dorgan brothers.

Weeks and months passed and Édouard didn’t drink a single drop. He had to have something to do all the time. When there were no customers he’d sweep or dust or do crossword puzzles — anything. Every night when the store closed, Simone came to pick him up and took him straight home. Except on Monday and Wednesday, when it was Monsieur Vinet’s turn to wait for Édouard outside the store to take him to Mass, as he called it — actually, to meetings of Alcoholics Anonymous.

Years passed without the slightest hitch. Not a drop, not even on New Year’s Day. Édouard became again the excellent salesman he’d once been, bought a nice little house in Pont-Viau and was an exemplary father and husband who never missed his meetings on Monday and Wednesday with Monsieur Vinet, or failed to help anyone he could help.

“It won’t last,” Cécile said whenever his name came up. “Believe me, it’ll never last.” It was as if she was angry with him for being successful.

Édouard did indeed have a relapse twelve years later. Twelve years! He had managed to stay sober for twelve years, but that didn’t stop Cécile from repeating, “I told you so,” to anyone who’d listen, and even to those who wouldn’t. Never in front of Louis, though.

When Édouard slipped, he fell a long way — or perhaps we

should say he went a long way. All the way to the Saint-Jean-de-Dieu Hospital, in fact, where he was interned for more than a month in an attempt to cure him with heavy doses of words or shots or pills, I don't know which.

"If the first time was the Dorgans," he said when he go tout, "this time was my Second World War."

Roland Vinet was waiting for him at the door. To take him to Mass, to tell him that everyone's entitled to make a mistake, that even Christ fell three times. He helped him hang on for seven or eight years, till the next relapse.

Seven or eight years isn't negligible. There would be more relapses later on, closer and closer together, and many remissions, and everyone would finally get used to it. People said that Édouard was unstable, or overly sensitive, or that he was like some couples who need fights so they can have reconciliations — except that his fights were with himself.

Simone had her own highs and lows, she took some well-earned conjugal breaks, but she always went back to her husband.

And every time Édouard fell, Monsieur Vinet was there to help him. Always.

• • •

When Édouard took his first "vacation," Léo decided to stop drinking too, out of solidarity but also out of concern for his own health: the doctor's been talking about it for a long time now, he said, maybe it'll help me with my memory problems. . . .

He stopped drinking just like that, all at once, with no

outside help and apparently no difficulty: he simply forgot that he liked it.

Now when they played cards on the first Monday of the month, everyone drank ginger ale, even Louis. But he'd sometimes linger in the bathroom, where he always kept a little mickey cool, in the tank. He'd have liked to stop drinking too, but in his case it was, let's say, a little more complicated.

• • •

Monsieur Vinet died at the age of sixty-six. His heart.

I didn't get to know him well when I was young. For me, he was a friend of my father's, a man from another age, a gentleman who wore a hat. But as my father insisted, I felt I had to go to the funeral parlour, with my brothers. And I wasn't sorry. Uncle Édouard was there and he told us his story, of which we knew only little bits at the time. There were also some cousins there that we hadn't seen for a long time, and lots of other people Monsieur Vinet had helped over the course of his life. Monsieur Vinet had known dozens of Uncle Édouards, and they were all there to bid a final farewell to this chubby little man who was so good at imitating the rip of a pair of pants. And they all remembered that imitation, of course, and thought about it every time a new visitor came and knelt at the coffin. Never in all my life have I laughed as much as I did that night.

His name was Roland Vinet. Monsieur Roland Vinet.

28

ORGANIZATIONAL CHART

During the fifties and sixties, Fillion et Frères is a solid enterprise, a prosperous business whose name is highly regarded throughout the city, at least in the French-Canadian part — but even so, it's not Rockefeller or Eaton or even Dupuis Frères. In any case, the fact that your name appears in big letters on the front of a store doesn't mean you're rolling in dough. And the furniture business, like so many others, is subject to seasonal fluctuation. While the fall is quite a good season, sales drop after Christmas and don't come back until March, when a truly insane period begins that lasts until June, ending abruptly with the last wedding; after that, you twiddle your thumbs till September. Who, after all, would think of buying a sofa during a heat wave? Under such conditions it's hard to hold onto your staff. Fillion et Frères isn't the government, able to pay employees to do nothing for six months of the year. It's not surprising, then, that the store has seen dozens and dozens of drivers and delivery men whose careers were brief. Delivering sofas up spiral staircases is great exercise for the biceps and the dorsals, but it's rarely seen as a lifelong occupation. Those who didn't opt for an out-and-out change of career would try to find a stable, steady job, unionized if possible, whereas the dream of those with a true trucker's soul was to take an eighteen-wheeler down the roads to Florida. Drivers and delivery men were only passing through, with the notable exception of Monsieur Demers, who worked for Fillion et Frères all his life.

It was also very hard to find good salesmen, and even harder to hold onto them. If peoples have their own distinctive characteristics and features, the same is true for occupations, and salesmen often have unstable temperaments. Sometimes they have to be let go if their breath smells like turpentine, or if they think they're irresistible — which inevitably happens as soon as they have any success — and start chasing women. The most successful want to be paid on commission, something Louis always refused to do. He made it a question of principle. To begin with, it was because he wanted his customers to come back, and for that to happen, in his opinion, it was essential they not feel hounded by salesmen. For Louis, though, there was more, much more, than this merely commercial consideration: the thought of any relation between how much you earn and how hard you work struck him as not only immoral but indecent. At the very least, there should be no connection. The employee must always do his best, regardless of his salary, because that's his responsibility — to his boss, of course, but also to his customers, and even more to himself, because there's nothing like the feeling of a duty fulfilled. That was how Louis had behaved when he worked for Lunn, and it was how everyone should behave in all circumstances and that was that, and it should apply as much to a sweeper as to a doctor.

The salesmen would learn their trade at Fillion's and afterwards, as soon as they'd become as vain as salesmen, they'd move on somewhere else to sell cars, insurance or cheap furniture; and when they'd earned a little money, they would buy themselves gold pens and click them in their customers' ears while saying *proactive*, *paradigm*, *proactive*, *paradigm*.

It was terribly hard, then, to hold onto salesmen, with the notable exception of Monsieur Paquin, who worked for the Fillions all his life.

Such a business didn't need an army of secretaries, either. One was enough, especially if she was utterly devoted to the family. The one at Fillion et Frères was called Mademoiselle Thibeault.

Monsieur Paquin, Monsieur Demers, Mademoiselle Thibeault. Two men from another age and an old maid with a long nose. They certainly deserve to have a few words devoted to them.

• • •

Monsieur Paquin had started his career selling shoes and he'd definitely have spent his life in the field had he not been afflicted with chronic back pain. He worked for Trans Canada, just next door to Fillion, and at lunch hour he'd often come in and try out one of the armchairs, chatting with Louis while he rested his back. The two men soon realized that they shared the same values where business ethics were concerned, so it was quite natural for Monsieur Paquin to start "fitting backsides instead of feet," as Monsieur Vinet put it.

Monsieur Paquin was a short round man with a strange resemblance to the accountant, but he was less picturesque. In fact, he was so discreet that it was easy to forget him, so he'd regularly make us jump when he spoke to us. We called him the invisible man, and we suspected that his suits were made from the same fabric as the sofas. Monsieur Paquin was part of the furniture, you might say.

His only distinguishing feature was his moustache, the smallest moustache I've ever seen — hardly more than a pencil line, from a well-sharpened pencil at that — but also the most expressive. If a customer walked in you'd see it quiver, while our invisible man was transformed into Sherlock Holmes.

"That's a teacher," he'd whisper to us. "Classical college. French teacher, I'd say. Forty. Lives in Rosemont. Just came into a large sum of money. An inheritance, something along those lines, and he wants to put some of it into new furniture for his living room . . ."

When the customer had left the store, he'd show us the bill with a knowing wink, while his moustache fell into line with a satisfied smile: the man had purchased living-room furniture, he lived in Rosemont and Monsieur Paquin had established while chatting with him that he did indeed teach French and Latin at the Collège Sainte-Marie.. . .

Then he'd go back and melt into the landscape while we stood there gawking.

We — that is me, my brothers and my cousins — all worked for Fillion et Frères at one time or another, on weekends or during summer holidays. Usually we worked on deliveries, but sometimes we served an apprenticeship in sales, without much success, as it happens, despite our excellent teachers. Customers don't trust young furniture salesmen — what did we know about different kinds of wood, what did we know about comfort? — and we sensed, too, that our fathers had higher ambitions for us. . . . It was with tremendous relief that we went back to delivering mattresses, though we did miss Monsieur Paquin's demonstrations.

The guy certainly had his tricks. He followed the news closely, for instance, so he'd know for a fact that teachers had recently won a significant retroactive raise. And who could say whether the French teacher wasn't his neighbour or his cousin's brother-in-law? Still, his little demonstrations were so often successful that we admired him in the same way Dr. Watson admired Sherlock Holmes, minus the irritation. It was undeniable that Monsieur Paquin had exceptional powers of observation that enabled him to make some fine inductions — and not deductions, as Sir Arthur Conan Doyle wrongly believed.

He died at sixty-two. Discreetly, of lung cancer. That was a long time ago, but only recently did I realize that this man saw my father's life over the course of nearly forty years, and often for more than forty hours a week. That represents a lot more time than my brothers and I spent with our father, and probably more than he spent with Cécile.

Monsieur Paquin saw Louis arrive every morning, in a good or bad mood, and he was able to observe how he smoked his cigarettes, how he frowned, under what circumstances he scratched his head, how he reacted when customers were obnoxious or when he was worried about his brothers, how the temperature affected his mood, how much alcohol he knocked back depending on the gravity of the blows he'd taken. He was a witness to his gestures of impatience or resignation, to his doubts and sorrows, to all the little everyday acts that we accumulate like beads on a string, little nothings that make up our lives; for nearly forty years he saw, heard and felt all that, and then he interpreted, decoded, applied to all this his remarkable sense of observation, before dying at sixty-two of lung cancer. Maybe we ought to consider taking cigarette manufacturers to court and accusing them of destroying, along with certain lives, the human equivalents to the library of Alexandria.

• • •

If someone had drawn an organizational chart of the store — not that anyone had time to waste on such a thing — they'd have had to put Léo in a square right at the top, on an equal footing with Louis and Édouard and maybe even a little higher, since he was the true founder of Fillion et Frères, as they never failed to point out. Beneath his name would have been written "Director of Dispatching Services" or something of the sort; then there'd be a sheaf of short lines linking it to other, smaller squares, among which would be found the name of Monsieur Demers, who wasn't a director or deputy director or assistant anything, but simply a truck driver.

A truck driver who was practically never on the road during peak traffic periods, as he was too busy dealing with invoices and customer relations, hiring and training temporary deliverymen and doing a good part of the bookkeeping.

A truck driver who had his own office at the very back of the warehouse, an office that was always spotless — you would even see plants there, at a time when men would never give a thought to anything so useless — with filing cabinets, an adding machine, a typewriter and, on the wall, a huge map of the Island of Montreal and the surrounding area. It was in front of the map that he explained dozens and dozens of times to Monsieur Léo, his superior, that addresses weren't arbitrary numbers but that they followed a certain system:

"First of all there's Saint-Lawrence Boulevard, which divides the city in two, into east and west. Picture a man who parts his hair in the middle, Monsieur Léo." (He always spoke formally to his boss, but over time the "Monsieur Fillion" was transformed into "Monsieur Léo." Working together for thirty years entitles you to certain familiarities.) "Saint-Lawrence Boulevard is the part. To the left is the west end of the city. Close to St. Lawrence, the numbers are small. After that, they go up and up and up all the way to the West Island. Now, to the right of the part, it's the same thing. We call that the east end of the city, and the numbers go up and up and up all the way to Pointe-aux-Trembles. If somebody says 9000 Sherbrooke Street East, that's a lot farther east than 5000

Sherbrooke Street East, say, or 2000 Sherbrooke Street East.. . ."

"I know that," replies Léo, irritated at having these things explained to him as if he were a child.

But Monsieur Demers goes on with his explanations. He's already shown Léo hundreds of times and he knows that Léo knows. The problem is that Léo knows now. In a while, when he's behind the wheel of his truck, when he's back in the real world, with real streets, real roadwork and real detours, he'll get lost, guaranteed, and he'll phone Monsieur Demers to ask him where he's supposed to go and what exactly he's supposed to do with the yellow copy of the bill. And so Monsieur Demers explains, over and over again, without ever showing a hint of irritation. I've never known a man so calm and patient.

"South to north is even easier. The river is zero. Then it goes up and up and up to the Rivière des Prairies. If you've got an address like 9750 Saint-Hubert, let's say, that means it's quite a lot farther north than 3000 Saint-Hubert. . . . And since Clark Street goes from south to north like Saint-Hubert.. . ."

Léo looks conscientiously at the map, then at the bill, then at the map again. He gets into his truck, drops the bill onto the seat next to him and starts to drive. But suddenly he'll see a cat cross the street, he'll see a bird or a cloud, and he'll forget what he's doing there, he'll forget his work and maybe even his name. Léo is Léo. And he's the boss, so no one's going to stop him from making deliveries if that's what he feels like doing, or from going out by himself. In any case, he always comes back to the store — eventually.

Later, during the seventies, when business quiets down, it

will be a lot simpler: the delivery department will consist of Monsieur Demers, who'll drive the truck and look after the bills and customer relations, and Léo, who'll do whatever he can to help his employee.

I've never understood what an organizational chart is good for.

• • •

When addressing Mademoiselle Thibeault, the secretary, it's very important to emphasize the "Mademoiselle." For her, the title is a source of great pride. She always corrects customers when they say "Madame," but that doesn't often happen: skinny, of indeterminate age and with an endless nose, she has the look of a "Mademoiselle." It's not a question of beauty — Margot is ten times uglier, yet everyone calls her "Madame" — but of attitude, I imagine, or bearing, or bone structure — she's pointed all over, a real bag of nails — or of who knows what unconscious signals that the body sends out; the fact is, you call her "Mademoiselle" spontaneously, and that's another of life's minor mysteries.

Monsieur Vinet loves to tease Mademoiselle Thibeault by imitating the bell on her typewriter to make her jump to a new paragraph, and Mademoiselle Thibeault so enjoys being teased by Monsieur Vinet that I suspect her of making her own contribution by letting herself fall for the trick a little too easily; but never mind, it's the result that matters, and the result is that, every time, she bursts out into a great horsy laugh that's a thousand times funnier than all Monsieur Vinet's jokes.

Mademoiselle Thibeault worked for Fillion et Frères all her

life, first as secretary-receptionist, then as secretary-receptionist-saleslady when business was slowly declining, and finally as part-time secretary-receptionist-saleslady-cleaning lady when business became really sluggish at the end of the seventies. Such devotion obviously gave rise to rumours, most of which had Margot as their source: apparently Mademoiselle Thibeault was secretly in love with Louis or Édouard — Léo was never mentioned — or the two of them together, and she'd spent her life shilly-shallying, never able to decide and never admitting her love. . . . Since I have no way of knowing if there's a shred of truth to these allegations, I'll say no more. It's Mademoiselle Thibeault's business and no one else's.

What I want to say — to relate, rather — is a minor anecdote about something that happened around ten years ago, again in a funeral parlour. The coffin was Édouard's; he had died some time after my father, to the amazement of everyone, especially his doctors. It's hard to say what he died of, in fact, as he suffered from a combination of so many maladies. It was Simone, his widow, who came up with the ideal formula: he died of complications, she said confidently. Yes, complications.

At that point nothing was left of Fillion et Frères, not even the premises, which had been subdivided many times for many purposes. The store didn't go bankrupt, by the way. They simply closed the books for lack of customers, and for lack of Fillions to keep it going.

So we're at the funeral parlour. Handshakes, various emotions, sobs and laughter intermingled. Cousins, Aunt Simone, Léo and his Béa, Monsieur Demers and his Pauline, lots of people we hadn't seen for ages. And Mademoiselle Thibeault, still just as skinny, still as much an old maid, still as much a "Mademoiselle." By nature curious and, interested because it's my job, interested in the role that secretaries play in organizations, I chat with her for a while and offer to drive her home at the end of this pleasant evening.

I'd have liked to ask her some questions, but she doesn't give me the time, she's too happy finally to be able to talk about this and that, to recount the golden age of the Fillion brothers, Monsieur Vinet's gags and Monsieur Léo's "absences," the good old days when people knew how to build quality furniture that would last a lifetime, *not like this Swedish rubbish that you have to assemble yourself and that provides jobs for all sorts of people except our own. . . . My, this car is comfortable. . . .* (I don't dare tell her it's Japanese; I'd rather let her talk, fascinated by the way she keeps changing the subject, like a hare on the run.) *I used to drive when I was young but I couldn't now with all those buttons, I wonder if it's all for the best, it's like telephones, before they were all the same, black with dials, and they worked. . . . Would you like to come up for a coffee, Monsieur Fillion?*

"I'd be delighted, Mademoiselle Thibeault. But I'm afraid my wife will be jealous. . . ."

"You silly thing!" she giggles, nearly blushing.

But she doesn't burst out laughing, God be praised. Maybe she's learned to restrain herself since those days.

As I step inside the little apartment where Mademoiselle Thibeault has always lived, I realize that I never wondered if this woman lived somewhere. She was so much an old maid, so associated with the store, forever glued to her chair behind her little desk, making the bell ring on her typewriter or sealing envelopes. . . . When she left the store at night, you'd see her walk to the corner with her little old maid's purse swinging from her arm, and then she'd disappear. Women like her don't live anywhere.

She opens the door of her tiny apartment on Berri Street and time stops: an Arborite kitchen table and chairs that go *whhsshh*, an antediluvian sofa and armchair that look brand new, protected by lace doilies on the arms and backs, a standing ashtray that serves for storing knitting needles and the weekly *TV Guide*, glass-fronted cabinets keeping the dust off some china cats she got as premiums in boxes of tea, and everything spotless, like a museum — even the smells, which are guaranteed authentic to the period. . . . Mademoiselle Thibeault lives in a miniature Fillion et Frères. Worse, she still works there: next to the telephone — black, with a dial — that sits on a small table is a block of blank invoices from Fillion et Frères, the big furniture store for the French-Canadian family.

"We changed all the invoices when the phone company gave us a new number," she says quickly when she catches me looking. "They don't think about that, the phone company, they don't think about the trouble they cause. . . . It was your father who gave them to me. . . ."

She says *we*, when the phone company gave *us* a new number, and she practically apologizes for recycling old invoices, as if I might accuse her of stealing them. . . .

I sip herbal tea and look around the museum while Mademoiselle Thibeault goes on talking; I look at the furniture and I think, there must still be hundreds of these little museums, hundreds of Fillion et Frères still hanging on, scattered through old maids' apartments or retirement homes, in bungalow basements or summer cottages. A store is like a small universe: it's born, it expands, then it contracts and sometimes all it leaves is unexpected traces. . . .

"It's amazing how much you look like your father. You don't mind me saying that, I hope?"

"No, not at all. . . ."

29

How Well Do You Have to Do to Be Doing All Right?

"There's times I wonder how well you have to do to be doing all right. Business is slowing down, that's for sure, but we still have a better life than lots of people: we've got a nice house in Saint-Lambert, new furniture, a new car, television, an automatic washing machine. . . . We're living better than plenty of people in Canada, to say nothing of the Chinese; we're living ten times better than my father could have imagined, but that doesn't seem to be enough for Cécile. She says that we never take holidays, meanwhile Hélène and Thérèse are visiting Europe, apparently it's beautiful over there. . . . So I tell her that, yes, my sisters go on trips, and good for them if they can afford it, but we mustn't forget that they've got only two children, it was a personal choice, to each his own, we mustn't judge. . . .

"She says sure, to each his own, but still, there's the question of money. If we weren't always so strapped. . . .

"All right, let's talk about money. What we have to do is expand. The Plaza Saint-Hubert is fine but it's time we thought about opening branches in the suburbs. We have to follow our customers, we have to adapt. It's now or never. But that means reinvesting all our profits, even borrowing. Then maybe in a few years we'll be able to pay for some travelling, and we'll take the children. . .

"I don't even have time to finish my sentence before she gets angry: you aren't going to give me less money, we already live hand to mouth, you're always working, you arrange things so you're never at home and it's impossible to find reliable help nowadays, we'll be robbed, I guarantee.

"I say okay, all right, we won't open a branch. But what's the answer? After all, I can't turn myself into a doctor or a movie star. . . .

"So then we don't talk about the store any more. Cécile sulks in her corner and she comes back with whatever springs to mind. The willow tree, for instance. I planted a willow because they grow quickly and because the children need shade. She agreed. But now she complains that it's growing too fast, the grass is covered with dead branches that get caught in the rake and it's obvious I never rake the lawn. . . . I tell her I work every day except Sunday, and Sunday, I work in the basement, so where would I find time to rake. . . . She interrupts: exactly, how come the basement isn't finished yet, it's been going on for months, there's sawdust all over the place, it's easy to see you aren't the one who cleans up. . .

"I try to explain as calmly as I can that making bedrooms for the children is a lot more complicated than we thought, I have to be electrician, plumber, carpenter, plasterer and mason, I spend half my time looking for tools, and there aren't that many Sundays in a month, and when I also have to take the mother-in-law for drives because she's bored. . . .

"So then the pressure goes up some more and the kettle boils over. Cécile says it's not her mother's fault, why did I bring her up, and if she'd known having children was so much trouble, if she'd known she'd have to go without all the time, she'd have thought twice before she got married.

"I work six days a week, I give her all my money, on Sunday I cut the grass or shovel the show, and after that I break my back trying to finish the basement and I clean up the sawdust, most of it anyway, and there are times when I ask myself, how well do you have to do to be doing all right? I'm not talking about making her happy, that would be asking too much, I only wish she'd stop complaining for once, just for once. Have you got any ideas? Do you know how well you have to do to be doing all right? You work like a slave to give your wife and children the best of everything, you buy them a beautiful house, you move them to a little corner of heaven on earth and she tells you she's bored. You give her this and she wants that. You give her that and she doesn't want it any more. And when you go to bed at night, she complains about the sawdust, or else she reads romance novels and heaves these great sighs. . . .

What does it take to make a woman happy? Do you know?"

Louis keeps spinning the ashtray around and around. He feels bad for telling his brother all this, it's sometimes been hard to get the words out, he'd like to take back half of what he's said, but at the same time he feels relieved, so relieved.

Sitting on the corner of the desk, Édouard hasn't budged while Louis has been pouring his heart out. He hasn't moved a hair, not even to tap the ash off his cigarette. He hasn't moved and he hasn't said anything and he still doesn't say anything when the silence stretches out; he tries to think, but mainly he's moved by the fact that his brother has talked to him about all this, that he's talked about it to *him*.. . .

"I think I've got an idea," he says finally to Louis, who is tearing a corner of the pizza box into small pieces before making them disappear inside the ashtray.

Louis stops tearing his cardboard and looks at Édouard, who frowns as he lights a cigarette. Louis is convinced that his brother knows things about women that he doesn't, secret things. He certainly knows how to talk to them, otherwise his Simone would have left him long ago. And then he was almost a priest, don't forget, they must study human nature in the seminary. . . .

"When you sell an armchair," says Édouard, "you don't just put it in the window with a price tag. You pay attention to the lighting, to the layout, you select the colours. . . . Same thing with women. Your problem is, you count too much on logic and not enough on the trappings. What you have to do, Louis, is change your strategy. Everything you've just told me, you're going to tell her. But differently. And you're going to work on the atmosphere. . . ."

• • •

As he's crossing the Jacques-Cartier Bridge, Louis feels daunted, unsettled, vulnerable — so much so that he wishes he could turn back; it isn't normal to go home on a Saturday afternoon without warning. Cécile will have a fit. Nor is it normal to obey Édouard, who kicked him out of the store. Yes, he really did: plunked his hat on his head and pushed him all the way to the door, repeating that there isn't a soul during July in any case and no, he won't forget to turn on the alarm system and yes, he'll do the bank deposit and he won't forget anything, but go, Louis, go home, this is your brother talking, your associate. . . .

Édouard, all alone in the store. . . . And what if he finds the little mickey's hiding-place? He wouldn't do that, no. These days we can trust him. . . .

Louis drives more and more slowly, anxious about going home; he thinks about Lunn, who found it hard to get used to the customs of a new country, and tells himself that he feels just as much a stranger in his own house. He goes home later and later at night, he finds pretexts for staying at the store. . . . Yes, he ought to talk about it, definitely, Édouard's right, but how should he go about it?

He thinks about Cécile, whose life isn't always easy; it's true that it must get boring being alone at home with the children: the washing, the cleaning, the responsibilities. . . . And then the births, they disrupt the body, it's normal for them to upset the moods as well. Not to mention her periods. . . . He has to understand, or try to understand: how would he feel if he had a visit every month from an aunt he doesn't even know? Yes, maybe that's it: the blood blurs her vision and she can only see problems, instead of what's going well.

Louis starts; the sound of a car horn has just jerked him from his reflections. It isn't normal to drive so slowly on the bridge, you're right, sir. But it also isn't normal to be daunted by the thought of going home in the middle of the afternoon. It's not normal to feel like a stranger in your own house.

• • •

"What are you doing here?" asks Cécile, her eyes bulging. (She's so concerned that she hasn't even taken off her apron or hung up the phone.) "You aren't sick, I hope? Did you have an accident? What are you doing here in the middle of the afternoon? Who's going to close up the store? And what's *that* supposed to be?"

Louis answers all her questions, confusedly, beginning with the most awkward: that is a bouquet of flowers. And he's home early because he has decided they're going out tonight. The two of them. Without the children. We can ask your mother to stay with the children, or Béa. . . . No, I'm not sick. And I didn't have an accident. Édouard. Édouard will close up the store.

• • •

They ate at the American Spaghetti House that night. In a romantic little room with a candle on the table. "Bring me your finest wine," Louis said, handing the list back to the waiter without even looking at the prices. A fellow's entitled to play rich once in his life, especially when he's supposed to be a businessman.

They talked a lot that night. At the end of the meal they told themselves that it was going to be hard but that, if each of them was understanding, if each of them made an effort, they'd travel another stretch of the road, that it was worth the trouble, that there was really no need to complicate their lives. . . .

And over the years that followed, they did make efforts. Big efforts.

30

IMPALA

Business is slowing down, particularly during the summer, but that's not necessarily bad, especially now that Édouard is reliable again; Louis and Édouard have decided to give themselves one Saturday afternoon off every two weeks during the summer. Léo can't do that, as Saturday is the best day for deliveries, but he doesn't complain; he gives himself a Monday afternoon now and then, and even the supreme luxury of a Thursday evening.

It's a Saturday, then, at the beginning of July. Louis's Saturday. He leaves the store right after lunch and gets behind the wheel of his 1960 Chevrolet Impala, the model with the big gull's wings in back — in those days, engineers weren't forbidden to show imagination. Though she's new, the Chevy already knows the road like an old horse, and she crosses the Jacques-Cartier Bridge by herself. Louis likes this route: first you drive under some criss-crossed steel girders to leave the city and its smoke, touch down on Île Sainte-Hélène, then you drive through another, smaller tunnel of steel beams. A light structure that seems to have been put there solely to remind you of the first one. After that, you fling a quarter through the window, as if to pay for the right to have access to the suburbs, and there's calm, the countryside, peace.

Louis decides not to put the Chevy in the garage. In the summer he doesn't mind washing his car himself, so he can detect rust spots before they go through the metal, and also for the simple pleasure of standing in water, making bubbles and playing with the children.

It's 1960. Jocelyne, Christiane, Benoît, Louise, Yves and Marc-André. Short of a miracle, there won't be any more; Cécile has undergone the big operation. They're all there, along with their friends from the street, tying beach towels around their necks to play Superman on their CCM tricycles, or rocking their dolls under the branches of the willow tree — *next to the root is the kitchen and on the other side is the living room and we're rich* — or rereading their Tintin books for the tenth time, imagining that the willow branches are waterfalls and on the other side of the falls is the Temple of the Sun. Louis, who spent his own childhood in the greyness of sheds and lanes, has given his children trees, space and light.

He changes his clothes, munches a sandwich Cécile has fixed for him and goes back outside and settles in the yard. He washes the Chevy, then finds something to putter with outside now that the basement's finally finished — as far as anything in a house is ever finished, of course. He's already built a garden shed for the lawnmower and the garden tools, he's made a picnic table and a sandbox and now he's making Adirondack chairs. For the pleasure of it, because he feels like it. Because puttering around is a state of mind. Because the children come up to watch, curious, and he can finally win them over by showing them how to use a level and a square, a plane and a mitre box.

And then he puts his tools away and opens a beer, and it's the fine chaos of a late Saturday afternoon in July: a child asks why there's a boat on the label of the beer bottle, another wants the aluminum foil from the cigarette package for his collection, other children arrive and run off right away. They're always running, as if they want to do everything at the same time. They never stop, except maybe Jocelyne, the eldest, who has to learn to walk slowly when she's helping her mother set the table. A summer evening. An evening in July. They barbecue hot-dogs, then they let the time pass and that's all.

Later, when the children are asleep, Louis will clean the barbecue grill; then he'll walk around his house. He's always enjoyed walking around his house at night. He looks at the foundation to be sure there aren't any cracks and he checks the weather-stripping around the windows, but those are just pretexts. He just likes to walk around his house. He likes the idea that he can walk around his house, on his own property; he likes to tell himself that it all belongs to him, that it's a just reward for his efforts.

And then he goes back to sit in the yard, and he opens a few bottles of beer with little boats on their labels. Children in pyjamas, smelling of soap, will come and kiss his prickly cheek before they go to bed. Good night, sleep tight, don't let the bedbugs bite.

The bedroom windows light up, then go out one by one. After that it's dark, really dark, it's night.

Later, when all the children are asleep, Cécile will finally come outside and join him.

She'll complain a little, for sure, she'll say that her feet hurt or she's worried about their oldest girl who has a tendency to talk back to her mother, she'll go on about the youngest children's indigestion, about the hydro bill, she'll say, you could drink a little less, honestly, but Louis will only half listen.

He'll look at this big solid house, he'll tell himself that the children can sleep here in peace, that they're safe and sound. He likes the peace of the suburbs, and he says so to Cécile.

"It's nice here, isn't it? The peace and quiet. . . ."

The trouble with a remark like this is that takes just one sentence: afterwards Louis has nothing more to say, so he falls silent.

Rather than reply, Cécile goes on talking about the price of laundry detergent, and grass stains, and the oldest girl who always does exactly as she pleases. . . .

Louis would like to interrupt her: why don't you answer me, Cécile, why do you pretend you don't understand? It's nice here, isn't it? Tell me it is, tell me you're happy. . . .

As Cécile doesn't understand this kind of question, Louis doesn't really feel obliged to listen to her talk about her little worries.

He drinks his beer and gazes at the stars.

31

SECRET BALLOT

"If a total idiot has the right to vote," says Édouard, "I don't see why women shouldn't have it."

"We aren't talking about the right to vote," replies Monsieur Vinet. "We're talking about a woman with children who wants to go back to the job market. And I say that's not where they belong. And people shouldn't complain afterwards if there's unemployment."

"Why shouldn't we talk about the right to vote? The point is whether women are full-fledged citizens, whether they're equal to men or not. We're talking about human dignity. If women have enough judgement to vote, they can also be MPs or ministers or even prime minister. It's a right, a sacred right. I would remind you that Mussolini and Hitler were men, and we know what they did. If women have enough judgement to become prime minister, they must have enough to be doctors or lawyers, right?"

"Or lady truckers?" scoffs Monsieur Vinet. "Or garbage-women? Or girl soldiers while we're at it?"

"Why not, if that's what they want?"

"You can't be serious, Édouard! A lady soldier! In the trenches with the men! With a flame-thrower! A machine-gun! *Ratatatatat!*"

Édouard takes a drag of his cigarette, chews his lip, frowns. . . . Monsieur Vinet has scored a point, and Édouard, too proud to admit it, would normally give a flippant answer or change the subject surreptitiously, or mount a fresh attack in another key. . . .

"Okay, maybe I'm pushing it. Dialectics are like the tide, sometimes they take us a little too far. . . . Still, if there were more women in the job market, and particularly in politics, the world might run more smoothly."

Louis says nothing. He looks, he listens. He likes the way his brother argues, though he's not taken in by his wiles: the more cornered Édouard feels, the more he resorts to an old *curé's* wise words and parables. But he's clever and, while he does use big words, at least he uses them properly. And the way he accepts criticisms and uses them to bounce back. . . . Édouard is nearly as convincing as Philippe was when he wanted everyone to join him and go off to fight Hitler. Monsieur Vinet has his skills too, of course; he'll get the laughers on his side, for sure, but he knows how to draw out the suspense.

It's a Monday morning in September and there's not a shadow of a customer in sight, so they're having a chat before they start their week, settled comfortably in the colonial living room. That's one of the advantages of being your own boss: not only do you not have to pretend to be working all the time, you can join in the debates that make society move forward.

Léo enjoys these impromptu discussions too, even if he always has to do some strange gymnastics. His head moves not only left to right and right to left, as at a tennis match, but also up and down; he feels he has to agree with each of the arguments because they all seem equally valid, equally logical to him. Sometimes, when things go too fast or when he's overflowing with contradictions, he'll snort like a horse and move his head diagonally, as if to confuse himself even more. That people are able to form a clear picture of a certain subject, whatever the subject, is beyond him.

"Dizzy, Léo?" asks Édouard.

"A little. I'm wondering how you do it. . . . One thing I know, though, with you guys I'll never come down with a stiff neck. . . ."

Monsieur Vinet uses the diversion to recommend a new angle of attack.

"In any case, I hope there'll never be women priests," he says finally, fidgeting on his chair as if he were enjoying his next argument in advance. "'I can't decide which soutane to wear today; a mauve stole would go with my complexion, but not with my chasuble. . . .' Can you imagine that, Édouard? Seriously? Ten o'clock Mass would start at noon! And the secrecy of the confessional? Do you know even one woman who could keep a secret, Édouard?"

The men snicker, not so much at Monsieur Vinet's remarks as at the reaction of Mademoiselle Thibeault, who's pretending to be typing letters in her corner but isn't missing any of their conversation, and has just burst out in her horsy laugh.

When she recovers and starts typing again, the men all at once feel embarrassed, as if the bell on the typewriter has signalled the end of recess; there they are, all four of them, chatting away while the secretary works. . . .

"Anyway," says Édouard, "the test is conclusive: these chairs are comfortable. Once you're in one, you can't get out. . . . Good buy, Louis. They should sell."

"Were we doing a test?" asks Léo. "I didn't know. . . ."

"Sure we were, Léo," Édouard replies, patting his shoulder. "You know the Fillion brothers never stop working. . . ."

"Oh, okay," says Léo, who obviously hasn't understood a thing but gratefully accepts the pat on his shoulder.

• • •

For the rest of the day, Louis files invoices, looks at catalogues, goes through his mail, answers the phone, daydreams. He places orders, negotiates a line of credit with the bank, answers a few customers, daydreams some more. It's one of those Mondays, a day when you work but you aren't really there, when you do the little routine things without thinking, when you accomplish something even though, when evening comes, you'll have a hard time saying exactly what you did all day. It's not at all unpleasant; on the contrary. It's a day made of cotton batting, of flannel, of clouds. As if he's brought along a swatch of the fog that covered the Jacques-Cartier Bridge this morning.

He often thinks back to the conversation in the colonial living room, and he feels a little dishonest for observing the debate as a mere spectator when he was the one who started it. He wanted to get used to an idea. Rather, to get used to the idea that Cécile will soon be back in the job market. She's been talking about it for months, bound and determined to come up with arguments that Louis doesn't want to hear.

"What do you fellows think about women working?"

Édouard and Monsieur Vinet threw themselves onto this like cats on a ball of wool, and Louis watched the show, amused but no further ahead. That's what he was thinking about all day, in frayed wisps of thought.

Hitler and Mussolini were men, said Édouard, and we know what they did. Maybe. But Churchill and Roosevelt were also men. And Eva Braun was a woman. . . . Sometimes you have to take these discussions for what they are: opportunities to bring out certain values, pleasant diversions, that's all. It's not nothing, but it's not much help when you're really looking for answers. There are days sometimes, foggy days, when the grand principles seem so abstract, so useless. Your thoughts are either too far away or too near. As if there were no way of thinking right in the middle, at the very spot where detail is attached to theory so that it's no longer a detail, and the theory serves some purpose. It's complicated, all that. . . . The right to vote? Louis doesn't see any problem: if women work and pay taxes, we aren't going to stop them from choosing the people who'll be spending their money. And if they vote, they also have the right to run for office, to become ministers or even prime minister, there's nothing wrong with that. After Hitler, Mussolini, Stalin, Mao, Franco and all the rest, we could give it a try, just to see. Maybe it's time to let go of the grand principles and look after certain details, such as the right to live in peace, for instance. Maybe Édouard is right. Maybe. In any case, it sounds good.

And if women can be MPs or ministers, schoolteachers or doctors, they can also work in factories, even in peacetime. Why not? That's the problem when you start reasoning with what-ifs: you inevitably get around to saying that all women ought to have the right to work, and Cécile is a woman, therefore. . . . But it's there, right there, that logic goes into a skid. There's one detail that doesn't want to be attached to the theory, something that says no, no and no, out of the question.

"And why not?" asks Cécile.

"Because of the children," Louis replies, because it comes to him spontaneously.

But Cécile has an answer to everything:

"The youngest's in school, the older kids will look after him, your supper will be ready on time, don't worry, it's just a part-time job, the children won't lack anything, it will give us a little more money. . . ."

"But we aren't short of money! We've got everything we need, we're richer than. . . ."

"It's not about money," replies Cécile. "That's not why I want to work. It's so I can realize my potential."

She wants to realize her potential! That's the best one yet! She wants to realize her potential by becoming a cashier at

Steinberg's! *Three cans of peas for sixty-nine cents, one sliced bread for twenty-two cents, how much is the celery this week?* Potential! Since when do you work to realize your potential? You work to survive, to feed your family, because it's your duty, because it's something we have to do — not to realize your potential. Where did she come up with that one? Did my father think about his potential when he left for the factory? Or my grandfather when he milked his cows? Did Philippe think about his potential when he went to get killed in the skies over Germany? No, Madame; he did his duty.

She mounts a fresh attack, saying it's normal, all women want to work now, Simone works and she seems happy and your brother doesn't seem to be complaining, why not talk to him about it?

Louis talked to Édouard, he even talked *privately*, as they say. And his brother confessed that he was reluctant at first but he doesn't regret it; since Simone has been working, she's more cheerful, it's as if she's been rejuvenated, she's even friendlier, more good-natured, as if she's . . .

"As if she's realized her potential?"

"That's it, exactly! Yes, realized her potential. And in every sense of the term if you see what I mean. She's even got her appetite back for doing certain things. . . ."

Okay, fine, thanks, Édouard, we can do without those lewd winks of yours, and thanks again for the masculine solidarity.

Since that time Cécile, who has always called Édouard irresponsible, can see only his good qualities: "Édouard's smart, I've always trusted his judgement. . . ."

So she wants to realize her potential. Nobody knows what

it means, exactly, but it sounds good.

And then she mounts a fresh attack, on new ground as usual: one night, very late, she finally lets drop that she wasn't made to spend her whole life at home, that she doesn't like herself, she doesn't want to become like her mother. . . .

Now, that's something Louis can understand; women age badly, especially after the big operation. Putting on weight and spending all day on the phone isn't the most thrilling prospect. . . . Working, even just a few hours a week, gets your feet back on the ground, puts you in touch with reality. Maybe women need to let off steam. Maybe it disturbs their mechanism to twiddle their thumbs in the house all day. In the past they had twice as many children and ten times as much work, but today, with automatic appliances, they press a button and, bingo, the job is done. Maybe they need to work off the bitterness they used to put into wringing out the washing. Maybe they're simply afraid of getting bored. So they talk about potential, because it sounds better.

But there's still something in him that says no, something very profound.

"What will the neighbours think if they see you working at Steinberg's? They'll say that business is bad, that I need my wife's salary to support my family. . . ."

"What will people think of you!" Cécile repeated. "That's what's really bothering you. What I feel doesn't matter. . . ."

And then the conversation turned sour. Cécile talked a lot and, while she talked, Louis was thinking. He was thinking that he'd worked all his life, sixty hours a week, to do what a man has to do, and he'd managed to buy a house for his family, a lovely house in the suburbs, a big house you could walk around, and he'd gone on working sixty hours a week to furnish it, to pay for the children's clothing and their food, the doctor and their private schools, their bicycles and skates, a piano and piano lessons, and he'd paid for it all without grumbling, without complaining, because it was his duty, because he couldn't imagine life otherwise. And just when he had succeeded, just when he could tell himself that he'd accomplished what he thought was most important in a man's life, he was being told no, it's not enough, it's nothing at all, what's important is Cécile's potential. . . . That's just a little frustrating, Cécile, do you understand? Just a little humiliating. We aren't allowed to change the rules of the game like that, in the middle of the match, on the pretext that we want to realize our potential! How will we know what's right if the rules keep changing all the time?

That's what Louis was still brooding over at breakfast, that's what he was getting ready to say when Cécile caught him unawares. When a woman's got something in her head, you never know on which side she's going to attack.

"It's just a part-time job," she told him, all sweetness and light. "It could help pay for a cottage. . . ."

"If I need to have my wife pay for a cottage, I'd just as soon not have one."

"You don't really mean that, Louis," Cécile replied.

The worst thing was, she was right.

Crossing the Jacques-Cartier Bridge that morning, Louis heard a little voice from on high telling him it would be a lot simpler to give in. To capitulate, yes, because there was nothing else he could do. After all, he wasn't going to tie Cécile down or shut her away in her kitchen. Sometimes it takes more courage to capitulate than to fight, the little voice added, and Louis could have been hearing Édouard make one of his *curé* speeches. All right then, he'd make the best of a bad job, as they say. He'd try, at any rate. But don't expect him to take Cécile out for dinner to celebrate!

But then, what if it was just a caprice, a whim, a woman's fancy? Maybe when she got tired of her potential, she'd come back to the house. . . .

"What do you think about that, Léo?"

"About women working?"

He's surprising sometimes, is Léo. The day is nearly over, it's six o'clock, they're closing up the store, and he finds it completely normal to pick up a conversation they started this morning, as if nothing had happened since then. What fog does he live in while he's waiting?

"Theories, you know. . . . Béa would rather stay home and that's fine with me. But if she wanted to work I'd let her. As long as it didn't bother anybody. . . ."

Thanks, Léo. That's what I wanted to hear.

• • •

It wasn't a caprice or a whim. Cécile worked as a cashier part time, then full time and then she was promoted to head cashier, and by the end of her career she had a management position at company headquarters.

Louis didn't suffer too badly. Later on, he even had to admit that he'd benefitted from it and that, all in all, it was a good deal. When Cécile had gone back to the job market, the business had started to decline so quickly that Louis needed the extra income to stay afloat till he retired. In fact, that extra income was very quickly higher than his own. Though that didn't change what he called it: it was still extra income, and it helped pay for nonessentials.

If his hot meal sometimes wasn't ready right on time, Louis didn't complain. In any case, Cécile wasn't a very good cook and her food was too often seasoned with exasperated sighs. Ordering in Chinese food now and then wasn't so bad.

If Louis had been able to foresee how much Cécile would be transformed by working, he'd have accepted with far better grace. But how could he have known? Not that he'd use the word *potential* — let's not get carried away — but still, the transformations were to his advantage. When his wife came home at night she'd find fault with her bosses, her colleagues and her customers, she'd complain about her shoes hurting her feet, about the background music or the ventilation, punctuating her laments with a vast range of sighs. Louis would listen abstractedly, secretly satisfied; now he was no longer her principal enemy.

32

Wrapped Up

Louis had rarely felt more remote from Cécile than when she came home from her first day at work. Her first evening, actually. Half-evening, even: she'd worked one Thursday night from six to nine, but she talked about it till midnight and again the next morning as soon as she got out of bed, and it would never end. The slightest uncalled-for remark by a dissatisfied or grouchy customer, the least sidelong glance from her boss, the smallest run in the nylons of the head cashier merited not only being reported but also commented on, analyzed, criticized. As if each of these trifles had to be wrapped up in a dozen layers of paper and tied and trimmed with ribbons before it could finally be abandoned along the way. Cécile couldn't bear the thought that these trifles might be pointless.

She had to point them out, one by one. It was her life's work.

Louis listened to Cécile's detailed account of her evening's work, half preoccupied, half annoyed. All his life he'd done nothing but work. And he'd accumulated thousands of these trifles without ever thinking it was worth reciting them. Now all these anecdotes of Cécile's were taking on the air of exploits, and every day of her work was transformed into an epic. It was just a trifle frustrating.

• • •

Only once does Louis feel even more remote from his wife. It happens many years later, on the way out of the funeral parlour after Annette passes away.

Louis and Cécile are making their way unhurriedly back to the car, which is parked a few blocks from the church — the church he went to as a child, where he had his first communion and his confirmation, where he attended numerous ceremonies during which, to dispel his boredom, he so often studied the paintings and statues that covered the walls and pillars, never able to decide if those saints and gods were his friends or his enemies, if they were there to help him or doom him, to understand him or judge him. Now that his mother is dead, now that she has heaved her last sigh, he takes one last look at those statues and paintings and he sees them for what they are: effeminate Christs, faded Virgins, anonymous, interchangeable saints, hollow, lifeless statues that seem lost in this huge church, as if they've had nothing to do there ever since God deserted it.

Louis and Cécile walk slowly along the icy sidewalks without saying a word.

Louis is tired, rattled, stunned. He walks slowly, letting his mind drift, and he feels light or, rather, absent. Outside this world, where nothing can affect him. For the time being, he doesn't feel sad. That will come later, he knows from experience that grief never comes when you want it, but right now he's somewhere else. He's thinking about the perfectly calm sea he spied off the coast of Newfoundland, that perfectly motionless steel-grey sea, and then about the English nurse who was bending over him when he woke up in the hospital. She had gorgeous blue eyes, and Louis had the impression that the blue was brimming over from her eyes. It may have been just a morphine-induced vision, but it's still one of the most beautiful things he's ever seen.

Then he thinks about Juliette, who has just come back from the Philippines and helped their mother during her last moments. Juliette, thin, gaunt, so thin that when you look at her you think her nuns' clothes must weigh more than she does — Juliette will always give that impression, till the end. Just looking at her makes Louis feel soothed.

You can feel sad coming out of a funeral parlour, or happy, or relieved, or overwhelmed, or outraged, but you can also feel soothed, that's what he's discovering, what he's thinking about. Light and hollow, like a statue. Light, empty, fragile. He walks slowly, feeling no obligation to talk, letting his mind drift and trying not to slip on the icy sidewalk.

"She suffered a lot, your mother," Cécile says finally; she

can't cope with silence. "I'm sure it wasn't a lot of fun every day, with your father. . . ."

Louis lifts his head, takes a deep breath and says:

"Life wasn't always easy for him either. . . ."

He has spoken softly, calmly, with no thought of starting an argument — that would hardly be fitting — but simply because it seemed self-evident, because it didn't take anything away from anyone, because it deserved to be said.

Cécile stops short.

"You can't seriously think that, Louis! *Surely* you don't think there's any comparison!"

She's angry, very angry, and Louis will never really understand why. That man whom Annette spent her life discrediting, whom Cécile now allows herself to judge though she didn't even know him, was his father, after all. And why is it so important to compare them? Is it really essential to know which of the two suffered more, as if it were a competition? What follows is a tumultuous argument that sheds no light on anything, and that afterwards remains in suspense, like so many other things.

33

Cubes of Glass

"Listen here. They're all cows. All fucking cows. But why insult cows, cows at least give milk."

"Sure, sure, Édouard, we know. . . ."

"No, that isn't true. We men, we know it, but those cows, they don't know. . . . And even if we know, we still get caught and you can't tell me any different, Louis boy. Did you know that, Louis boy? Women from the Gaspé are all a bunch of. . . ."

"A bunch of cows, you already said that. And now you have to go home. . . ."

"You're wrong there, Louis boy, you're wrong: they aren't cows, Louis boy, they're pigs. Sows. Women from the Gaspé are all. . . . What're you doing, anyway, aren't you at the store?"

"No, I'm not at the store and neither are you, and it's precisely because you aren't at the store that I came to get you. . . . Come on, Édouard, don't go looking for trouble. . . ."

"What the hell are you doing here?"

The you in question is Léo. Léo, who stands there scratching his head, who doesn't know what to do, who lets Louis talk while he waits till he's needed. It will take the two of them to get Édouard home.

"Lemme finish my beer. . . ."

"Okay, but do it fast. . . ."

Édouard tries to bring his glass to his lips but it seems very complicated, and Louis looks around while he waits for him to finish. The owner pretends he's wiping the counter while he furtively observes the three brothers, a little uncomfortable. He knows his customers: when Édouard starts talking loudly, he always finds somebody to tell him to shut up, and that leads to trouble every time. So it's fine with him if the brothers can take over before things get any worse.

The owner knows his customers, and Simone knows her husband. She's seen it coming for a while now: his mood swings, his aggressiveness, his absurd remarks, deliberately incoherent — Édouard adores playing the one nobody understands — and the pointless arguments over trivialities; he was just looking for a pretext to start drinking again. They had one of those arguments last night — what was it about? He probably doesn't remember himself — and Simone knew this morning what was going to happen. "Don't call me at the store," he said, rushing out of the house and not looking her in the eye. "I'm meeting with a supplier."

Simone waited impatiently till eleven o'clock, when she called Louis.

Louis too had seen it coming: Édouard was chain-smoking, pacing, jumping at the slightest opportunity to judge everyone. And Louis had been suspicious the day before, when Édouard warned him that he might take the morning off. Édouard had got so tangled up in his lies and excuses that Louis felt apprehensive; surely he isn't going to start again, after four years of abstinence. . . .

Louis didn't need a picture. He just had to hear Simone's voice on the phone to know what he had to do: call the Quintal tavern, mobilize Léo. . . .

While Édouard sucks on his beer, the other customers, their backs to the wall, are deeply engrossed in their saltshaker or their glass or the big jar of pickled eggs on the counter, or the TV set suspended in the corner that usually no one watches unless there's a hockey game, or the sailboat on the Molson clock, the sailboat that will never be able to leave port and pass through the cubes of translucent glass that let in only a pale, watery light. The men are looking everywhere but at them, yet they aren't missing a thing. Louis too is looking elsewhere, and wishing that his name were Gélinas or Morin or Frenette, anything but Fillion, especially not Fillion of Fillion et Frères. . . . "They're all cows, nobody's ever understood you, we know that, Édouard, you're absolutely right, now finish your beer. . . ."

"Fucking cows," says Édouard one last time before he

collapses onto the table and knocks over his glass, which Léo catches before it falls.

And then he falls asleep.

"Fucking old cows," say Louis and Léo softly, to help Édouard sleep, and they repeat it again and again, like a lullaby, with no thought of reminding their brother of his grand speeches about women's dignity. This isn't the time. All that matters is to get him home.

This time it's not too serious. You couldn't call it a genuine relapse. When Édouard goes drinking at Quintal's, he knows perfectly well that the others will soon be there. If he'd really wanted to drink, to seriously drink, he'd have gone to another neighbourhood where nobody knows him, and he wouldn't have been seen for the rest of the week. No, it's not a genuine relapse. Just a slip-up. Tomorrow morning he'll be fresh as a daisy, and he'll come up with an eloquent apology. After that, he'll have a long talk with Monsieur Vinet, they'll go to some meetings and things will be better. Right now, though, he has to be taken home and put to bed.

Louis puts his arm under Édouard's shoulder and Léo does the same on his side, and they lift him fairly easily — Édouard has never been very heavy — and drag him to Louis's car.

Docile, even complacent, Édouard lets them carry him. Yes, complacent, and doubt brushes Louis's mind while he's carrying his brother; Édouard seems really happy, satisfied, as if he's plotted everything so he'll find himself here, arms outstretched, being carried by his two brothers.

• • •

When the other customers see the door close behind the Fillions, they'll go back to their drinking. They'll think differently, and they'll talk to their glass or their saltshaker or, if they're lucky, to another customer who won't listen to them.

When Louis steps inside a tavern, he hears these men thinking as clearly as he hears his customers thinking when they circle an armchair or a kitchen table. No doubt that explains why he doesn't places like this, and never sets foot in one — except to find Édouard, of course.

Louis also drinks, but not in the same way.

34

THE EMBARKATION

When you really like liquor, you have to drink alone. And Louis wants to drink. He wants to drink because the abyss is too deep, because the mystery is unfathomable and because he's looking for peace. To stay sober for years, like Édouard, is something he couldn't do. Not even for a day, in fact. Not if it means falling again, even farther, anyway. . . . Louis wants to drink, but responsibly, which is no small matter. To do that, you have to be alone. When you let yourself be led into bars and taverns, you're always a victim of your own politeness, and you quickly find that you've travelled too far and seen nothing of the landscape. That spoils the effect, besides costing twice as much. Bad move. Whereas drinking alone. . . . Drinking alone means giving every mouthful time to make its way, it means choosing your own ship, as well as your cruising speed and each port of call. The effect is so fine, so soothing, that it's criminal to throw it away in smoky bars where you never go anywhere.

The embarkation begins at the store, around four o'clock. Louis opens the filing cabinet, pours himself the first sip and the motor starts up. There's oil in the machine, the gears are cleaned out, a gentle warmth sweeps over him. Now it's a matter of keeping the fire going. He'll return to the filing cabinet between customers, and each time the warmth will be more gentle, more penetrating. Another sip when the doors of the store are shut, to greet the end of the day — the seven thousand six hundred and twenty-eighth, let's say — and to forget it. And, why not, another sip for the road; the Chevelle isn't really a good car. For a while now, the American army seems to have been conducting secret experiments on Detroit engineers to amputate any imagination they might have, and 1970 is a particularly terrible year. The Chevelle is a square box, very ugly, but not ugly in a way that can be charming. Not only are these cars ugly, you just have to give them a tender look and they rust. The only way to make driving them pleasant is by pouring, not chemicals into the gasoline, but a few sips of liquor into the driver's stomach. Then the suspension becomes less stiff, the power steering more powerful, and while the motor is still just as sluggish, it's easier to put up with. Even the music coming from the radio — whatever music you can pick up between the two metal structures of the Jacques-Cartier Bridge, that is — seems more harmonious, as if the alcohol has driven away the static.

Feel a bit peckish when you get to the house. Settle into the Adirondack chair, congratulate yourself because the rounded seat and the angle of the back are perfect — why don't sofa manufacturers copy them, why insist on making seats flat? — and take advantage of the vast armrests that let you set a bottle of beer on one side and a glass on the other. Sit there and don't do anything but slowly drink your beer, savouring every sip, lifting your glass to the sun now and then to enjoy the dance of the bubbles.

When the weather won't let you drink outside, sink into the most comfortable armchair in the living room, which belongs to the father by divine right, pour yourself a beer that scents the room with its bitter perfume, then go through the newspaper, nibble a few peanuts, light a cigarette. . . . It's only outdoors that Louis can drink, just drink. Indoors, he has to surround himself with props that he abandons one by one for want of decent armrests. Drink, just drink, but take another few peanuts anyway, because how can you stop, and another drag on the cigarette, because how can you stop, and because beer tastes so much better when it's fragrant with salt and tobacco.

At night, after supper, treat yourself to another beer outside if it's summer, and stretch it out until long after sunset. If you sit it in the grass, the bottle will stay cool. Or make yourself comfortable in the living-room armchair if it's winter, or, even better, in the La-Z-Boy in the basement, and just sit there. Turn on the TV and don't move. A little drink and the Canadiens finally start playing decent hockey. Yvan Cournoyer serves up his best feints to the other side, Jean-Claude

Tremblay sends him his smartest passes and Ken Dryden stops the pucks with more panache. A little more alcohol to better appreciate Jacques Normand's humour on "Les Couche-tard," then a little more to help you tolerate the news. Why these wars, famines, earthquakes, crimes, frauds, lies? Why does God, who's supposed to be all-powerful, allow it? And why send His son to die on the cross? Does He want to show us that He can be even more cruel than humans? Alcohol doesn't give you answers to these questions, but it sometimes lets you go beyond words to get a glimpse of a glimmer of light in the distance, to catch sight of the tip of the tail of a mystery at the very moment it's running away. You don't understand any better, but it's easier to accept not understanding.

Then turn off the TV and go through the paper. Try to take an interest in economics and politics, which offer us such small mysteries. Start the same article for the third time, then give up. Take a chance on the crossword puzzle, but skip too quickly from words to emotion and from emotion to memory. Drop the paper, take another sip to see how far you can go without the help of words. Think about God and mystery, about blue skies and oceans, let peace settle in on its own instead of looking for it, then finally find it, as if by chance. Now try to hold onto it, just hold onto it. It's a matter of dose, of concentration, of attention, and it warrants applying yourself; it's hard to get there and so easy to go too far. . . . You have to be alone, otherwise you'd never get there.

Drink alone. Not to be happy, that would be asking too much of life, but to be better able to put up with it. To feel all right for a few hours. Just all right. Drink alone to yourself mostly above the waterline. Or to survive till your thirtieth mission, after which you can finally come home.

• • •

The best beer is the beer you drink at the cottage. Maybe it's the fresh air, or the scent of the spruce trees, or the influence of the stars, no one really knows, but every bottle opened at the cottage takes you to peace more quickly and keeps you there longer.

You settle in on the veranda, turn your chair towards the far end of the lake, open a bottle and just hear the *psschhht* and already you're happy, ready to embark. If you're alone it's perfect. And if you're with someone else and that someone else is Léo, let's say, it's even better. If Léo wants to drink too, you won't complain. If he doesn't, you can anyway, without feeling guilty; Léo doesn't judge. He doesn't even know what judging is. And drunk or not, Léo is always Léo.

Settle in on the veranda on a Saturday night and tell yourself, tomorrow's Sunday and the day after is Saint-Jean-Baptiste Day, or Labour Day, or Thanksgiving, you can stay up late, so hand me another beer, Léo, would you. . .?

And Léo just has to reach out his arm; he's put a fridge on the veranda so there'll always be cold beer within reach. The fridge goes back to the early days of Fillion et Frères, when they still sold appliances. This one never worked properly, but they had to take it off the customer's hands, as he had bought a new one. Léo couldn't resign himself to selling it for scrap for five dollars; it was a handsome piece, this fridge, with round corners and chrome trim, like an object from outer space.

"What did you do to make your fridge keep beer so cold? It's exactly the right temperature. . . ."

Louis knows the story because he's heard it twenty times, but never mind; Léo is so proud when he tells it.

"I took it apart and put it back together, that's all. When I finished I had dozens of screws and bolts left over, all kinds of things, I didn't even know what they were for. When I plugged it in it started to shake, it shook so hard I was afraid it was going to blow up. And there was a smell of burnt rubber. . . . Maybe it just fixed itself, did the soldering it needed. . . . And then it calmed down and it's been purring away in its corner ever since. Ever since, it keeps beer cold and never gets tired. Must be twenty years now. . . . Twenty years of running properly. Maybe it just wanted somebody to pay attention to it. . . ."

And Léo looks at his old refrigerator, eyes filled with tenderness, as if the appliance had a soul — which is quite possible, after all.

"The best thing about it," he goes on, "is that it never vibrates. Not at all. I could build a house of cards on top and it wouldn't fall over. Never try that with a modern one. . . . Another beer, old Louis?"

"Why not?" Louis replies, thinking that there aren't many people on this planet who'd even think of building a house of cards on top of a fridge; that alone makes it worth drinking to Léo's health.

And then fall silent, watch the sun go down behind the spruce trees at the end of the lake and let your mind wander. When the sun sets between the pink clouds, finally see the wheezy, shaky old Lancaster that got lost in time after losing its way in the sky over Germany. Salute the tail-gunner before he goes back to his own world.

"Are you thinking about Philippe?" asks Léo, who has seen Louis gesture vaguely in the direction of a cloud.

"Did you see him too?"

"Yes. He looks good, I thought. . . ."

"Very good. He was a hell of a good big brother, our Philippe. . . ."

"Yes, a hell of a good big brother," Léo echoes.

"He had imagination. . . ."

"Lots of imagination," repeats Léo, who enjoys this ritual of fraternal litanies.

"He was ingenious, he was brave, but . . ."

This is the first time Louis has ventured that but. And so he lets the silence stretch out while he waits for Léo to repeat that but in the form of a question, as any normal person having this conversation would do, but Léo isn't familiar with this kind of code; if Louis wants to go on talking, he'll talk. And if he'd rather keep quiet, that's his business.

"But sometimes he was . . . a bit of a pain in the neck, don't you think?"

"More than a bit! If you want the truth, old Louis, I'll tell you, there were times when he was a big pain in the neck. I've never understood why it was so important for him to play big brother. . . ."

"Me neither, Léo, me neither. He could've been happy just being a Fillion, that was enough. . . ."

• • •

Yes, drink alone. Because it's so good. But drink with your brother too, now and then. Because it's good for you.

35

Léo's Cottage

Louis dreamed about a cottage. He'd been dreaming about one forever. He'd take a few steps into the forest and right away he'd be in the countryside, with streams and ponds, rivers and unspoiled lakes, so many lakes that they wouldn't even have names. If he walked directly north and never turned off, he'd cross through Mont Tremblant Park and then, after two thousand miles of lakes and forests, of tundra and ice, he'd come to the shore of the Arctic Ocean. Throughout the journey he'd see deer and caribou, foxes and polar bears, squirrels and thousands of birds, but never another human, not even a trace. Two thousand miles without meeting a single customer, without selling a single piece of furniture.

He never went to that frontier, of course, and I wonder if

he even walked anywhere but on the dirt road that circles the lake. It was enough for him to know that he could have done it: he just had to turn his chair to face north to organize expeditions to Jack London country. He'd be breathing the same air, the northern air that makes your thoughts so clear, and in the evening he'd gaze at the same pole star beyond the northern lights.

Sunday morning at dawn he'd open the veranda door and set out down the little path that wound through the ferns, and at the end of it there would be a lake — his lake. Then he'd sit on the floating dock to watch the family of ducks sail through patches of fog, and he'd take that priceless image home with him and it would last all week. To the left of the dock would be a beach the size of a handkerchief, not even big enough for building a sand castle, but it would still be a beach, a sand beach. . . . (*You call that sand? If you ask me it's mud. If you think I'm going to put my feet in that. . . .*) On the right, a few waterlilies for the frogs' concerts, and a Verchères rowboat that would take on water a little and would have slightly rusty oarlocks, but a wire brush and a little paint would take care of that, hard work never hurt anybody, and even if the oars went *creak creak*, would anybody mind?

So there'd be a Verchères rowboat to go to the far end of the lake, where you could see the big rocks and where there must be loads of bass. On the way there he could troll, which might rouse the appetite of a grey trout deep down in the lake. And even if there weren't any trout or bass, even if there was nothing but sunfish and catfish, he could still take the boat there, just row peacefully in the evening after supper, wander in silence far from the store, from customers, and never be disturbed by the telephone. Peace. Total peace. Blessed peace.

A cottage for the children, so they can get to know Madame Raccoon and her family of burglars, the bats that camp in the attic, the skunks and porcupines, the owls and woodpeckers, and the deer they might by chance see at dusk, the deer that would stand there frozen, motionless, for three seconds that would last for three eternities, and then disappear into the forest. The rustling of dry leaves, then silence, then the urge to thank the Good Lord. . . . (*And the blackflies, what about the blackflies and mosquitoes . . . ?*)

And the blackflies and mosquitoes, yes, if that's the price you have to pay. Blackfly season doesn't last all that long, let's not get carried away. A cottage for the silence and peace, for the cool, quiet nights, for the fresh air that makes you dizzy; a cottage for the children, most of all, so they can enjoy that peace, so they can have what's best in this world, so they can feast on wild raspberries and climb trees, so they can be pirates or Indians, prospectors or explorers, so they can find treasures and fish for crayfish, so they can learn to swim and to sing together in the evening around a campfire. And the best thing of all is that the cottage exists. It really does exist in real life. A very simple cottage built of pine boards. . . . (*That's a lot of work, it'll need painting every year. . . .*)

Every five years, that's all. And it's not such a terrible job if everybody joins in. It's even a good way to get some sun. A fine, plain old cottage made of pine boards. (*I'd rather have a new one, it would be a lot less trouble if you ask me. . . .*)

A fine old cottage that's tried and tested, that has worked

well. A new one wouldn't have all these improvements, like the veranda, really, look at this veranda, the screens are practical during the blackfly season, the veranda so big we can all sit here for meals or to play cards on rainy days, or Scrabble or Monopoly. And a new cottage wouldn't have this good old wood stove. (*Do you really like making toast on a wood stove? Really?*)

This wood stove that also works on electricity, and these cupboards overflowing with dishes, enough for an army. . . . (*As long as your soldiers like chipped plates and rusty knives.*)

And this good old mismatched furniture that we're giving a second life. . . . (*The furniture no one in the city wanted.*)

And the sheets and bedspreads and even the dishtowels. They may not be new, but it still beats having to buy everything (it's not a bad idea to anticipate criticisms).

We were talking about peace just now, about peace and children, how did we get onto dishtowels? We were talking about a fine old cottage that's tried and tested and that really does exist, a cottage we could get for next to nothing, since it belongs to Étienne's cousin Théo and Théo hasn't been here since his wife died, and he's too old to enjoy it anyway and he'd like it to stay in the family. An old cottage we could get for a song, with the furniture and dishes thrown in, not to mention the Verchères rowboat and some fishing rods, the axe and two cords of wood and all the tools in the garage. Think about the children, Cécile. . . .

"*It's your cottage after all. . . .*"

That's probably the most enthusiastic remark she's made on the subject. Her tone is like that of a mother giving in to the whims of a child: *You can keep your hamster but you absolutely can't let him out of his cage. . . .*

Since she's started working (and it's a habit that will become more and more pronounced as she rises in the ranks), Cécile always speaks in italics, with her mouth puckered as if she's been eating sour cherries. She's like that at home, anyway, and even more at the cottage. At work, apparently, she is radiant, relaxed, her potential fully realized. But that's another story, and my sisters could probably tell it much better than I can.

• • •

The cottage adventure lasted for just two summers. The first summer Louis spent sawing, nailing, planing, sanding, gluing, painting, fixing, straightening, patching and sweating — but a beer tastes so good at night when you've got sawdust in your hair and your hands are rough, and it's so good to swim in the lake when you've spent all day sticking asphalt shingles onto the garage roof, and you feel so powerful when you split a log with just one stroke of the axe, and afterwards you sleep so well. . . .

"*If you think I'm going to travel a hundred miles so I can clean up your sawdust and wash dishes by hand, if you think I enjoy being eaten alive by blackflies and swimming in mud, and I get worried sick when the children go out in the boat, and when are you going to fix that boat for heaven's sake? Go ahead, take the boys if you want; I'm staying here with the girls. . . . It's your cottage, after all.*"

By the end of the first summer, Cécile is only going there every other weekend. She'd rather work. Louis doesn't understand; she prefers the air of the supermarket to that of the north; the sound of a cash register to the songs of birds. She calls that realizing her potential. . . .

Still, Louis should have known. At the very beginning of the summer he'd invited his mother to the cottage. Annette was very old then and didn't often leave her retirement home. But she remained true to herself: *Why on earth would you heat with wood when you could have electric radiators? Does it make any sense to chop wood by hand, like in the old days? You must really enjoy making life hard for yourself! And would you take a look at that old wooden furniture. . . . Looks poor if you ask me. And you haven't got a TV set? Not even a telephone? Why not sleep outside while you're at it? When do we go back, Margot?*

In contrast, Madame Desmarais would have liked to be invited more often, but not for the cottage, for the drive; she'd commit every sin in the book if it meant she could take a long trip in the car. As soon as Louis turned the key in the ignition she'd start talking, as if her mouth were an extra cylinder and her tongue a piston:

"Hang out the washing by the side of the road, have you ever seen such a thing, not too bright if you ask me, with all the dust from the road, they may be too poor to buy a dryer but some poor people have got common sense, really, I can't believe. . . . What's wrong with that clock? It can't be two-thirty, we just left. . . . I have to say, this is a nice car you've got. You ought to be happy, my girl, having a husband with such a nice car; your father never had one like this. . . . Would you look at that beautiful lawn. . . ."

Louis always stopped halfway on the pretext of filling the gas tank: in fact, it was so he could fill his ears with silence.

When they got to the cottage, Madame Desmarais would shut herself inside and not come out till Sunday morning, to go to Mass.

"Why don't we go to the church in Saint-Donat for a change? That way we could take a car ride. . . ."

• • •

When it was Léo's turn to come, he didn't hesitate for a second; there was a lake, a rowboat, fishing rods. He headed for the big rocks and came back with a dozen bass, which Béa hastened to cook on the wood stove. A treat.

• • •

"They're predicting good weather for the weekend. . . . If I had a cottage I think I'd go there. . . . Don't mind me, I'm just thinking out loud. . . . And even if it rains, the fish bite. . . . Did I tell you that Béa really likes your cottage? It's true the northern air is good. . . . Okey-doke, I'm going back to work. . . ."

It was only when Louis bought his cottage that he discovered an unexpected side to Léo's personality: his brother was capable of being impatient and even so agitated that he got on Louis's nerves. If Louis went two weeks without asking him up, he'd come and talk to him ten times a day:

"The bass must be biting now. . . ."

Louis muttered as he pretended to be filing invoices, unable to make any kind of reply till he'd talked to Cécile but already guessing her reaction: *It's not enough to see him all week long, now you have to put up with him at the cottage. . . . If you think I feel like sitting around with Béa, being bored to death. . . .*

As the cottage was on a very big lot, there was talk of Louis ceding part of it to his brother so he could build something. *I know perfectly well,* Cécile said, *your brothers have always been more important than your family. . . .*

You can't impose peace on someone who doesn't want it. Cécile hated the cottage and everything it represented, and her feelings intensified from one weekend to the next. So there was no point insisting. But when Louis wanted to share that peace with Léo, who knew how to appreciate it, it only brought trouble. As he couldn't see the sense of charging into every wall that destiny set in his path, at the end of the second summer Louis decided to sell Léo the cottage. It was undoubtedly one of the most surprising decisions he'd ever made, and certainly the wisest, because it made everyone else happy: Cécile would never have to set foot there again, Léo and Béa would be eternally grateful to Louis for letting them have this little piece of paradise, and they'd always welcome him there with open arms. Even his children would benefit from it, though in an unexpected way.

36

EGGBEATERS AND MIXERS

On Saturday afternoon, when it's time to go up to the cottage, I pile into Uncle Léo's car every chance I get. My brothers and my cousins prefer Louis's car: it goes faster so they'll get there sooner. But I still prefer Uncle Léo's, not so much so I can breathe my girl-cousins' perfume, as my brothers maintain, but so I can observe this family that's so similar to mine and yet so different. And every time, I come back more troubled and at the same time reassured.

• • •

"Don't forget to turn left after the church," Béa reminds Léo.

Léo, who still manages to get lost on the way to his own cottage. Léo, who never takes offence at being brought into line by his Béa.

Béa, who can watch the road and her knitting and keep an eye on the youngest children at the same time.

Béa, who can give Léo information without making a big deal of it.

Léo, who drives slowly, so desperately slowly.

Béa, who opens her window to breathe the northern air and smiles.

Everything seems clear and limpid, with no sardonic insinuations, no remarks in italics. There's no escalation of resentment, and the children don't feel as if they're witnessing another episode in the Cold War. So it can be done.

• • •

Léo in the Verchères rowboat. Léo, who shows us how to select the best worms and wrap them around the hook till we can't see any metal. Léo, who teaches us to be quiet and wait. To pay attention to the slightest shudder, the slightest jolt. . . . But the best hooks and the best rods don't change anything: the pike and bass are only interested in Léo's worms. How do you do it, Uncle Léo?

"It's like your father," he replies. "When a customer's ready to buy, he knows. We've all got our own talents. . . ."

Léo doesn't teach any lessons, he doesn't preach, but you see him smile when he pulls out another bass and you think, maybe that's the trick: you just have to find your own talent.

• • •

On the lakeshore, Béa fishes for minnows with a dishtowel.

Béa, who isn't afraid of crayfish, frogs and snakes, who isn't even afraid of toads.

Béa, who swims and all you can see is her smile above the water.

Béa, who bakes raspberry upside-down cakes that fill the whole cottage with their perfume. On the way home the car will still be scented with wild raspberries.

Béa, who smells of raspberries even in the city.

• • •

Léo, who speaks to Louis as he's preparing the fish:

"You know you can come up whenever you want, it's your cottage as much as mine. . . . I'll never be able to thank you enough. . . ."

"You don't have to thank me," replies Louis with a shrug. "This cottage has always belonged to you, it's obvious. It belonged to you even before it was built. . . . Maybe even before Jacques Cartier discovered Canada. . . ."

"Aren't you getting carried away?"

"Not all that much, Léo, not all that much."

• • •

"The living room's the ocean and it's full of sharks and you have to walk on the islands and the first one that falls in the water is dead."

And all the cousins, boys and girls alike, walk across the armchairs and sofas and never step on the floor. The cottage is also boredom, and you find whatever you can to keep you busy on rainy days. All the cousins walk over the armchairs and sofas, and leave behind sand, dead leaves and pine needles. And Béa doesn't say a word.

On Sunday before we leave, out will come the broom and the dustmop, the rags and the dusters. When everyone pitches in it takes ten minutes. And everyone will pitch in, cheerfully. So it can be done.

• • •

Aunt Juliette, so frail, Aunt Juliette adrift in her nun's robe, Aunt Juliette, whom my father went to pick up at the hospital. We settle her on a lawnchair and she does nothing all weekend but look at the far end of the lake.

"Thank you, Léo. Thank you, Louis. And thank you, Béa. I've never seen such a beautiful sunset."

Béa, who is happy to welcome Juliette and treats her as if she were a precious stone.

• • •

Léo, to Édouard:

"Look, Édouard, you're my brother and you know you'll always be welcome, but to be blunt, Béa and I would prefer you to come with Simone, because . . . because accidents like what happened yesterday happen more often when you come on your own, and then Béa has to clean up, she doesn't complain, that's not what I'm saying, it's just that . . . It's no fun, Édouard, it's no fun for you, it's no fun for anyone. . . ."

Édouard, who swears that he's going to stop drinking, he promises, and Léo, who doesn't believe a word. And then Béa, to whom Léo reports the conversation with his brother:

"You were right to talk to him, but you mustn't get mad. It isn't his fault, it's a sickness. . . ."

And I, who thought everything was our fault, always.

• • •

Béa in the kitchen, fixing the evening meal. The sound of the wooden spoon in the mixing bowl, the sound of the mixer or the eggbeater, the whisk or the potato masher, the sound of saucepans and kettles. . . . With Béa, those sounds never seem like reproaches.

Léo, who comes to get a bottle-opener and, while he's there, plants a kiss on Béa's neck. Béa, who shudders, who wriggles, and you can tell that her whole body is smiling.

A ten-year-old who happens to be there and watches the scene, incredulous.

He goes back to his games but he doesn't forget.

37

The Nine Floor

"Sell the store? Why not sell our mother while we're at it, or our brothers or our children or our own hearts? What are you talking about? Fillion et Frères is a business, yes. Among other things. But it's a business that's called Fillion et Frères, and that's the point. . . ."

"No problem; actually, it's the name we're interested in. Look, Monsieur Fillion. . . ."

Though he's reacting abruptly, Louis enjoys listening to business proposals, which inevitably end like this. People talk to him about mergers, banners, economy of scale and expansion, but all he wants to hear is that ultimate compliment: it's the name we're interested in. The furniture is bought on credit, the space is rented; the name is the Fillion brothers' only capital. And if they sold it to people named Smith or Cohen or Filiatreault?

"If Fillion is a good name, it should go on being good for Fillions."

"At least think it over, Monsieur Fillion."

And Louis does think it over, sometimes; it's true that competition is massive. The Americans are coming on strong with unbeatable prices, while the Europeans are taking over the high end. All that's left for an independent is the middle, which in business is always the hardest position to be in: if you're neither this nor that, you're nothing. Styles change too quickly. And as soon as you make a little profit, the government invents a new tax.

"It's getting harder and harder to stay independent, Monsieur Fillion. You have to regroup, you need volume to get good prices. Talk it over with your brothers, Monsieur Fillion, talk with your children. . . ."

Talk it over with his brothers? Louis sometimes imagines the look on Léo's face, his dismay: "Sell the store? You can't be serious, Louis. What would we do?" Good question, Léo. It would give us a very meager income while we wait for our pensions, and we're past the age to start over in a new field. Look for a job? Selling furniture at Eaton's, maybe, or driving a truck for Pascal's? Some promotion!

Talk with the children? What for? They may work at the store during summer holidays but they'll never take over from their fathers. Those children are going to stay in school as long as they want, and it won't be so they can work sixty hours a week selling furniture at the Plaza Saint-Hubert. There won't be any Fillion et Fils, no sir. Cécile would die of shame. . . . But that doesn't mean I'll never sell. Come back and see me in ten years, then we'll talk.

Ten years later it would be too late. They should have sold in 1965, when there were all kinds of quiz shows on Channel 10 that offered a jackpot of *this magnificent living-room suite courtesy of Fillion et Frères. Fillion et Frères in the Plaza Saint-Hubert. Fillion et Frères, superior quality at a reasonable price. . . .*

"You have to hit them hard," say the advertising people: "At the Plaza you smash prices, you demolish them, you crush them, you grind them, you pulverize them. . . . Television's no place for subtleties."

But Louis resists: "In the long run, flashy ads don't pay. People end up thinking the merchandise is poor quality. No matter what price they pay, they feel as if they've been had. *Superior quality at a reasonable price*. I insist."

"Whatever you say, Monsieur Fillion. It lacks punch, but you're the one who's paying. . . ."

"*Superior quality at a reasonable price*," repeat the stars of Télé-Métropole who address the viewers directly from Fillion et Frères, the big furniture store in Plaza Saint-Hubert. Louis doesn't like these grossly sensational manoeuvres. He feels his store is being invaded.

"The lights, the cameras, the stars — sure, they draw people, but I'm not convinced it's a good idea. . . ."

"I've never seen anyone so behind the times! This is the twentieth century, Monsieur Fillion! Your store is known all over town now, you've never had so many customers, but you're still doubtful!"

Lots of customers, right, but not many more buyers, muses Louis, who's in a better position than anyone else to verify the first law of advertising: What it costs, we know. But what it brings in. . . .

What it brings in, for the moment, is wind in our sails. Plenty of wind: in 1965, I'm our class hero because all my friends see my father's store on TV every day and they assume I'm a millionaire. In 1965, the Fillions are visited not only by TV stars but also, driven there by the same wind, representatives of the Chamber of Commerce, aldermen, MPs. The Fillions are solicited, praised, treated with respect. They're given to understand that the mayor is interested in their opinions, and apparently the minister. . . . In 1965, the elder Madame Fillion doesn't know whom to call first when she learns that Anita Barrière in person has come to her sons' store, and even Cécile lets herself get carried away with bursts of pride when she talks about the store: *I've always believed in my husband, he always had to be pushed but it paid off.*

"Don't you think we're moving a little too fast?" Louis asks sometimes. "Don't you think we should slow down a bit and see where this is taking us?"

"Of course not," reply the ad people and the marketing specialists. "This is just a start!" add the representatives of the plaza's Retailers' Association, who never miss a chance to point out that everyone benefits from all these customers. "We have to succeed, it's our mission," point out some — who haven't forgotten the secret handshake. "We have to take the plunge, we mustn't be afraid of success," responds in chorus the entire Fillion family, which includes distant cousins whom no one knows but who still let themselves be driven by this wind: it's so good to feel it blowing in your hair when you walk with your head high. And in this chorus Louis sometimes thinks he can hear Philippe's voice (*Keep it up, Louis, prove to them that I was right*), and Étienne's (*Success is something to be savoured, like revenge*).

Louis forgets his fears and takes the plunge. As the experiment with advertising wasn't completely negative, he decides to make a big move by joining forces with a supplier in Saint-Jérôme to offer a Newlyweds' Special: furnish your whole house for just nine hundred and ninety-nine dollars and ninety-nine cents! Twenty-four pieces, everything you need to furnish three rooms — for under a thousand dollars! All you have to supply is your love!

The offer is appealing, the TV show is popular and the camera spends longer on the price than on the furniture. It works. It works beyond all expectations: some customers order by phone without even seeing the furniture. Louis insists that they come to the store so they at least know what they're buying, but it's no good; in those years television still has such an aura that customers seem to think nothing bad can come from it. Hasn't Anita Barrière herself called it an excellent buy? Didn't she say it *on television*? If you can't trust Anita Barrière. . . .

At the same time, Fillion et Frères reserves the back page of *La Patrie* and *Dimanche Matin*. Since photos always give a pitiful impression of fragility, they ask a draftsman to use his artistic vision to reinforce the legs of a table and give the armchairs some depth. Which obviously doesn't stop the real chairs from being terribly fragile, but it's still a good deal *for the price*, says Louis, who is constantly justifying himself. "What can I tell you, the customers want it. True, the legs are fragile, but it's the same everywhere. Look at cars! One rainfall and they rust, but nobody complains. People want something new, always something new, and so what if it breaks, that way they can get something else new. True, I'd prefer it if customers took their time, I wish they'd spend longer on the main floor of Fillion et Frères, where there are never any reductions, where there's no compromise on quality. But the customers don't even look at the good, solid furniture. They climb straight up to the second floor, what Léo calls the *nine* floor: nine ninety-nine! Nineteen ninety-nine! Ninety-nine ninety-nine! Nobody's obliged to buy. Times are changing, you have to adapt. . . ."

But selling poor-quality furniture that has to be delivered, then taken back to the factory to honour the guarantee, then delivered to the customer a second time, is never good business regardless of the price, regardless of the volume; a few years later, when the customers want to replace their furniture, they'll go to the Italians for a leather sofa, they'll buy cardboard boxes *made in Malaysia* from the damn Swedes, but they won't go back to Fillion et Frères.

It was not good business and Louis knew that from the beginning, but the money had to come in to pay for the rent and the advertising, and the heating, lighting, and taxes, and the children's clothes and their education and their doctors' bills, and Édouard's salary even when he wasn't working, and the allowance for Annette and Madame Desmarais, and he was fed up with being told that he was behind the times, and who knows what tomorrow will bring, and show me someone who turns up his nose at money so we can have a little talk, just the two of us.

Yes, they should have sold in 1965, when volume could create an illusion and the name Fillion et Frères still had a certain value. Later on, there wouldn't be any more offers to buy or associate or merge. Customers would desert the Plaza to get their feet stepped on in one of the suburban malls, on the pretext that parking was free and so what if you had to walk three kilometres to find your car. Then the employees would leave, one after another, and there would be no one left in the store except the three Fillion brothers and their last handful of employees, who would hold out together through the seventies, that terribly hopeless, terribly long decade.

Fillion et Frères would be a quiet place then, where time passed very slowly. The Fillion brothers would wear outmoded clothes, their store would smell of old dust and their showroom would display furniture that was solid but out of date, furniture that would still please an aging clientele.

Time would pass slowly and the Fillion brothers would twiddle their thumbs, but they'd never play cards during business hours; that would show a lack of respect towards the store, towards the name Fillion et Frères. They would read *Le Devoir*, they'd do crossword puzzles, they'd worry if Édouard took a little too long when he went to the drugstore to buy stamps and they'd listen to the open-line shows on the radio, repeating time and again their beefs about youth, feminists, judges and unions — all of them more or less responsible for the degeneration of society and the decline in sales of colonial-style furniture.

Often they had to pinch pennies, but they'd hang on to the very end, till retirement age. Then they would close the books, though not before they experienced one last explosion of customers, one final period of abundance — at least apparently.

That would be the ultimate sale, the big closing sale, the big party that went on for one whole week at the very beginning of the eighties. A big party: that really was how Louis, Édouard and Léo had envisaged it. A big party with balloons, pink sandwiches, flutes of champagne, confetti, and the Fillion brothers would be in their Sunday best. They would entertain family, former employees, satisfied long-time customers; people would exchange old memories, trade handshakes. Then they'd close the books, give the keys back to the landlord and treat themselves to one last drink, maybe even to a fine bottle.

That was how they'd envisaged it, but they were wrong. There wouldn't be any satisfied long-time customers or former employees or family. Only sharks, rats and vultures: and I step on your feet and I give you a shove and I pull an arm off that chair and I demand an extra discount and I bargain, I haggle, fifty percent isn't enough, I want free delivery, I insist on a guarantee. . . .

No, it would be not a party but a bloodbath, a massacre, the Normandy landing. And that was just fine; when he was finally retired and someone asked if he missed the store, Louis would say no, not at all, with the look of someone who's never heard such a ludicrous question.

38

A Good Life

"We never learn," says Louis. "I made the same mistake as Monsieur Lunn, exactly the same mistake. It's as if I spent my whole life reminding myself, 'Watch out for the hole!' and ended up falling into it. . . ."

"It isn't your fault, Louis, it really isn't," replies Léo in a faintly irritated tone. "Anyone else would have done the same thing. And everybody was proud when they saw the ads on TV, everybody. You weren't on your own, Louis. The business was called Fillion et Frères, remember. . ."

"I should have been careful. If I'd stuck to my guns. . . ."

"By the way, have you ever noticed that a cloud often comes out of the bottle when you open a beer? You see it in the ads. In real life too. Not all the time, but nearly. It goes *psschhht* and then there's a little cloud of smoke coming out of the bottle. . . . D'you know why that is?"

"It must be vapour, I guess. The pressure. . . ."

"No, that's not it. It's a kind of present from the bottlers. A present they put in their bottles. See, it's like the prizes in boxes of Cracker Jack."

"A bonus?"

"Here, I'll explain: every time I open a beer, I tell myself, the cloud of smoke is the past. Look at it and it's already gone. But you've still got your whole beer to drink. . . . Do you follow me, Louis?"

"Absolutely, Léo, absolutely. . . . And what do you say we check out that theory of yours?"

Léo gets up slowly, goes to his old refrigerator, opens the door, shuts it, comes back and sits down, smiling. . . .

"Haven't you forgotten something?" Louis asks after a while.

"The beer! And I was telling myself. . . ."

"Never mind, I'll get it. . . ."

They open a beer, look at the cloud of vapour and then at the spruce trees at the far end of the lake. There are long gaps in their conversation, long gaps that neither of them feels obliged to fill. There's the northern air to do that, and the sunset and the stars.

"Still, we've had a good life, don't you think?" asks Louis a few moments later, after watching another cloud of vapour fly away.

"A very good life," replies Léo.

"We've created jobs, we've supported our families, we've brought up our children. . . . Not everybody can say that."

"Nope, not everybody."

"We've got nothing to feel guilty about."

"Absolutely nothing."

"We've had successful lives."

"Very successful. We did what we had to."

"We did what we had to and we did it well. We always did the right thing. At the end it was harder, of course, but the children never wanted for anything. We made money when they were young, when they needed it. After that they could stand on their own two feet. We've had a good life, old Léo, a very good life. What do you think?"

"Same as you, old Louis."

"A very good life," repeats Louis again.

They're sitting in their Adirondack chairs, looking at the far end of the lake and telling themselves that they've had a good life, yes, a very good life. Towards the end they have a tendency to repeat themselves a lot, which is perfectly normal. After all, someone has to tell them: yes, they've had a very good life.

39

Fillion and Sons, Fillion and Daughters

Jocelyne, Christiane, Benoît, Louise, Yves, Marc-André. They're all alive and they're college or university teachers, proofreaders, officials in the Department of Human Resources Development or psychologists. Léo's and Édouard's children have taken the same path: there are nurses and union officials, aid workers and computer scientists, journalists and administrators, but no one who has anything remotely to do with business.

Nor has anyone joined a religious order and left it. The Fillion sons and daughters are nearly all married, divorced and remarried, and while they're perpetuating the Fillion name, they're doing so timidly, as if on tiptoe: their children are called Fillion-Allard or Ménard-Fillion, and very few of them know that the words *brother* and *sister* can be plural.

They live in Longueuil or Saint-Lambert, Sainte-Foy or the Plateau Mont-Royal, their cars are Japanese or German and, when they travel, it's to Europe rather than Florida. No statues of the Virgin or crucifixes in their houses, but Italian leather sofas and furniture from kits.

They don't suffer from any serious illnesses or major handicaps, aside from a penchant for the bottle, chocolate or tobacco — all kinds of tobacco, all kinds of chocolates — and a strong tendency to talk about their childhood to listeners who are all the more attentive because they're paid to be. The Fillion sons and daughters like to talk, the men as much as the women, and they talk all the time, as if they had two generations of silence to catch up on; they talk all the time, with a marked predilection for everything their parents never talked about: sex, relationships, fear.

Among the Fillion brothers and sisters, as everywhere else, friendships are forged and broken, unions are created and undone, there are fallings out and reconciliations, but regardless of whose home they're at, whether it's over bagels and lox or barbecued hot dogs, there's always a bottle of wine on the table and someone who wants — in order to comprehend it better — to rewrite once again the history of the Fillion family, which is constantly being revised and corrected.

Most often it's enough to repeat the same anecdotes, with minor changes, but sometimes they feel the need to start from the top. This general review happens every five years on average, sometimes a little more often — when a Fillion son or daughter becomes a parent, for instance, or when a new love requires them to revisit their past once again.

Each time it's a grand trial with the same witnesses called to the stand to tell the same anecdotes; their memories are sometimes sharper or more elusive, and it just takes some new lighting or re-editing and to create a completely different story. When these same witnesses are transformed into judges, they are sometimes cruel, sometimes benevolent, as if they were sitting either at the court of the Inquisition or in Youth Court. But their favourite role is that of advocate: they like to talk and they engage in lengthy speeches for the defence, invoking, depending on the period and the fashion, Marx or Marcuse, Freud or Jung, Simone de Beauvoir or Germaine Greer. They talk about complexes and frustrations, self-image and male chauvinism, and someone will always point out that *we mustn't lose sight of the fact that all this is taking place within a context, isn't that so*, and imagine he's said something very profound.

Always the same witnesses, the same judges and advocates, but the verdict will be different each time: the wrongs switch from one side to the other, without nuance, or the two parents are judged equally guilty or innocent. But no matter what the sentence is, it will never be served; that's already been done.

• • •

One of the Fillion sons is a university professor. Of Management, to be precise. Businesses, like families, are cells, organisms that are born, live and die. Some are more successful than others and it's not without interest to attempt to understand the reasons. They multiply, they withstand attacks by employing various strategies, and the most effective strategies aren't necessarily the most rational ones. Financial firms, it must be said, are the ones that most resemble sects, or introverted families. All this is absolutely fascinating and it can lead to a very satisfying university career, but it's not material for a novel, I'm well aware of that. Still, I wanted to say a few words on the subject, even if it's just to point out that there's more to management than bookkeeping, and to situate the narrator of this tale.

It often happens that the narrator is invited to attend symposia and to present papers all over the planet, which is not the most unpleasant aspect of his job. He talks about strategic alliances, the new economy or restructuring till he senses the first signs of drowsiness in the audience. He'll go on with his gibberish for a few moments, aware of the hypnotic powers of his speech — to each his talent — and then pretend to deviate from his text and, on the pretext of illustrating his remarks with examples, begin to talk about his father, who had a furniture store in Montreal, a store where one Monsieur Vinet, accountant by trade, was particularly effective in human resources management, where a Monsieur Demers taught his hierarchical superior how to read the map of the city, where a Mademoiselle Thibeault and a Monsieur Paquin worked to earn a salary, yes, among other things, but only among other things; and he'll explain that it was there, in that business, that the narrator learned to be wary of graphs and organizational charts, to look more closely at what goes on beyond the numbers, to study aspects that don't fit any theories, to take an interest in all those little things that slip along the most tenuous of threads, little things that life consists of, and that all this is what we lose sight of at times, and it's what we should be trying to safeguard. . . .

There are always a few in the audience who come up to see the speaker at the end, to talk with him not about strategic mergers but about their fathers who had a hardware store in Illinois, a machine shop in Clermont-Ferrand, a restaurant in Charleroi, a barbershop in Milan.

And they'll all get together in a little bistro that isn't part of a chain, they'll drink wine or sake, observe the boss leering at the cashier while his wife leafs through her celebrity magazine. After that they'll tell each other about Fillion et Frères, Lincoln Office Supplies or the New Saigon Steak House before drinking a toast to their late fathers. And then they'll fall silent and go on drinking, fall silent while they go on talking to someone, over there. . . .

In an airplane one day, our speaker got the idea of writing it all down. To tell the story, that's all, without the pretext of a speech, without pretending to have any ideas to illustrate or defend. To put words into Louis's silence. To talk about him one way or another, and find another way to tell him that he had a good life, a very good life.

40

Nocturnal Adoration

It happens at the funeral parlour. An old lady no one knows goes right up to Louis's coffin without speaking to anyone. There's something very dignified about this old lady no one knows, but at the same time terribly vulgar, like all old ladies wearing too much makeup.

The wife and children of the deceased exchange a questioning look: no, none of them knows her. Neither do Léo and Béa or even Mademoiselle Thibeault, though she recognizes everyone, even some of Louis's childhood friends whom everyone has lost sight of for decades. The old lady heads directly for the coffin, sheds a few tears and offers a few prayers, then struggles to her feet and makes her way to the door.

I may be imagining, but it seems to me that Cécile shoots her a look filled with venom. Intrigued, I go up to her; this woman isn't going to walk out just like that, without telling us her name, without even signing the register. She moves slowly so I have no trouble catching up with her as she arrives at the door.

She tries to open it, unsuccessfully; it's so hot inside the funeral parlour and so cold outside that the pressure seems to have sealed the steel door permanently. As she already needs all her strength just to wear her coat and carry her purse, she'll never get it open.

"Here, I'll give you a hand, Madame . . . Madame . . . ?"

It's no good, she doesn't want to give her name. I open the door but it's so cold outside, and so dark, and the lady is so old and so alone and so pathetic, that I tell her: "Wait a minute, let me drive you home; I was leaving anyway. . . ."

She protests a little as a matter of form, but two minutes later she's comfortably ensconced in my car, which will soon be filled with her perfume.

"You're Benoît, aren't you, the one who teaches at the university? Your father was so proud of you. . . ."

She still hasn't told me her name but she has given me her address: Chateaubriand Street, very close to Fillion et Frères. I take my time getting there. Mainly because the streets are slippery, but particularly because I know from experience that people talk differently when they're in a car. Especially at night. It probably has something to do with the fact that they're looking straight ahead at the road and not at the other person. They're more apt to call up memories, to explore their own world out loud.

"Were you a customer of my father's?"

"Yes, you could say that. And Louis . . . and your father was a client too, you might say. . . . Oh my, I've heard so much about you and your brothers and sisters, I feel as if I've always known you. And your voice. . . . Has anyone ever told you that you've got your father's voice?"

"A few times, yes. . . . You were . . . a friend?"

"A friend? Yes, I think you could say that. . . . Actually I. . . ."

Just as we pull up in front of her place her voice breaks. Luckily, there's a parking space across from her house. I hurry to open her door and offer to escort her up the stairs, which must be slippery. . . .

"You can come up if you want. . . ."

She wants to talk to me, I can tell, and that suits me fine; I want to listen to her. An old lady who seems to be my father's age, who claims to be his friend, who lives so close to where Fillion et Frères used to stand. . . .

"It's not what you think," she says when we're finally inside her tiny apartment cluttered with knick-knacks and flowered cushions, and she's offered me a glass of Diet Coke. . . . "No, it's not what you think. I've been in that trade — the one you're thinking of, yes, don't deny it, I know what I look like. I even piled it on a little thick tonight, just to annoy your mother. . . . I was in that trade when I was young, so it doesn't bother me that . . . I needed the money. A rough period. And I was still doing it when I went to Fillion et Frères to buy furniture. It was near the end, but I was still doing it. . . . Louis understood right away that I had a business, like him. That man was so quick to understand, even if he didn't talk much.

I needed furniture, he needed me, so. . . ."

"I'm not sure I. . . ."

"It's not what you think, even if he deserved it, and even if I'd have done it for free. No, it's not what you think. And I want to tell you, so you'll know what kind of man he was. If you don't know, nobody ever will."

She filled my glass of Diet Coke and I didn't protest — my throat has never been so dry.

"He'd come to see me every week, on Thursday, right after dinner. Every Thursday for. . . for, my goodness, nearly thirty years. He'd sometimes come at night too, but more rarely. He'd sit here" (she points to the empty spot on the sofa where she's sitting) "and he'd talk to me. About this and that. About his customers and his brothers, about his memories of the war, about shoe-polishing cannons and about his friend Bonin, the one who died in England. About life. . . . And he'd talk about his children too, he always spoke so highly of you, always saying how proud he was. And he'd also talk about Cécile. But that. . . . When he'd finished talking he'd take off his shoes and stretch out on the sofa. He'd always ask my permission first, in case I didn't want him to. I always did want him to, but he'd ask my permission anyway. He was such a courteous man, and thoughtful. He'd stretch out on the sofa and I'd sit here. He just wanted to rest his head against me. He just wanted to . . . to snuggle, that's all. To sit close, to feel safe. Sometimes it was for a few minutes, but other times he needed to stay longer. I'd run my hand through his hair the way you'd do with a little boy who's sad, but that was all. He never asked me for anything else. When he came at night he wouldn't talk. He just wanted to lie down and snuggle. He called it his 'nocturnal adoration.' Often he'd cry. He'd cry like a child, and dear God but it seemed to come from far away. Then he'd get up and he'd be like new. He'd say he was restored. . . . He'd get up, he'd lift his shoulders one after the other, pull in his stomach, put his hat back on and he was Monsieur Fillion again. He paid me at first but not at the end. I didn't want him to; it may sound funny but it was good for me too. And I didn't want anyone paying me any more, especially not him. . . . He finally went along with it but he was always giving me presents, he couldn't help himself. Ends of lines, he'd say, seconds, so he said, but though I'd look and look I never found any flaws. . . . Your father was a generous man, but I'm sure you know that as well as I do. So yes, you could say we were friends, I think you could say that. . . . That's what I wanted to tell you, Monsieur Fillion. I wanted you to know."